DEDICATION

This book is dedicated to the faith and obedience of my Pastors, David and Rhonda Knox, who set out for Paraguay in obedience to a dream, not knowing where they would be going or where they would be ministering. The Holy Spirit arranged their itinerary, and many lives were changed by the power of God, including theirs. Rhonda's dream planted the spark of this story in my heart, and with the help of God, I was inspired to write this book.

I would also like to dedicate this book to Peter and Evie Ratcliffe, who also set out for Paraguay with David and Rhonda Knox. Based on a one week trip, and seeing how eager God was to move, they answered His call. They went back to their home in Oklahoma, sold all they had, and moved their family of six, with one on the way, to rural Paraguay. There they share the love of God with everyone. They are making a difference in every life they touch.

Lastly, this book is dedicated to all missionaries who have been called by God to step out in faith and venture into the unknown. Great will be their reward.

ACKNOWLEDGEMENTS

Saying thank you is too small a word for the gratitude I have in my heart for all who have helped me in this endeavor. I especially want to thank my friends Lore Swingle, Elsie Hoffstatter, and Brenda Livingston, my sister Cathy Ryan and her husband Dick, and my husband's cousin, Frank Rattacasa. Their comments and encouragement helped me finish this book, and bring the editing up to a much higher standard than I was capable of on my own. My friend Lore started me down this road. All through this process, she was there for me with suggestions and expertise that I did not possess.

I want to thank my husband Mike, who not only helped and encouraged me, but was willing to drop what he was doing to come to my aid and help me find just the right word when I had writer's block. He has been my sounding board. I have read this entire book to him in order to get the perspective of someone who knew my heart and the message I was trying to convey.

I also want to thank all of my family for their input and encouragement in this project. Only God knows the lives that will be touched by this book and the eternal consequences of it.

PREFACE

Almost everyone you talk to who knows that Jesus is coming back, believes that He is coming back soon. Just as the characters in this book received a call from God, I was also given a call to write this book, to encourage believers, and to fulfill God's quest to persuade unbelievers.

While I was attending church during a Sunday night service, a minister began to speak to my pastors and encourage them. He told them God was going to open the doors of South America for their ministry. It was then God gave me the embryo of an idea for this book. I belong to a small church, but it is heavily involved in world missions, and our pastors have followed the hand of God into foreign nations all over the world.

A week or two after this visit, my pastor's wife had a dream that the country of Paraguay was calling them. When she shared that dream with the church, that embryo began to grow.

In response to the dream, and being obedient to what they sensed that God was asking them to do, they purchased tickets to Paraguay. After making a few phone calls to virtual strangers telling them of their intended arrival, they landed in Paraguay two weeks later. God used their trust in Him and their obedience to pave the way for Him to move.

Another couple went with them, whose hearts were also for missions, and a minister and friend who translated for them. Many doors of ministry opened while they were in Paraguay. They saw the Hand of God move in miraculous ways. Upon returning home, the couple who accompanied them sold their home and most of their belongings, and moved their entire family to rural Paraguay.

As the above events took place, the embryo of this book continued to grow and I began to write. I cannot tell you how the story will end other than Jesus will be coming back. I have no outlines, except the titles of at least three books, The Call, The Quest, and The Coming.

Every time I sit down to write, I feel as though God gives me ideas. I'm sure I'm not the only one who has had this experience, but what astounds me that I was sixty-seven years old when I wrote this first book.

I invite you to come with me on this journey. I promise you will be entertained; I know you will be ministered to. It is my hope that this book provides an impetus for you to seek Him out.

Footnotes have been inserted along the way as scriptural references to the thoughts, feelings, or events that are happening in the book. I encourage you to look them up and let the Word encourage those who believe, and give God the opportunity to minister to those who don't.

I don't claim to be an "end times" scholar. This book was not written to be a text on Eschatological events, but my hope is that those who do read it will be urged to do as He said and prepare for His coming.

CAST OF CHARACTERS

Akeem Farzhi   Friend from Iraq, lived with Josh thru college

Angie Pritchard   Jim Pritchard's wife

Audrey Hathaway   Jim Hathaway's wife who frequents Bekah's shop

Axel   Member of Manu's tribe mentored by Daniel

Bekah Ryan   Main character- focal point of dream

Carlos Rampone   Haydon Carlton's "handyman"

Chabuto   Manu's step-mother

Ciba   Village woman seriously gored by wild boar

Constanzia   Edwardo's wife, a/k/a Connie

Daniel Albright   Joe's brother, missionary in Northeast Paraguay

Edwardo   Young pastor Daniel mentored in Paraguay

Emilio   Baby in a basket sent downriver by young mother to escape being a burnt offering to an evil god

Erecia   Young nursing mother – helps Noemi feed Juan

Ernesto	Wild boar hunter
Esteban Montero	Bounty hunter in Paraguay
Fuego Zangersen	Bekah's father's second wife – her step mother
Gabriella Zangersen	Bekah's father's first wife and her mother
Giancarlo	Member of Manu's tribe mentored by Daniel
Haydon Carlton	New York City jeweler
Isaac Klein	C.I.A. operative and friend of Josh's
Jean	Owner of Lobster Pot in Ogunquit, Maine
Jim Hathaway	Sargent of Maine State Police
Jim Pritchard	Bekah's lawyer
Joe Albright	Roberta's husband, Daniel's older brother
Jose	Owner of Excelsior-arms store in Asuncion
Joshua Randall	Stranger from Claremore, Oklahoma, first to have dream
Juan	Manu and Noemi's newborn son
Juan	Injured wild boar hunter
Kay	Part of a large prayer group in Maine
Lara	Connie's 22 year old sister living with them
Leonardo	Ciba's husband, Manu's advisor
Luna	Bekah's half-sister
Maite	Member of Manu's tribe mentored by Daniel

Manu	Young chief of village
Mara	Riki's wife who was killed by wild boar
Maria	Edwardo and Connie's three year old daughter
Mario	Young man Daniel mentored
Nana Sarah Zangersen	Bekah's late grandmother
Noemi	Manu's wife
Paloma	Helper girl given to Sherry from Manu
Paulo	Edwardo and Connie's six-month old son
Penny	Works at Eye of the Needle, Sylvia's granddaughter
Philippe	Young man Daniel mentored
Renato	Foreman of Bekah's apple orchard, from Paraguay
Riki	Villager whose wife was killed by a wild boar
Roberta Albright	Part-timer at Bekah's "Eye of the Needle"
Sandy	Part of a large prayer group in Maine
Sherry Albright	Daniel's wife/missionary/nurse midwife
Shirley	Part of a large prayer group in Maine
Suma	Village girl sent to help Noemi
Sylvia Jessup	Part-timer at Bekah's "Eye of the Needle"
Ted Ryan	Bekah's ex-husband
Young Woman	Sent her child down the river in a basket in response to dream from God

PROLOGUE

The young woman clutched the screaming infant to her chest. He was wrapped in the skin of a wild boar to keep him warm. She was dressed in the style of her people, a skirt and tunic top; but the quality of the clothes told its own story, and the current condition of them, torn and stained, told another.

She was probably the younger wife of a chief or of a wealthy elder of the tribe. It was not uncommon for men of high stature to take a young wife when they were older. She was battered and bruised from struggling through the tangled vegetation of the dense jungle, afraid to go down the many trails that led to the river for fear of being caught. She was no more than a child herself; childbearing started young in these remote tribal villages. A woman's worth was judged by the number of living children she had birthed, living being the definitive word. Infant mortality was extremely high, the main reasons being disease and poor diet; the other being the situation that was unfolding at this very moment.

It was the time of year when a distant, barbarous tribe living deep in the jungle came scavenging across the lush landscape. They sought the infant children of the smaller, peaceful tribes that inhabited this area to sacrifice to their bloodthirsty gods. They had been performing this deadly ritual for more than current memory served. They ravaged these tribes and killed and mutilated those who opposed them, picking a different tribe every year to assure their supply of infant sacrifices was not depleted.

It had been ten years since her village had fallen prey to their devastating brutality. She had been a young girl the last time they had struck, but she remembered the death and destruction that had been perpetrated. She remembered the heat of the roaring fire and the screams of the infants as they were thrown into it to appease the evil and murderous gods of this warlike tribe. She remembered the sobs of her parents as the warriors ripped her small baby brother from her mother's arms. She still remembered the sound of his screams as they carried him away. Some things are never forgotten. While growing up she had prayed she would never be one of those parents, but if she and her son did not get to the river quickly, circumstances suggested she would.

She thought of the other young mothers of the village, friends she had sat with as she nursed her son. She felt guilty for not having warned them, but knew she could not risk being deterred from her objective. Now she was being chased through the jungle by the object of her fear, and she needed to reach the river before they reached her.

This warlike tribe was led by an evil witchdoctor who believed human sacrifice not only empowered the tribe, but also empowered him, strengthening his powers with each additional child that was sacrificed. It was said that voices spoke to him, encouraging his blood thirsty savagery and his continual need for further sacrifices. Every spring, the men of this tribe were ignited by his frenzy. They had been on this rampage for many years, and so far, it seemed to be working. No one had been able to stop their carnage. They kept getting stronger and stronger.

Before the birth of her son, the young woman had experienced a dream that told her an attack was imminent, and to begin to prepare a way of escape. She did not know who the dream had come from, but some instinct told her that it was from one of the unknown gods they worshipped. This unknown god said he would answer her prayer and spare her child. She carried his talisman with her now, which she had stolen from her shaman's collection hanging near the temple in her village. She had always had an affinity for this particular god. She enjoyed hearing the stories, no more than legends now, of how he came to save his people.[1] She only hoped he would be true to his promise and save her son.

In obedience to the dream, she had fashioned a basket of reeds to take the child downriver. She had done so in secret, fearful someone might try to stop her. She was putting her child in the hands of her God, and if He was listening, she hoped He would hear her prayer. As she ran, she was begging Him to help her get her son to safety.

She could not pray for her village. The sights and sounds she had seen and heard robbed her of any faith she might have had. Someone had to oppose this barbaric tribe, but she knew it would not be her. She had neither the weapons nor the strength. What was needed was a savior. She had called out to her unknown God, but did He hear her? Was He even listening? In this life, it did not appear that she was to partake of the redemption she had prayed for, but she was determined that her son would. He was going to go free. Her God had shown her in a dream what was required of her, and she had been obedient to do all she had been shown.

Her breath was becoming louder and harsher as she continued to run. The acrid smell of smoke burned her throat, and the yelling and screaming in the distant village haunted her

---

[1] Luke 19:10

thoughts. The jungle spread before her, its dense canopy shutting out most of the morning sun.

Her bare feet were bruised and bleeding from tripping over the many rocks, tree roots, and twisting vines that traversed the jungle floor. She paused to catch her breath and get her bearings. No one appeared to be following, but she knew that could change at any moment. She couldn't see through the dense jungle, and the smoke was thickening. The wind had picked up, and sparks and burning leaves were being blown across the canopy, dropping down to the ground below. Looking about, she could see small fires starting up in several spots. The only saving grace was that the jungle was green and the air was humid. Fire had a difficult time taking hold under such conditions.

She ran as though the devil himself was chasing her, as indeed he was. The forces of darkness were converging and gathering strength for the fight that was coming to them. Satan had his army on Earth, and he was whipping them into a raging fury. His evil and viciousness were being expressed not only on this small village but also throughout the entire earth. In other parts of the world Satan was using people to bring death and destruction to the helpless. It was almost as though he knew his time was near, and he was garnering his forces for a final offense.

Several of the attacking tribesmen had broken off to pursue the fleeing girl. One had seen her slip through the group of warriors that surrounded the other mothers and their babies. These warriors cared nothing for her, but her child was the prize they coveted. Whoever presented the sacrifice of a living baby to the witch doctor had the promise of his strength and prosperity being increased tenfold, or so the witch doctor said. Their progress was inhibited because they were not only chasing her, but also fighting each other. Each one strove to reach her first. It was this distraction that bought her the time she needed to reach the river.

She continued on, though more slowly. Her strength had been depleted by the initial run to escape, and her breath was becoming more labored as she persisted. She looked down at the small infant she was carrying. His crying had subsided to a soft whimper. Her heart ached, knowing that she would not be there to see him grow. But there was a job to complete, and if she wanted to succeed, there was no time to waste on grieving over what could not be.

Moving across the carpeted jungle, the ground beneath her feet became saturated, announcing her closeness to the river. She kept glancing behind her, hearing angry voices and running footsteps. They were closing in. She needed to move faster. Physically and emotionally exhausted, she put one foot in front of the other. She continued to call out to her God. "Please," she begged, "please save my child."

She came to the river and reached the pile of rocks where the basket was hidden. In desperation, she tugged it from its hiding place, knowing she did not have much time, and that her life was forfeit, but she fought bravely for the life of her son. She would die, but he must live. The unknown God had promised, and she had obeyed.

With no time for even a last hug, she placed the baby in the basket and laid the talisman next to him. Lowering the basket, she launched it into the river. The swift current drew the basket quickly out of reach, propelling it down river.

She could tell by the sounds behind her that time was running out. At that moment, she cried out in pain. A small dart had imbedded itself in her shoulder. She felt a burning, and then numbness traveled down her arm. She looked over to the right and her worst fears materialized. There stood her pursuers. Two warriors with blackened faces and bloody hands advanced toward her. As the poison entered her system, she fell to the ground and muttered one last prayer, thanking her God for the safe- keeping of her son. The last sounds she heard were the screams of frustration from the raging warriors. She did not fear for herself. Death was taking her; but even as the life force drained out of her, she did not struggle. Her God had been faithful and her son had escaped. Laying her head down, she took her last breath, knowing she had given her son a chance at life. She was at peace.

It was the time of the year the river flowed swiftly, swelled by the seasonal rains. The basket traveled uninhibited for many miles with its small bundle. The hand of God rested upon him as it had upon the child Moses. Birds of prey flew overhead watching the struggling infant. He was helpless, but protected by the grace of God, and none dare approach.

After two days, the basket came to rest in a tangle of reeds. The child had arrived at a safe haven just as God promised. God is always faithful to perform His Word. The small infant began to cry, alerting those nearby of his presence.

BOOK ONE - THE CALL

CHAPTER ONE

OGUNQUIT, MAINE

JUNE 5

Bekah picked up her head and scanned the evening sky. Dusk was approaching, and the western sky was painted with a palette of colors in varying shades of gold, pink and lavender. The rays of the setting sun streamed through a profusion of wispy clouds, looking like Heaven's glory coming down to earth. The two towering pine trees that sat in each corner of the yard framed the spectacular sunset. They stood like two dark, brooding sentinels sent to guard the Garden of Eden. The breeze whispered peaceful songs across the leaves of nearby trees, and the soft scents of summer beguiled Bekah's senses.

This was the time when day transformed into evening and when buried thoughts and feelings rose to the surface. Tonight Bekah had a multitude of them. To her, it seemed more than her fair share. She bowed her head in prayerful contemplation of her current situation, trying not to let the worries of the day distract her from the intense beauty of the sunset before her.[2] She

---

[2] Matthew 6:26

thanked God for all His blessings, His love for her, and the knowledge that her steps were ordered of the Lord. [3]

Bekah was hot and tired. She had been working in the garden since lunch. Sweat trickled down her forehead into her large brown eyes, the salt stinging them and causing tears to run down her troubled face. Her blouse was damp with sweat and covered with dirt.

Gardening was a dirty business. For some reason, weeds seemed to grow better than tomatoes. Her hands and nails were filthy and her face was streaked with dirt. Her back and shoulders reminded her she was no longer a teenager. Bekah was slight of figure, measuring three inches over five feet. She had thick, wavy, dark brown hair, with a scattering of bright silver running through it, even though she was only thirty-seven. She wore it long mostly, flowing free, unless it was very hot or it got in the way as it did today. Gardening and long hair did not co-exist. Today she had gathered it up and twisted it, catching it in a large clip; but soft tendrils had come loose and were plastered to her sweat-streaked face.

Bekah looked down at the large basket she had been carrying. Her efforts in the garden were fruitful, probably due to her praying over it. These days she prayed for and over everything, thanking God continually for His faithfulness.[4] She knew beyond a shadow of a doubt that any success she achieved, large or small, was due first to God's grace, second to her obedience, and third to hard work.

At harvest time most of her tomatoes were bright red, but some were yellow, purple and orange. They were usually blemish

---

[3] Proverbs 20:24
[4] 1 Thessalonians 5:18

free, and varied in size. She also grew the marble sized grape tomatoes that rarely made it to the table. They were so sweet and juicy they tasted like candy, and she usually ate them as they were picked. Medium size Romas that were thick and meaty were used for canning, making spaghetti sauce, salsa, and an array of other things her imagination came up with.

Cooking was one of Bekah's passions, and her garden fed that particular passion. She canned and froze much of her produce and gave away boxes and boxes of it. She had established a mini food bank at her store in town. Times were hard for scores of people, and she felt as though she was making a difference. Many times she would come home and find strangers working in the garden, giving back in whatever way they were able.

She also grew broccoli, zucchini, and various kinds of peppers, eggplant, asparagus, potatoes, peas, cabbage, cucumbers and green beans. Several herbs also grew there which she used very effectively. Having an abundance of rosemary, she cut some to put in a vase. Her whole kitchen would smell of it, a very pleasant smell indeed. Most of tonight's harvest would be left in the enclosed porch, adding to the growing pile of vegetables that needed to be processed. The early crops were coming in. The big harvest would not begin until the end of June. Bekah would usually find something to take in to go with supper, but tonight was different.

Her Nana Sara had finally breathed her last at ninety-five years of age. Her funeral had been this morning. Neighbors and friends had come over after the funeral and had prepared enough food to last Bekah several days. Nana had been loved by many and her funeral had been well attended. Bekah knew almost everyone in attendance, but there had been a few strangers whom she had not had a chance to talk with before they left.

Nana had enjoyed life to its fullest, and spent each day thanking God for all her blessings. She had been alive a long time and did not let go of life easily. Nana had a stroke ten days ago, and had fought death to the very end. Bekah had spent most of the last ten days at Nana's bedside. Bekah had a feeling gnawing at her that Nana was trying to tell her something. Nana couldn't talk or write, she couldn't even scratch her nose, which she had been prone to do when she was thinking. The stroke had left her almost totally paralyzed from the shoulders down, and the ability to speak had also been lost.

Bekah tried reading to Nana to calm and comfort her. She had always loved to hear Bekah's voice, whether talking or singing, but peace appeared to escape her during these last days.

Bekah had begun to sing when she was small child. Memory after memory came flooding back to her of her standing by the piano as Nana played and she sang. Bekah had started singing special music at church when she was only three years old. Nana said she had perfect pitch. Whatever it was, when Bekah sang, people closed their eyes, imagining they were in heaven listening to the angels sing. Today Bekah sang at Nana's funeral. Nana's favorite hymn was "In the Garden" and that melody had been running through Bekah's mind all afternoon as she worked the rich, moist soil. Her tears added additional moisture to it as she progressed up and down row after row of plants.

Bekah had no memory of her parents. She had no recollections of them interacting with her. No memory of hugs or kisses, of trips to the park or bedtime stories. Her parents were killed in a car accident when she was a small child. That's all she

4

knew about them. Their picture sat up on the mantle over the large stone fireplace, but they were strangers to her.

Nana Sara had been there for her as long as her memory reached back; though Nana shared her memories. That was the problem though; they were Nana's memories. They did not elicit any emotional response from Bekah. Through the years, Nana's love became enough. It was just the two of them, and Nana had a lot of love to give. Bekah had never felt deprived.

The whole town had turned out for the funeral this morning. It had been a beautiful, sunny day, just the kind of day that Nana loved. "The hotter, the better," she would say, and she got her wish this morning. For the beginning of June, it had been especially hot, reaching a record ninety degrees. For Maine that was hot; even at the height of the summer.

Most of Nana's friends were already gone; ninety-five was very, very old. Nana had been laid to rest out under her favorite apple tree. As Nana's age took her into her nineties, she had pointed out to Bekah where she wished to be buried, and Bekah took care of all the arrangements necessary to grant that last request. Bekah had stood there thanking God for the breeze running through the trees this morning and for Nana Sara finally being at peace.

Bekah and Nana had lived on the family apple orchard; one hundred acres of softly rolling hills, planted with hundreds of apple trees. There were several varieties and all were wonderful, juicy, sweet and crisp. Just thinking about them made her mouth water.

The church they attended set out a lovely brunch for her and Nana's friends, but it had been a long time since the funeral brunch. As if in agreement with that thought, her stomach let out a long, low growl. There was a tremendous volume of food in the fridge. She remembered the tray of lasagna and thought a salad would go great with it. That would more than satisfy her hunger.

Slowly Bekah got to her feet. She would shower first and then eat. Food was always important to her. She loved to eat and loved to cook, especially for large groups of people. It was very rare that there were just the two of them for dinner. Though having no biological family, she had a large church family, and a small business family who loved her almost as much as Nana did – "No," she reminded herself, "now it was as much as Nana had."

Bekah took care of the orchard and the employees it involved: her foreman, Renato, and several seasonal employees. In addition, she owned and managed a small needlework store in Ogunquit called, "The Eye of the Needle". She had two part-time employees, Roberta and Sylvia. All her employees were considered family; but more than family, they were close friends.

As she thought of the gathering this morning, it had been apparent that it was a celebration of Nana's life, but even the burden of a funeral couldn't dampen Bekah's appetite.

Looking in the basket, Bekah picked out some lettuce and spinach leaves, and a few radishes. She looked forward to later in the season when the tomatoes would be ready to pick. Her mouth watered at the thought of one of the large yellow heirloom tomatoes she had been experimenting with.

She wasn't sure it would tolerate the temperature extremes of coastal Maine or if the bugs would like it too much. She tried to grow as organically as possible, and with the new bug resistant varieties, it was possible, but an heirloom had none of those capabilities and they sometimes needed a little chemical help. She wasn't hard-nosed about it, but preferred to live as chemical-free as possible.

CHAPTER TWO

OGUNQUIT, MAINE
JUNE 5

Bekah stretched to get the kinks out of her sore muscles. She caught sight of a dark sedan parked down the road, wondered whose it was and what it was doing there. No one lived close by and she didn't recognize the car. There weren't many strangers that came through the area, and the orchard was a dead end. It was an area you came to on purpose, not by accident.

Bekah went upstairs to shower off the dirt and sweat of the afternoon. She wished she could wash away the grief that was in her heart, but some stains required special treatment. She asked the Holy Spirit, the Comforter, to help her in her time of grief.[5]

Two hours later, Bekah walked down the stairs, listening to them creak and groan as she descended. Walking into the living room, she glanced up at the mantle. There was a picture of her and Nana taken last year at a local baseball game. Nana had been given the honor of throwing out the first pitch.

Bekah had only meant to shut her eyes for a few minutes, but instead had fallen fast asleep, and had slept for over an hour. This was unusual for her; she wasn't normally a daytime sleeper. What was more unusual was the dream she had. The memory of

---

[5] John 14:16

it was still with her, and her heart was still racing. She didn't often remember her dreams, but this one was fresh and vivid in her mind, as though planted by God.

As she struggled to make sense of the dream, she heard a car driving into the yard. Looking out the window saw that it was the same black sedan that had been parked down the road earlier. She turned on the front light to get a better view of the stranger getting out of the car, since it was now dark and the yard was in deep shadow.

The car door opened and a tall, dark haired man in a somber black suit got out. Bekah remembered him from the funeral. He was one of the people she had not recognized at the time. She had wondered who he was, and why he had been there. Now she wondered why he was here. He walked slowly up to the door, as if giving her time to look him over and evaluate her situation.

"It's strange," she said to herself, "I should be afraid, being all alone now, but I'm not." She opened the door and they stood there looking at each other. No one said a word. The crickets were the only ones making noise at that moment.

Suddenly, he seemed to gather his thoughts and he spoke. "I have a message for you," he said in a low voice, not much more than a whisper, "It concerns the dream you just had."

"How do you know about my dream?" Bekah questioned in a stunned voice. Uneasiness began to grow inside her, bringing fear as a friend.

"Don't be afraid," the man said, as if sensing her response, "I was told to bring you this message from the One who gave you the dream. He said to tell you that He has a plan and purpose for

9

your life and that now was the time for it to come to pass.[6] He said you now have the time, and the means to carry out the call that He has placed on you, and that you were born for such a time as this."[7]

Those were the exact words that she experienced in her dream. Before she could think any further, he began to relate to her more of the substance of her dream. He spoke with such detail; it was almost as if he had dreamed it himself. "You had the same vision Isaiah had. You were in the temple and saw a vision of God and you humbled yourself and confessed your sins. But unlike Isaiah, you did not need to have a coal touch your lips. You have already been cleansed by the shed blood of Jesus,[8] but just as Isaiah said when God asked, 'Who can I send?' you said, 'Send me.'[9] Now that you have agreed to go, God sent me here to tell you that you have been called to a quest. I was also called to support you in wherever this quest takes you, and whatever you will be doing."

Bekah was still standing in the doorway staggered at all he had said to her. Her mind was in such an uproar, that at that moment, she was not capable of coherent speech. He, on the other hand, continued speaking to her, choosing to ignore her silence. "I also had a similar dream. God directed me to come and tell you my dream so that it would be a confirmation to you."

"Stop," Bekah whispered. "This is too much of a shock, too much for me to take in. It's late. I'm tired, I'm hungry, and I need the turmoil inside me to subside a little before we talk about this

---

[6] Jerimiah 29:11
[7] Esther 4:14
[8] Matthew 26:28
[9] Isaiah 6:1-9

dream any further. It's going to take me a few minutes to decide whether to let you in. For all I know, you might have read the obituary in the paper and decided to come and rob me now that I am alone."

The stranger said, "Let me introduce myself. My name is Joshua Randall and I'm from Claremore, Oklahoma. I want to tell you that you're not alone. God said in His Word He would never leave you or forsake you.[10] He also said He's closer than a brother."[11]

Joshua paused and Bekah relented. "Well, I can't leave you standing on the steps Mr. Randall. You might as well come in."

Bekah stood aside and let the stranger enter, her mind still reeling from the shock of what he had said. He followed her into the kitchen and sat down in the chair she indicated. She sat down and looked over at him. "Well, Mr. Randall, what else do you have to say for yourself?"

---

[10] Hebrews 13:5
[11] Proverbs 18:24

CHAPTER THREE

OGUNQUIT, MAINE
JUNE 5

Speaking quietly he reiterated, "As I said, my name is Joshua Randall and I'm forty-six years old. I was born and raised in a small town outside of Tulsa, Oklahoma, called Claremore. I attended Oral Roberts University and graduated with a Master's degree in Biblical Studies and Sociology. I have been on staff at a local church in Claremore, and head of their Mission's Department for the last five years. During that time I have put together and led three trips to the Amazon region of South America, and two trips into Paraguay. I wrote my doctoral thesis on unreached people groups of South America." Joshua paused and looked carefully at Bekah, assessing her response to the information he had related thus far.

Determining that she was still attentive and appeared willing to listen, he continued with his story. "In both our dreams, we were told by God that He had received an urgent call for help from a young woman who was a member of a desperate tribe of people living in the South American jungle. They appeared to be under attack from evil forces and were crying out for help. Our God heard their call and has decided that the fullness of time has come,[12] and since we volunteered to go, He would take us up on our offer."

As Joshua paused to take a breath, Bekah cried out in an outraged and indignant voice, "What do you mean I volunteered to go? All I did was have a dream! Granted, it was a terrible nightmare, but nightmares can't be from God. They bring fear and God

doesn't do that. He brings love. In addition, volunteering in a dream doesn't count, and my dream had more to it than that. Terrible things happened in my dream, things I would just as soon forget. I want to get rid of the fear, not dwell on it. I never said I would go anywhere."

Trying not to lose control, Bekah closed her eyes, leaned over, and put her head in her hands, seeking answers to the scenario being presented to her. She whispered a short prayer. "Lord, I know You said You would never allow anything to test us more than we can bear, but this seems to be an exception.[13] Was this dream really from You?"

Suddenly, in the depth of her being, a gentle voice whispered, "Be still and know that I am God."[14]

"How can this be God?" she argued with herself, "God wouldn't ask me to do this. I've never even been on a mission trip. Surely there is someone more qualified than I am to fill this position."[15]

Again the voice spoke, but louder, and more compelling. "Be still and know that I am God."

---

[12] Matthew 24
[13] 1 Corinthians 10:13
[14] Psalm 46:10
[15] 2 Timothy 3:16-17

"God," Bekah cried out from the depth of her being, "If this really is You, You are going to have to do more than speak to me in my head. I'm going to need some pretty convincing confirmation that this is all true, and that I'm not just paranoid. I don't want to believe this, but if this dream really did come from you, I don't have a choice. I must obey."[16]

---

[16] 2 Corinthians 13:1

CHAPTER FOUR

OGUNQUIT, MAINE

JUNE 5

As Joshua sat and listened to her cry for help, there was an unexpected knock on the door. Bekah jumped, startled at the interruption. Getting up, she walked into the hallway, wondering who could be knocking at this hour. She opened the door and was surprised to see Renato standing there.

Renato was the foreman of the apple orchard, and he had worked there as long as Bekah could remember. In a way, he was the father she never had. When she was little, she took all her problems to him. His was the arm she leaned on and the shoulder she cried on. He was like a member of her family.

She loved this older man and valued his counsel. Nana's death had been as much a blow to him as it was to her. At times, Nana had been jealous of Bekah's relationship with Renato, but Nana was too good a person to let jealousy infringe upon it.

Now Renato stood at the door, his dark eyes troubled. He was running his hand through his thick gray hair and chewing on the stem of his ever present pipe. She inhaled the familiar smell of the tobacco. Its rich aroma seemed to settle upon her and bring her a measure of peace, just as it had done when she was a child; for that alone, she welcomed his intrusion.

"I'm sorry to bother you Miss Bekah," he said quietly. "I saw that you had company, but I needed to come speak with you right away. This could not wait."

Bekah wondered what could be so urgent that it couldn't wait until morning. "Come in, come in and tell me what's troubling you." Bekah worried that at sixty-seven, the work at the orchard might be more than Renato could handle. Was the strain of it all beginning to show and she had just refused to see it?

"Miss Bekah," he began, "I was watching television, trying to relax after the funeral, and fell asleep. I didn't sleep long, but while asleep, I had a very unusual dream. I dreamt I saw God in His temple. He called to me and said He needed my help. He said you needed my help, and that I should come see you right away. God also showed me other things in the dream, some that were very troubling. I don't understand what He wants us to do."

Stunned, Bekah stood in the doorway for a moment not knowing how to respond. In more turmoil than she had ever been in her life, she grabbed Renato's arm and pulled him into the kitchen. Pointing her finger, she raised her voice in frustration. "This is Joshua Randall. He showed up here this evening claiming he had a dream from God four days ago. He advised me God sent him to confirm the dream I had this afternoon. God asked him to find me and help me get started with a quest that He has called us to. Did you hear that? God has given us a quest. At first I thought my dream was just a by-product of stress and sadness. All of us have had strange dreams at one time or another. Then Mr. Randall shows up and relates his dream to me, which comes as kind of a shock. I was still unwilling to believe and asked God to give me some kind of confirmation. Now, here you are with the same dream. I guess we are all going to have to sit down and resolve whether God is speaking to us, and if He is, which seems to be the case, what is He saying?"

As Bekah sat down at the kitchen table again, trying to untangle her fears and emotions, the phone began to ring. "What now?" Bekah thought. "I'm going to let the answering machine pick it up," she said. "Too much is happening all at once and I don't want to talk to anyone else. I don't need any more stress tonight."

Then she heard a loud voice shout over the answering machine. "Bekah, Bekah, are you there?"

Bekah stared at the phone in shock. She hadn't heard this voice in a long time, but recognized it immediately. It was the voice of Ted, her ex-husband. She may not have seen him in almost ten years, but some things you never forget.

They had married young, both unbelievers at the time. They had each been searching for fulfillment and Bekah thought they were looking for the same thing. She found hers in her faith, in dedicating her life to God. Ted found his in high finance. He wanted to get rich, and dedicated his life to that purpose.

Bekah had thought maybe it was her new faith in God that had caused the rift in their marriage. Maybe Ted was jealous of time spent away from him while she went to church, bible studies and prayer meetings. But it wasn't that. He rarely noticed she was gone. He had another god he worshipped. He put all his time, effort and imagination into attaining wealth, and he was very successful at it. So successful that it became his god. He loved money and thought about it constantly. He thought about how much he had, how much more he wanted, and how he was going to acquire it.[17] Finally, he just stopped thinking about her completely.

They had a quiet divorce. Bekah didn't want anything from him, except to get over her hurt and rejection. Out of guilt, Ted wrote Bekah a $100,000 check to help her start a business and support herself. Her little needlework store, "The Eye of the Needle," was the result. It had been a good investment, and she had done very well with it.

Bekah's mind, having taken a quick trip back in time, was jolted back to the present by hearing Ted continue to yell, "Bekah! Bekah! For God's sake, if you're home, will you pick up the phone and answer me. Bekah! Bekah!" he shouted louder, "Answer me, it's important! God told me to call you. I'm supposed to tell you about this strange dream I had!"

Bekah couldn't have been more stunned than if a van pulled up and told her she had won the Publisher's Clearing House Sweepstakes. "OK God, thank You for the confirmation," she said to herself, "but this is turning into a real mess, especially if Ted is involved."

Ted was still there and still hollering into the phone, "Please answer me!"

Bekah picked up the phone. "I haven't said anything to you yet because I don't know what to say. You're the fourth person to have a strange dream, myself included. I don't know what is happening, but people seem to be having similar dreams from God and He is referring them to me. I just can't talk to you now. I have too much to think about and it's been a long day. Call me tomorrow morning and we'll talk. Maybe, by then, I'll know more about what's happening. I've got to go. I promise we'll talk

---

[17] 1 Timothy 6:10

tomorrow." As a side thought Bekah added, "We buried Nana today, in case you didn't know."

Bekah hung up the phone before Ted could reply. She knew it was rude, but social niceties were the last thing on her mind. Why would he have a similar dream? This certainly can't be from God if he's involved. Bekah brooded, but only for a moment. She still had Renato and a Mr. Joshua Randall to deal with and she was exhausted, both emotionally and physically.

As she walked back into the kitchen, Bekah's mind was still on Ted's phone call until she realized that both Mr. Randall and Renato were talking quietly. Without further thought she assumed they were talking about her. All her insecurities were on high alert after talking with Ted. She charged into the kitchen looking for a fight.

"Wait just a minute!" she said with a raised voice; her temper finally surfaced. It had been held in check all evening due to the seriousness of the topics they were discussing and the fact that God was involved in the events. It is not a good idea to lose your temper when you're dealing with God. You might say something you will regret later. But her frustration level was over the top and she threw caution to the wind.

"It seems to me," Bekah fumed, "that given the nature of what is being discussed, you should both wait to include me in the conversation instead of talking about me. You both have been sent here to help me, and before anyone makes any kind of decision or determination about what is going on, I need to be involved. I just got off the phone with Ted, my ex-husband, and it seems as though he had a similar dream also. Before we go any further, I want a few more questions answered."

Bekah paused to take a breath and Renato broke in and said, "Miss Bekah, we were not talking about you, we were praying for you."

All the bluster left her like a deflated balloon and Bekah was immediately contrite. Bekah sat down and apologized. Then she opened her heart and voiced her fears. "It's difficult for me to tell you about the rest of my dream. I'm not making excuses about my behavior, but the dream really scared me. The thoughts it evoked brought fear to my heart. I'll describe my dream to both of you and then you can tell me what you think.

"I dreamed of a jungle village that had come under attack by a large warlike tribe. A significant number of warriors from the attacking tribe were herding a small group of women toward a roaring fire that had been started as soon as the attack began. All the women had small babies in their arms. The women were screaming and clutching their babies while they fought to escape. It was as if they knew what was going to take place next. The warriors, indifferent to their struggles, held them in place with their spears. The rest of the village was contained on the other side of the fire. They were also struggling and fighting, but they had no weapons and the long spears of the attackers kept them at bay also. It appeared as though several of them had already been killed. There were a number of bodies lying on the ground.

"Just then a large and powerful man in a painted mask came forward and spoke to all the people that were assembled. I could not understand what he said, but his words reverberated through the crowd."

Bekah paused and looked up at Joshua and Renato. There were tears running down her face. "This dream was bad enough when I thought it was just a nightmare. But now that I believe it was a dream from God I have the horrifying feeling that the things I saw in the dream were real. All the babies were ripped from their mother's arms and brought before the man in the mask. He performed what appeared to be a religious ritual over the babies and then they were thrown into the fire."

Bekah shuddered. Breathing deeply, she tried to maintain her composure. Her heart was racing and the horror of what she had seen was causing her to sob. Renato reached over and took her hand, giving what comfort he could. Bekah took another deep, shuddering breath and continued. "The screams started to die down as shock set in. Then a group of warriors moved through all the dwellings, searching them for anything of value. When they had finished, they set fire to the whole village and left behind a people bereft of hope."

Bekah finished and her control broke. She began to sob inconsolably. Renato stood her up and wrapped his arms around her, speaking to her in a low voice. He too had tears running down his face. "I understand what you are feeling sweet Bekah. It seems a burden too heavy to bear. Maybe that is why Joshua and I are here. I don't know about him, but I had a dream so similar it could not be a coincidence. It breaks my heart thinking about it. If God is somehow calling us to help in this situation I don't know what else we can do but volunteer. Joshua, would I be wrong in assuming that your dream was very similar?"

Joshua stared at both Renato and Bekah with a very sober expression. "You're right. I had the same dream. Something terrible appears to have happened, and for some reason God has asked us to help."

CHAPTER FIVE

OGUNQUIT, MAINE
JUNE 5

Joshua began to share his story. "I had my dream four days ago. Bekah, God told me you lived near the southern Maine coast, and that the ancient guardian, whom I discovered was your grandmother, Sara Zangersen, had just died. God said, 'Now was the time for her charge to come forth and take up the call He had put on her life.' I had to figure out the rest. I didn't even know your name." Joshua paused and considered what to say next. "You have to realize that this dream was a shock to me also. I feel that God has spoken to me before on several occasions, but never like this, and never with so much mystery. Before, He had always been pretty specific about who, what, when, where and why. Well not always why. I don't necessarily need to know all that, but this dream and the fact that I had to search you out, really had me confused. The full content of the dream left me in turmoil. I've never been placed in a situation like this. I'm glad that we have confirmation from some other people that this is genuine."

"Thank you." Bekah acknowledged. "I have to apologize again. I wasn't thinking of anyone else's confusion and concern. I was just focusing on mine. Why don't we try to relax a little and eat some supper?" Bekah dished out some of the reheated leftovers and turned to serve them. Renato went to sit down at the table and then stopped. "What's the matter?" Bekah asked.

"I just saw Joshua sitting in Nana Sara's chair. With all the turmoil of the dream, I forgot about Nana Sara. The realization just hit me that it's not her chair anymore. We won't be having her special chocolate cake or fried chicken on Sundays anymore. We won't hear her humming, or playing the piano ever again. On a nice day, with the windows open, I would sometimes hear her play and you sing. I will miss that so much," Renato said with a sigh. "Even though she was old, she was still such a powerful presence in this house."

"I know," Bekah agreed, "I can't believe she's gone. I have no one now. I have no family."

Renato went over and stood looking down at her. He took her hands in his, and in a voice filled with love, he said, "Miss Bekah, you have always been part of my life. Now, if you will have me, I will become your family, and I pledge my life to you. I also have no one now but you. In a way, Nana Sara was like a mother to me. Now, I will be a father to you and you will be my daughter. I could not love you any more, even if you were a daughter of my flesh." Renato took Bekah into his loving arms and she sobbed upon his shoulder, just as she had done as a child. Now, just as then, he comforted her.

Bekah raised her head from Renato's shoulder and said, "I don't know how bad your week has been Mr. Randall, but both Renato and I have just buried a loved one and then had this horrifying dream. If I can speak for us, we're both spent. Let's just finish our meal and we'll deal with the rest of this tomorrow." They all sat down and began to eat in the silence of the room; the noise of their thoughts, scattered as they were, sounded loud in their heads.

"I understand the stress you have both been through, but please, call me Josh or Joshua," he said. "It's been a strange and stressful week for me also, so I'll be on my way. I was staying in Ogunquit, but checked out of the motel this morning. I thought if I needed it, I could get a room closer to you and your orchard. If you can give me directions to a nearby motel, I'll come back in the morning."

Bekah thought a moment, considering options, and then said, "Josh, I have a spare room. It's kind of unusual, but given the circumstances, you're welcome to spend the night. Then we will all be here in the morning to talk and plan."

"No", Renato interrupted, "That would not be right for him to stay here, but he can spend the night at my house. I have a spare room also."

"Alright," Bekah relented, "But I'll have breakfast here at eight o'clock. I don't understand all that is happening, but I have come to the realization that God is indeed calling us, and we need to hear exactly what He wants, and we need to do exactly what He has called us to do." She paused and asked softly, "Could we join hands and pray for God to lead and guide us in this endeavor?"[18]

After the prayer, the two men left and Bekah breathed a sigh of relief. She rubbed her neck and stretched her back, trying to work out the kinks and relieve the stress she had been feeling all night. She walked into the kitchen and turned off the coffee pot. She poured herself the last cup, not really wanting it, but she needed something to sip on while she tried to digest the happenings of the day and clean up the kitchen.

---

[18] Proverbs 3:6

It seemed so improbable that these things could be happening to her, but the fact that four people had had similar dreams of God calling them to action could not be ignored. She tried to think of a reason, other than the obvious, but nothing seemed to come to mind. Finally she got up and put the dishes in the dishwasher, rinsed out the coffee pot, and went up to bed. She didn't see how she would be able to sleep with so much turmoil rattling around inside her head.

The sounds of the soft spring night could not shut out the grief and emptiness she felt inside. Nana was gone and would not be coming back. Even the house seemed to groan in sorrow, aware that something or someone was missing.

Bekah knelt beside the bed to pray; something she was prone to do in times of great stress and confusion. "Dear God, I know Your Word says that all things work together for good, [19]but I don't see how any good can come of this. Please take the sorrow from my heart and the fear from my mind.[20] My desire is to serve You and only You. The Bible says that David encouraged himself in the Lord in a time of stress and great sorrow.[21] I need to do the same." Bekah took a breath and began to sing one of her favorite Christian songs and the melody and lyrics ministered to her grieving spirit.

She stood up and went over to the window. There was no moon, but it was a clear night and twinkling diamonds littered the sky. She stood there a moment and took in the beauty of God's creation. Then she walked over to her bed and lay down. She immediately sank into a deep and restful slumber.

---

[19] Romans 8:28
[20] 2 Timothy 1:7
[21] 1 Samuel 30:1-6

25

CHAPTER SIX

OGUNQUIT, MAINE

JUNE 6

Bekah opened her eyes to a room full of sunshine. If birdsong was a harbinger of what kind of day it would be, then today would be glorious. The birds were in rare form, and Bekah listened to them as they warbled, chirped and tweeted in a harmonious cacophony of song. She didn't know the words but tried to whistle with them, and smiled at the attempt until she caught sight of the clock on the nightstand. It was almost seven-thirty. Oversleeping was not usually a problem for her. She rarely used an alarm, but it appeared that today was an exception. Grabbing some clean clothes, she sprinted down the hall to take a quick shower.

At ten-till-eight, Bekah entered the kitchen with her wet hair still up in a towel. As she put water in the coffee pot, she heard a car come into the yard. "Just my luck," she thought. "They're early and I don't have anything ready." Bekah went to unlock the back door and let them in, thinking it was Renato and Joshua. She looked out the window, and a strange car was rolling up the drive. The dark windows prevented her from immediately recognizing the person in the car. To her surprise and chagrin, it was Ted getting out of the car. Bekah couldn't have been more shocked or irritated.

"Just what do you think you're doing here?" she asked crossly. Of all the people in the world she did not want to see, he would be in the top ten. She had not seen him for almost ten years, although she had spoken to him briefly several times. Given their history, and the current circumstances, he was more trouble than she wanted to deal with. She frowned at him as he walked toward the house.

He hadn't changed much since the last time she had seen him. She remembered it well. He had purchased his divorce with a one hundred thousand dollar check. He was still tall, dark, and handsome, except for his hair. It was completely silver. It somehow made him appear more caring and compassionate; whether he was or not remained to be seen.

Ted was getting his first impression of Bekah also. He took in her appearance and her posture and thought, "She looks great." His next thought was, "She's still mad at me," and he was right.

He reached out to hug her and she stepped back abruptly, "You haven't answered my question, what are you doing here? I told you I would call you this morning."

Ted started to reply, and then stopped. Another car was coming into the yard. He watched silently as it approached. Two men got out. He recognized one as Renato, but he did not know the other. Renato stood still for a moment as if deciding what to do, and then he came over and put out his hand. "It's been a long time Ted," he said.

Ted shook his hand and said, "Yes, but strange circumstances seem to have brought us back together again. It's good to see you Renato. The years don't seem to have touched you. You're looking very well."

Renato looked Ted over and replied, "You look to be in good shape, but you hair tells a story also. Have the years been hard?"

"No harder than most people experience. They've just been lonely," Ted replied.

Bekah drew in a breath, shocked by the admission she had just heard. Ted had never been one to share his feelings. Transparency was not one of his attributes. This was a side of him she had never seen before. She decided to say nothing. There was no sense in bringing up old issues. She had enough on her plate right now without dredging up the past. Bekah turned to Joshua who had been standing silently by the side of the car. "Ted, I want to introduce you to Joshua Randall. Joshua, this is my ex-husband Ted Ryan.

"Joshua was the first person to have this dream. I had it yesterday evening. Then I found out Renato had it also, and then you. Joshua stayed at Renato's last night. We were all going to meet at eight for breakfast, but I overslept, hence the towel." Then she whipped the towel off her head and shook out her long, dark hair.

Bekah led the way into the kitchen. "Why don't all of you come inside? Renato, you know where things are, will you start the coffee while I at least comb my hair and brush my teeth?" Without waiting for a reply, Bekah then turned and started back up the stairs.

Feeling refreshed, she went back down, but paused a moment to listen to the conversation taking place in the kitchen. Renato was asking Ted what he had been doing for the last ten years. Ted's response surprised her. "I was searching for something, I don't know what. But in the process I made quite a lot of money. I also finally realized that money doesn't always buy you happiness. I own a house in the Rockies, and a condo in New York City and Miami, a boat, three cars and the airplane I flew over on. I should be perfectly happy and I'm not. I don't know why I'm spilling my guts out to you. Let's just chalk it up to lack of sleep."

Bekah walked into the room and silence fell. She looked at each one of them and said, "Well I hope someone has made himself useful. Is there coffee?" Immediately, all three of them began to apologize at once.

"Oh Miss Bekah, I'm sorry, we got to talking and I forgot," Renato said sheepishly.

"Bekah, I was so busy listening that I forgot too," Ted said.

Joshua just shrugged and said, "No excuses, I'll make it next time."

Bekah cooked and the men attempted to get acquainted, asking small polite questions of each other, but nothing of consequence. While she was putting the food on the table she asked Renato if he would ask the blessing. They all joined hands and he prayed, "Heavenly Father, we come to You today, asking You to bless our time together. We ask for clarification of the dreams we have all had. We ask for guidance in what we are to do, and for understanding, patience and faith. Thank You for blessing this food and nourishing us with it. In Jesus' name we pray, Amen."

And each in turn said, "Amen."

Breakfast was a quiet affair. Ted asked about Nana and what had happened. He apologized for not keeping in better touch and said it would not be that way in the future. "Thank you," Bekah said, but didn't look up from her plate.

Joshua basically sat and observed the interaction between everyone. He had learned over the years that listening and observing provided as much, if not more information, than having questions answered. The trouble with questions was that you needed to know the right ones to ask.

CHAPTER SEVEN

OGUNQUIT, MAINE
JUNE 6

After clearing away the dishes, Bekah poured everyone a second cup of coffee and they turned their attention to the subject all of them seemed to have been avoiding. Bekah spoke first. "From what I gather, we have all had a dream that has brought us together." Before she could continue, the doorbell rang. "What now?" Bekah thought in exasperation.

Bekah looked out the window and saw Roberta and Sylvia, her friends and employees at her store, and Roberta's husband, Joe. "Looks like we have more company," Bekah said with a sigh, "and I'm afraid to guess why."

Bekah went to answer the door. An anxious group of people stood there and Roberta began to speak nervously, "Bekah, we're sorry to bother you this morning, especially after seeing you have company, but we had to come. This just couldn't wait."

"Don't tell me," Bekah interrupted, "Let me guess. You have all had a strange dream." The three of them stood there dumbfounded. They had not been prepared for this response. "You might as well come in and join the party. You're not the only ones having strange dreams. It seems God is putting together an unlikely team of players. We're just going to have to figure out what we're doing, where we're going, and how we're going to get there; a few of the minor details God has yet to reveal to us." Bekah paused as she surveyed the situation and then said, "Why don't the three of you go into the living room and sit down, and I'll get the others from the kitchen."

She walked back into the kitchen and asked, "Renato, would you and Joshua bring in two more chairs from the kitchen? It appears we have more company, and if I'm not mistaken, more dreams."

Walking back into the living room Bekah said, "I guess we need to make introductions, and then we need to share our stories and our dreams. Seven people seem to have had what appears to be a God dream. All of which, if things hold true to course, have amazing similarities. Also, everyone's dream seems to have a common denominator." Bekah paused and took a deep breath. She looked around at everyone and then uttered one word, "Me."

Bekah began, "I had my dream yesterday evening, and in it, just like Isaiah, I saw God. He told me about a South American tribe crying out for help. He asked me, 'Who shall I send?' and just like Isaiah, I said, 'Send me.' Now it's good and well to volunteer to go, but the question is to go where? Also, given the content of the dream, what does He want us to do? Now my question to all of you is what did God show you in this dream and what did He ask you to do? Please," Bekah asked in a subdued voice, "tell me about your dreams." Bekah stood there looking at everyone, knowing something like a miracle had taken place concerning their dreams, but unsure of all the particulars and the consequences.

The room was quiet for two heartbeats, and then everyone began to speak at once. A dream from God is an extraordinary thing, but when seven people have the same dream it's miraculous. The question now was how were they to proceed?

Bekah looked around the room at each person sitting there and her organizational skills kicked in. She held up her hands and said, "Wait a minute everyone. Let's stay calm. First, I'd like to ask each of you to introduce yourself. Not all of us know each other and this will help pave the way for us to work together as a team. Also, please share your version of the dream and what you think God was saying to you." She paused and looked at Joshua. "Since you had the dream first, please tell us what God showed you."

Joshua stood up and took a moment to look at each person sitting there. He wondered what God would have him say; then he decided to ask. He bowed his head and said in earnest prayer, "Heavenly Father, I don't understand all of what is happening here, but I do understand that it is urgent, and that You have brought us all together for what looks like a monumental task. I pray now for peace, understanding, and clarity of thought. I believe You have brought us together to advance Your Kingdom. I believe we are to fight the fight You have put before us, and to put on the armor of God. I believe we are to take a stand in the name of Jesus."[22] Joshua paused and looked up at everyone. "I would ask everyone to say 'Amen' with me if you are in agreement." And everyone did.

"My name is Joshua Randall. My friends call me Josh and I hope you will also. I was raised in a small town about thirty miles north of Tulsa, Oklahoma, called Claremore. I went to Oral Roberts University and did my doctoral thesis on unreached

---

[22] Ephesians 6:10-18

33

people groups. I am on staff at a local church in Claremore as head of their Mission's Department. During the last five years, I have led five mission trips to South America. Three of them were in the Amazon area, and two into the northeast jungles of Paraguay. While down there, we organized medical clinics, and built schools and churches. We've had a fair amount of success and I think we gained the respect and acceptance of the indigenous tribes we encountered." Josh paused and asked, "any questions so far?"

Ted raised a hand, "Yeah, I've got one. How did you fund these mission trips and how many people went?"

"Good question," Josh said. "We had anywhere from five to twenty-five people, depending upon our agenda. These trips were funded by garage sales, bake sales, assorted other fund raisers, and letters to friends, neighbors, and relatives. We asked for their support financially and in prayer. The church bought my plane tickets, but I had to fund everything else myself. I also work part-time as a contractor/builder, doing repairs, remodeling, and anything else that comes my way. Does that answer your question?"

"For now," Ted said with a thoughtful expression on his face. Even though he knew some of the people in the room, he had not seen or spoken to them for many years. Ted was sure their protective natures were fully engaged concerning Bekah. He had hurt Bekah with the divorce, and he was certain none of them had forgotten that.

Josh continued on, "I had my dream on June first, four days before everyone else. I guess the reason for that was so I could make my way to Maine and find Bekah. I believe I had the same dream most of you had. I had Isaiah's vision, of seeing God in His temple, asking 'Who can I send?' Naturally, when God looks at you and asks for a volunteer your response is, or should be the same as Isaiah's, 'Send me.'[23] I assume we have all been drafted into God's army, and there's no going to Canada to avoid it. The last person I know of who was a draft dodger from God ended up in the belly of a great fish.[24] So I thought it wise to volunteer also.

"As you were told in the dream, God received an urgent call from a young woman who was a member of a desperate tribe of people living in the South American jungle. In the dream they appeared to be under attack from evil forces and were crying out for help. God is calling us to be an answer to their prayers. Just as the apostle Paul had a dream, and was called to go to Macedonia, this appears to be our Macedonian Call.[25] Bekah, Renato and Ted all had their dreams yesterday." Josh looked over at Roberta, Joe and Sylvia and asked, "Did you have your dreams yesterday or last night?"

As one voice they answered, "Last night."

"I did not know Bekah," Josh said, "and God did not tell me her name when I had my dream, but He gave me a clue. He said, 'The ancient guardian is dead and now is the time for her charge to come forth. In Maine you will find your companions for this quest. Tell the one to whom I have specifically sent you that I have a plan for her life, and that now is the time to put it into play.' Bekah, God said that you now have the time and the means to launch the mission to which He has called you. You are to go forth in His power and might and set the captives free.[26]

---

[23] Isaiah 6:1-9
[24] Book of Jonah
[25] Acts 16:9-10
[26] Luke 4:18-19

"So I got tickets to Portland the next day and began my search. Thank God for the internet. I began searching the obituaries for recent deaths of people of extreme age. There were only three this week, and only Sara Zangersen fit the criteria. I read Bekah was next of kin. I'm sorry I intruded on the funeral Bekah, but I wanted a chance to see you before I approached you with my message. The rest I think you all know. If there are any questions, I'll try to answer them; if not, maybe Bekah should be next."

No one seemed to want to ask any more questions. Most people seemed to be operating on information overload, so Bekah stood up. She took a deep breath and began to speak, "Most of you know me pretty well, but I'll give Josh a little background. I was born outside of Los Angeles thirty-seven years ago. When I was two, my parents were both killed in an accident and Nana Sara came out to get me and took me home with her to Maine. I went through grade school and high school locally and then went to a small college just a short distance north of here. I graduated with a Master's Degree in Social Science. Ted and I married as soon as I graduated and divorced almost five years later." Bekah paused and looked towards Ted. "Anything you want to add to that?" she inquired.

He just shook his head, "No", not wanting to take a chance of saying the wrong thing and stirring up feelings that he hoped would stay buried.

Bekah continued on, "Concerning the dream. I had my dream the afternoon Nana was buried. Just as Josh said, I also had a vision of God in my dream and He asked me the same question, 'Who can I send?'

"There was a second part of my dream, and also Josh's and Renato's. It concerned a tribe of people that were being attacked by another larger tribe. This larger tribe was taking the infant children of the smaller tribe and offering them in a burnt sacrifice to their god."

Bekah looked at the group questioningly, "Have all of you experienced this part of the dream? If you have, it just confirms the necessity of our acting on what we know in order to answer the call God appears to have given us."

Bekah looked around and everyone seemed to be nodding yes, their eyes wide with worry and confusion.

"I'm sure this must be a shock to all of you; it certainly was to me. Let me share with you my dream, the whole dream, and then we can open everything up for discussion."

Bekah took a calming breath and repeated the part of the dream about seeing God in His temple. Then she began the story of the attack on the small village and the sacrifice of all the babies in the tribe. She did not look at anyone as she described the events she witnessed in her dream. She heard Renato praying for her quietly, and felt his comforting hand on her shoulder. Bekah could not stop the tears from falling. It appeared she was not alone in her sorrow. She heard quiet weeping and looked around at all the people gathered together. Everyone's face was wet with tears. After finishing the tale, she turned and asked Renato if he would pray and ask God's help in dealing with the emotional trauma everyone seemed to be experiencing because of the horror of the dream.

Renato did not move from her side, but squeezed her shoulder. He stood quietly with his head bowed for a moment before he began to speak. "Heavenly Father, for some reason we all don't understand, You have called the group of us on a quest. You have shown us a very disturbing dream concerning a tribe of people in a distant jungle who have been attacked. A sacrilege, an abomination, has been committed against them. Their babies were ripped from their mother's arms and sacrificed to evil gods. This is so horrifying to us that we are traumatized by the thought of it. We need Your help to come together and coordinate some sort of plan. Help us Lord to understand what this dream means and what You require of us. Also Lord we ask for Your peace to come upon us, to drive away the fear the enemy has tried to bring. Thank You Lord for all You do in our lives. In Jesus' name we pray. Amen."

Everyone just stayed where they were and welcomed the presence of God. Finally Bekah spoke up. "Well we've overcome a huge hurdle. I'm glad we know that God is with us and that we are not alone in this endeavor. Renato would like to speak next. Most of you know him, but Josh doesn't know any of us."

Renato stood up next and began to speak, "As Bekah said, most of you have known me for years. Josh spent the night, and we talked a great deal. I can tell all of you that though I don't know him well, God has shown me his heart, and I believe we can safely put our trust in him. As for me, I've been at this farm since before Miss Bekah was born. In fact, I was at her parents' wedding."

Bekah's head came up abruptly and she took in a quick breath of surprise. "Renato, you never told me that. Did you know my dad?"

Renato answered, "He was just a boy when I came to first work at the apple farm and I was a teenager. I watched him grow up. Did you know he met your mother while he was a missionary

38

in Paraguay? He married her there, but when they came back for a visit, Nana Sara wanted them to have a wedding here. In fact, they were married near the tree where Nana Sara is buried."

"Renato, why didn't you ever tell me this? I've always been curious about my mom and dad but no one has ever been able or willing to tell me anything about them." Bekah looked at him searchingly.

"Bekah, your grandmother made me promise not to talk to you about your parents. She wouldn't say why, just that she had her reasons. She was always very secretive about your parents and their death. I don't know why. Maybe you'll find out some information from all the papers she has in her desk."

Nana Sara's desk was like a museum, or maybe a time capsule. There were so many compartments and drawers full of papers, pictures and documents. "I'm sorry I never said anything to you, but I gave my word to Nana Sara. Maybe I can help you go through the desk and some of the contents may help answer any questions you have."

Bekah looked up and realized everyone was watching and listening to their conversation. "I'm sorry for interrupting, but this was such a shock. Renato, do you have anything else you want to say? You didn't say much about your dream."

Renato shook his head and said, "No, my dream was basically the same as yours. God told me of people needing help, and showed me the babies being sacrificed. God said He was sending you, but you would need help also. He asked if I would go and I said, 'Yes'.

"Miss Bekah. I told you already that I am pledging my life to you and that I would be the father you never had. I will go with you and try to protect you from any harm. With God's help I will succeed."

Bekah got up and walked over to Renato. She reached up and hugged him with tears running down her face. "I have always loved you and can't thank you enough for your support. I'm so glad God asked you to come with me."

CHAPTER EIGHT

OGUNQUIT, MAINE

JUNE 6

Bekah looked around the room and saw that everyone was touched by the intensity of the moment. She stood up and said, "Why don't we listen to one more person and then take a break. I'll make a pot of coffee and put out something to go with it." She looked around. "Who wants to be next?"

Sylvia stood and said, "I think it should be me. Let me introduce myself to those of you who don't know me. My name is Sylvia and I have worked with Bekah at her store "The Eye of the Needle" for several years. Not only do we work together, but we go to church together. I think that she would agree that we are more family than friends.

My dream was a little different. I also saw the sacrifices and they were terrifying then, but even more so now because I believe they were not just a dream, but reality. God told me of your dreams also, and the quest you will be going on, but He didn't ask me to go. He said that I should remain here and be your anchor, that I should be the one you keep in touch with here in the States. If you need anything I can make arrangements to get it to you. I will need to be in contact with you on a regular basis. I will also need to gather several friends I know who will commit to pray with me daily while you are away." Sylvia looked over at

Bekah and added, "Miss Bekah, I've worked for you for almost five years and we've spent a lot of time together. I feel like we have become very close friends. I want you to know that you are always in my prayers, so it won't be hard praying for you and everyone else involved in this quest. It's one of the things I do best. Also, it looks like all my computer experience will pay off while I shop for you, purchase tickets, or research any questions you may have."

Bekah got up again and went over and hugged Sylvia, "I appreciate your friendship Sylvia, and all your prayers. You are an inspiration to the rest of us."

Josh stood and looked over at Bekah and said, "This would be a good time for a break. We need to get something to eat and drink and then come back and continue."

Bekah nodded and said, "I still have a ton of food in the fridge Sylvia. Would you help me put some of the food out?" Sylvia smiled and she and Bekah went into the kitchen. Everyone else stood up and stretched. Most of them stayed inside and spoke quietly, but Josh and Ted walked out the back door. They walked to the corner of the yard where one of the giant sentinels stood, spilling its shade. They sat on a couple of rocks that had been pushed up through the soil by the massive tree roots.

Both were quiet for a few moments, listening to the wind rustle through the trees and the extraordinary symphony performed by the birds. Each bird played a different instrument, making up the orchestra that entertained them. Then Ted spoke first. "I'm having a hard time with all this. I can see why God has called all these people. He knows them and they know Him. I barely know Him, I don't know how to pray, and I know that Bekah doesn't want me here. I hurt her tremendously during our marriage and subsequent divorce. She must still hate me, and I definitely know she hasn't forgiven me."

Josh looked at Ted, and felt compassion rise up inside him. He saw the remorse on Ted's face and felt his sorrow for the pain and suffering he had caused. Just from casual observation, he could see that Bekah was definitely not happy about Ted's involvement with this quest. He felt that there was some healing that needed to take place in both of them and that maybe he could help facilitate that. "Do you know Ted that God has a plan for your life? He says that it's a good plan meant to prosper you. [27] Sometimes because of mistakes, failures, and sin in our life, we take a the wrong way around. But if we are truly seeking to do what's right and follow God, we eventually get where we need to be. I believe this is God's plan for your life, that He is leading and guiding you just like He is the rest of us. I believe that Bekah will come to recognize that also. Would you like me to pray for you?"

"Why would you want to?" Ted asked warily, "What's in it for you?"

Josh paused before he spoke. He could see and hear the hurt and defensiveness in Ted's words and posture. Then he replied, "I need you on the team. If God gave you that dream, then He needs you on the team. If He needs you, then we can't succeed without you. We'd be like a car with only three wheels.

"Understand Ted, we all need prayer. We all suffer from fear, past failures, and insecurities. It was very hard for me to come here and initiate this quest, but I didn't have a choice, and unfortunately, neither do you. You can fight it all you want, but you have been called. If you don't volunteer, you will be drafted, and you don't want to face the consequences of avoiding the

---

[27] Jerimiah 29:11-12

draft.[28] Come on, let's go back inside. We'll have something to eat, and then we'll deal with what we need to."

They both stood up and started back toward the house. Ted put his hand on Josh's shoulder and stopped him. "I want to thank you for listening. I'm not usually a cry baby, but seeing what I let slip through my hands, and having this crazy dream, has really shaken me."

"Don't worry about that," Josh said. "It shook me too."

As they walked, they passed Bekah's huge garden. It seemed hard to believe one person could take care of it all and have a business too. They walked up the steps into the enclosed back porch and saw all the vegetables waiting to be processed.

They both looked at each other and said, "How does she do it?"

Walking into the kitchen, they immediately saw Bekah putting together three trays of food. There was a tray of what looked like assorted homemade cookies, another of different cheeses and crackers, and one of assorted fruit, cut up into bite size pieces.

Bekah turned and saw Josh and Ted coming through the door. They looked at all the food that had been prepared and blurted out to Bekah, "How do you do it all? Where do you find the time?"

She looked up at them and answered, "Well I'm not Wonder Woman. These trays are from food left over from the funeral luncheon yesterday. Even I couldn't put something so elaborate together so quickly. Now, you're just in time. Will you help me carry these trays into the dining room? I'll get the milk and sugar and the coffee pot. Will one of you please get the cups

---

[28] Jonah 1:1-17

and spoons and napkins?" With that said, she picked up what she needed.

"It appears we've been drafted again," Ted said good-naturedly, "Although I don't mind. It's good to feel needed."

They both did their assigned chores, carrying what was needed into the dining room. With the three of them working together everything was in place, and Josh went to gather the group. That left Ted alone in the dining room with Bekah. For a moment he was silent. Then he said, "Bekah, I know this is hard for you, having me involved. I don't know why God chose me. I just want you to know I'll do everything I can to make things as smooth as possible between us."

Bekah looked up from the table, surprised at Ted's statement. She had never seen him humble himself to anyone. She heard everyone coming down the hall and replied quickly, "Thanks Ted, I appreciate that. Maybe we'll have a chance to talk later."

CHAPTER NINE

As the day moved forward, everyone realized that they needed to get back down to business and return to the living room. They were all dragging their feet trying to put off the inevitable, intimidated by the project God seemed to be placing before them.

They filed into the living room in somber silence, and then Ted immediately stood up and said, "I don't claim to know a lot about God and how He works, but I am convinced that these dreams were from Him and He would only show us something like the sacrifices of those babies if it was necessary. We don't need to discuss the horrible details, but just agree on the fact that it happened, and that God showed it to us for a purpose."

Josh got up and said, "Ted, you may not think you know God very well, but He knows you. You said just what we needed to hear. I believe He gave you those words. Don't disparage your lack of knowledge. I have a feeling we are all going to be learning continually in the days to come. Do you have anything else you would like to say?"

"Yes, I want to tell my dream next. It was somewhat different from the ones so far. I didn't see Isaiah in the temple. If I had, it wouldn't have meant to me what it did to all of you. I don't know much of the bible. But I do know that God spoke to me

46

plainly. He said that you all don't have time for cake sales or fund raisers, so He asked me to fund this project. I realize now that He has blessed me all these years in order for me to be able to help all of you.

"God told me that I've been on the fence too long and it was time to make a choice. Well, today I stand before all of you and tell you I have made my choice. I choose Him, and I choose to join with you and do whatever I can to make this endeavor successful.

"I know to some of you I've been a disappointment and a failure." Ted turned and looked directly at Bekah. "I know I've hurt Bekah and I ask her to forgive me. If I have hurt anyone else here, I ask your forgiveness also. God didn't tell me to go, but He didn't say not to. If you will have me, I would like to go, and to be part of the team."

Everyone was quiet for a moment and then they all looked at Bekah. Ted just stood there, his eyes on Bekah also. He knew the final decision would be hers, and though he was still not comfortable with praying, he uttered a quiet prayer to God. Not knowing what to say, he just said, "Help."

Bekah realized the ball was in her court. She had the power to say yes, or no. With all that was happening she recognized that she still nurtured some feelings of unforgiveness toward Ted that needed to be dealt with. Bekah stood and walked across the room toward him. She took both his hands and looked up at him. She saw the hurt in his eyes and realized they had both suffered hurt, and it was time to get past this issue.

"Ted," Bekah said, "I was hurt, and I did hold it against you, but now I realize I need to forgive you. It's the right thing to do and I should have done it long ago. I also ask you to forgive me for holding it against you all these years. My unforgiveness hurt both of us."

Ted looked into Bekah's face and saw her sincerity. He felt at peace with her. Something he had not felt for a very long time.

Bekah stopped and looked at the whole group. "If we are fighting any kind of evil force, we all need to be sure we don't have any unforgiveness in us. God can't work in our lives when we won't forgive.[29] I will leave all of you here to pray and to think about this while I go clean up the dining room."

Bekah walked into the dining room and Ted followed her. "Bekah," he said, "I know we can't go back. I've been through two marriages and am in the process of ending number three, but I hope that maybe we can be friends. Even though we haven't stayed in touch, I do think of you often. I really am sorry about Nana Sara. I know she meant the world to you. I promise I will never lose touch with you again. I know if you'll let me, I can be a good friend."

Bekah chose her words carefully. "Ted, I believe that whether I like it or not, you should go on this trip unless God says otherwise. We are all going to be working together for some time. I have no idea how long, but I'm sure that given time a friendship could grow. That's all I can promise right now. Too much is happening too quickly for me to promise more. I hope that doesn't offend you, but it's all I can give at the moment."

Now it was Ted's turn to take Bekah's hands. He felt her pull away slightly, but he held tight. "Bekah, I know I can never make it all up to you, but I promise you won't be sorry you gave me a chance." He squeezed her hands and let them go. Then he turned and walked back into the living room.

---

[29] Matthew 6:14-15

Bekah continued cleaning up the dining room. Renato wandered in and helped her carry the dirty dishes and food trays back into the kitchen. Then he loaded the dishwasher.

Renato said, "That was very generous to open the invitation personally to Ted. A simple yes would have sufficed, but you have always had a big heart, and a forgiving nature. I'm so proud of you, and Nana Sara would be also.

"We all need to keep Ted in our prayers, he's very fragile right now, very vulnerable. He doesn't have a firm foundation of the Word yet, but I will take him under my wing, feed him spiritual food, and help him digest it with love and understanding.

"It's not an accident he is here. God sent him to be part of this quest with us for a purpose, and I don't believe money was the sole reason."

CHAPTER TEN

OGUNQUIT, MAINE
JUNE 6

Bekah and Renato walked back into the living room. She looked at everyone and said, "Well, I guess Ted is coming, unless there are any objections." After a pause, Bekah continued on, "Roberta and Joe are the only ones who haven't shared their dream." She looked over at them. "Do you want to share together or separately?"

They stood up together, holding hands. Roberta looked at Joe and said, "Why don't you share Joe, since this involves your family." Roberta sat back down and nodded to him.

Joe had never been comfortable speaking in front of a group, and even though most of them were his friends, it made no difference. "For those who don't know us, my name is Joe Albright and this is my wife Roberta. I've been retire for a few years and Roberta works at Bekah's shop."

Joe began to speak slowly, "Roberta and I had the exact same dream, but it was different from the others. We woke up about 4:30 this morning knowing that God had spoken to us through this dream and but we were not exactly sure what we should do next. Just like everyone else, we were shocked by what God had showed us. We prayed and asked God for direction and felt like we were supposed to call Sylvia first. Even though it was only a little past five, we knew this was important and she wouldn't mind."

Joe looked over at Sylvia, she nodded encouragingly, and he continued on with a little more confidence. "Roberta told Sylvia about our dream. Sylvia told us she had just awakened a short time ago and had a very disturbing dream also. She said she would be right over. For those of you who don't know, Sylvia only lives two blocks away from Roberta and me. Anyway, when we started discussing our dreams, we could see that they had similarities and differences. Now we can see that they were also somewhat different from everyone else's.

"All three of us saw God in the temple and the killing of the babies. It was the most terrible nightmare I ever had. God didn't ask us to go, but we both volunteered. In Roberta's and my dream, God told us where the group will be going and at least two other people who will be helping us."

Joe stopped again and looked at Bekah questioningly. "Go ahead Joe; we want to hear the whole thing."

Joe nodded and continued, "God told us to call my brother Daniel, and his wife Sherry, after we talked to you. They are missionaries in northeastern Paraguay. God said He sent them a dream also, and that they would be part of our quest. We didn't realize so many people were already involved." Joe looked around again and asked if anyone had any questions.

Bekah stood up and said, "I bet if we had time, we could all come up with twenty questions apiece. Maybe what we should do is have a quiet time and see if God imparts anything else to us."

"Sounds good to me." replied Ted, "I want to take some time to look at the south forty. I've never seen such a big garden with only one person working it. One thing I can say for sure, no one should ever go hungry in this house." He laughed as he remarked, "There is even food hanging from the ceiling in the back porch!"

As Bekah, Sylvia and Roberta walked into the kitchen, Bekah said, "Sylvia, Ted's comment about the garden made me think. If we are going to leave for an extended period of time, I'm going to need someone to at least water it. The early crops are coming on strong, and the later ones are starting to come on also because of all the warm weather we've been having. Sylvia, would you consider staying here while we are gone and keeping an eye out? It's just the garden that needs tending right now, the apples are months off. Maybe some of our church friends could help or maybe Joe and Roberta's daughter. She's home from college isn't she, Roberta? I could pay her a bit if she's interested. I'm also going to need to hire at least one temporary helper for "The Eye". You can't handle that all by yourself. Then there's the food bank. It's summertime, and maybe one of the college kids at church would be willing to volunteer for a summer job, kind of like a home mission."

"My goodness, this project is requiring more and more planning," Sylvia replied, "and we're just getting started."

Ted walked in while they were talking and caught the end of the conversation. "Remember," he stated, "I can supply the funds for any extra wages. That's part of the job God gave me."

Bekah looked at him with an unreadable expression and answered, "Thanks, I'll let you know if I need help."

Bekah immediately felt the chastisement of the Holy Spirit speaking to her.[30] "I called Ted to be a help to this group of

---

[30] Hebrews 12:5-11

believers, and to be helped by them also. Do not let your feelings interfere with what I am doing in him and through him."

Immediately, Bekah asked Ted to forgive her for her attitude. "I've had unforgiveness towards you for a long time. The Holy Spirit reminded me to keep a heart of forgiveness, not just to you, but to anyone else who might have hurt or offended me."

Ted answered, "No problem. It's no more than I deserve, but I found out that Jesus took my punishment, and because of that, God forgave all my sins. You may not realize it Bekah, but you inadvertently showed me the way to forgiveness, and I will be eternally grateful."

With a look of complete surprise, Bekah questioned, "How did I help you? I wasn't even present in your life anymore?"

Ted responded, "When I moved out, I used one of our suitcases to pack some of my things. When I unpacked, I found your red leather bible, the one you scribbled in all the time. For some reason, I kept it. When my last marriage started to unravel, I started to read. I was grabbing at straws, and God was there to catch me. I went through it and read everything you had highlighted and all your comments. Your comments became almost as important to me as the Word of God; not so much for their spiritual value, but for the fact that they let me see you in a whole new light. Before I came to believe, your faith had been a very large thorn in my side. Now it has helped me to see how God's word works in someone's life."

Bekah was astonished. "Even then, God was bringing all of us together, working everything out to be able to have this team available to do His will. Ted, please believe me when I say I'm honestly glad you're here and a part of this quest."

Ted searched Bekah's face for any sign of sarcasm, but could find none. "Was she sincere?" he wondered.

Bekah did not avert his stare, but returned it with a soft smile. She stepped toward him, reached out, and gave him a brief hug. She stepped back and sighed. "I have to admit initially, I was against you coming. I felt threatened and defensive, but I believe God has revealed at least part of your heart to me, and I am relieved. You have changed Ted. I see a side of you that wasn't there previously, but has become more apparent during the time you have spent here."

He stood there startled at her response. Bekah saw his unease and patted his shoulder. "We have to get to know each other again before we can become friends, but I believe we are making a start."

Everyone returned to the living room and they spent over an hour praying and seeking direction from God.

A late lunch and was served and it was a pretty quiet affair. Everyone seemed to be lost in his own thoughts, content to just relax mentally, emotionally and physically while enjoying the good food and these moments of peace. With everything that was happening, it looked as though peace would be a welcome, but scarce, commodity in the coming days.

With the leftovers eaten and the dishes put away, they all went back into the living room and took their seats. Josh stood up and recapped the morning's events. "Well, we seem to have a direction. We know where to go and who is going. Now we need to talk with the people we will be working with. Joe, can you tell us about your brother and his family before we call them? Do you know where in Paraguay they live? I wonder what the weather is like there in June? Do you know what time it is in Paraguay?" Josh paused and waited for Joe to answer.

"They are way up in northeastern Paraguay. A river separates them from Brazil. My brother Daniel and his wife Sherry have been missionaries there for over four years. They have a small compound in a remote tribal village along the river. It is late Fall there now, but to us it would be rather comfortable. The summers are wet, hot and humid, but fall is not as wet and its cooler, days in the 70's and 80's and nights in the 50's and 60's. Remember too, since we are on Daylight Savings Time here in Maine, it is the same time in Paraguay as it is here.

"They have a satellite phone that was given to their ministry three years ago. We usually call them once a month, timing our call because the charge is per minute and it can get expensive. Costs vary as their rates are constantly changing, but we budget around fifty to sixty dollars a month and make sure we have a list of what we want to say before we call." Joe looked over at Josh and asked, "Is there anything else you want to know, or should we start working on our list of questions?"

Renato spoke up then, "I don't know if you remember, but I lived in northeastern Paraguay until I was a teenager and immigrated to the United States. I may not be able to answer all your questions. Some things change, but some things never do."

"That's right," said Josh. Do you know what part of Paraguay you came from?"

"I don't remember the name of the village," Renato replied. "Some villages don't even have special names, but are called by their place or location, or some descriptive thing about them, such as the village by the big rock, or the village by the falls. I do remember it was a small village of maybe fifty or sixty people.

I also remember stories of barbaric, warlike tribes attacking neighboring villages. That may be one of the reasons we left.

"We lived in the city for a time until my father and I could earn enough money to immigrate to America. My father had a cousin who spoke for us and we were allowed to enter. We later became citizens.

"His cousin lived in northern Maine, but it was much too cold for us up there. My father found a job in Ogunquit working on a fishing boat, and I worked in the apple orchard.

"When my father died, Nana Sara took me on full time, and gave me a place to stay. There was a small room off the old storage shed she converted into a sleeping area. She had an outhouse dug for the seasonal help which I used, and she allowed me to shower in the basement bathroom.

"When I became foreman, she built the house across the field for me. She gave it to me as a wedding gift when I married, along with the five corner acres it rests on. I own twenty-four of the apple trees in the orchard. Every year at harvest time she paid me five percent of the harvest as a bonus, in addition to my salary, and I allowed her to harvest my trees."

"I don't know if anyone else knows all of this. I have copies of all the papers that were drawn up by her lawyer. She must have copies also in her desk, or in a safe deposit box, if she had one."

"Wow!" said Bekah. "I had no idea of all that. I just knew you were around all my life and lived in the house in the trees. I didn't even know you were married. May I ask what happened to your wife?"

"She died in childbirth a few years after we were married. Nana Sara became my family after that."

Everyone was surprised by the revelations Renato had made. It appeared that he and Nana Sara both had some secrets.

"We seem to be learning quite a bit about each other today," Josh said. "I'm sure there will be more surprises before this is over. Why don't we spend some time in prayer? Then we can make up our list of questions for Daniel and Sherry. We can discuss anything pertaining to the trip, anything God has told us and any problems we have that might need to be addressed. Then we can call Joe's family in Paraguay and see what they have to say about this whole scenario."

CHAPTER ELEVEN

THE VILLAGE, PARAGUAY
JUNE 6

Daniel walked up the well-worn path to their compound. He had just docked the boat from his monthly trip to Puerto Bahia Negra. He usually brought Edwardo, the young pastor he had mentored, with him. Since Edwardo couldn't go this trip he brought Mario, another young man from the village who was a member of their small church. Daniel had been laboring with Edwardo for four years, but the work was hard, and so far, their rewards had been minimal. They only had ten or fifteen converts, but they were determined to continue and not give up.

It was an eight-to-ten hour boat ride from the village to Puerto Bahia Negra, depending upon how the river was running. It had been uneventful going down. The river could only be traveled by day, because there were too many obstacles in it to navigate in the dark. Daniel had to purchase all his supplies and then transfer them to his boat to make the twenty-five mile upriver run back to the village by the big rock in the river. This eight-to-ten hour journey downriver took Daniel through swamps, bogs, and hordes of mosquitoes. The run back upriver could take from twelve hours to three days, depending upon how the river was flowing. Thankfully, with the cooler weather, the mosquitos were less of a problem. It may be only twenty-five miles as the crow flies, but as the boat floats, it was closer to forty. Their mailing address was Puerto Bahia Negra, Paraguay, but if truth be told, they were probably over the border and well into Brazil. There were no boundaries or signs this far out other than the river. The northern border was anyone's guess.

When they arrived back at the village and docked, Daniel had asked one of the natives who sometimes worked at the compound to help Mario unload the supplies while he found Sherry. Naturally, she was in the clinic doing pre- and post-delivery exams. The native women came from far and wide to have Sherry deliver their babies. She had the best survival rate for mother and child, hands above any local shaman or witch doctor.

It didn't hurt that she also gave each mother a set of baby clothes for the new arrival. In addition, the people felt comfortable with her because she could speak their language. Guarani was the local dialect, and after four years, she was pretty fluent. Sherry had always had a gift for picking up other languages, and it certainly proved to be a blessing here. She also spoke Spanish fluently and could get by with Portuguese.

Daniel was grateful he caught Sherry between patients as she was washing her hands. He came up behind her and gave her a hug and quick kiss on the neck. She responded with affection. For a few minutes, they looked like two teenagers making out in the back room. They had been married ten years, but they worked at making it feel like ten days. They were very successful.

"Anything go on while I was gone?" Daniel asked. Living where they did on the edge of civilization, literally anything could happen.

"No," answered Sherry, "only two live births, mothers and children doing well. Oh, and there was rumor of some kind of attack on one of the rural villages way up the river. I didn't have a chance to investigate, but maybe you can ask Edwardo to look into it after you get everything settled."

"Good idea," replied Daniel, "I'm going to go down to the river and start filling the water barrels. I'm sure it will take more than a few trips. Did you need any help while I was gone? Did you have enough water? How about rain, did the rain barrel get any water?"

The river water had quite a bit of sediment. They had two barrels, one that they let sit to allow the sediment to settle while the other was in use. Both barrels had to be cleaned out on a regular basis, and the sediment was collected to be added to the garden. It was very rich in minerals and worked much better than commercial fertilizer. The rain barrel could not be counted on. Rain was sporadic in some seasons and the need for water at the compound was monumental. With all the nursing Sherry did, they went through a tremendous amount of water.

"Philippe stopped by several times and made a number of runs to the river to keep me supplied, but I'm sure we're nearly down to the bottom of the barrel. I received several meals from former patients, and that was helpful. Recently, I've been so busy that I haven't had the time or the inclination to cook.

"The villagers all know when you are away and they try to take care of me. I think the people of the village realize that we make a difference in their lives. In the four years we've been here, we haven't seen as many conversions as we would like, but these people accept us and appreciate what we do. God is working in their lives, and we're planting seed.[31] One day there will be a harvest; we just have to keep going and not give up.[32] I still have

---

[31] 1 Corinthians 3:6
[32] Galatians 6:9

some left over bread, fruit and cheese we can have for dinner. I shouldn't be too late finishing up here."

As he walked down the narrow path to the river Daniel heard the birds making their usual racket. They needed to be loud and boisterous to be heard over the insects. He was carrying two large buckets down to the river. Fetching water was one of his jobs, and he had to make the trip several times a day. He liked the first, early morning trip the best because it usually coincided with the dawn, and the splendor of it made him thankful to God for all his blessings.

He loved watching the sun come up; its beauty was always reflected in the swiftly flowing water. Even though he hadn't been present this morning, he knew beyond a shadow of a doubt that God had managed to outdo Himself again. He was convinced that God put so much work into sunrises because He enjoyed them also. Daniel continued walking down the path, noticing the encroaching vines and grasses. Weekly, someone had to go out and cut back the green jungle as it tried time and again to obliterate the path with its tangle of brush and vines.

Daniel paused for a moment as he remembered the strange dream he had sometime during the night while they were tied up at the small station about halfway home. It wasn't necessary to stop there on the way down because the current propelled them and they used less fuel, but on the return trip the boat was heavier and they were traveling against the current. They needed to stop and refuel, and it was safer to spend the night at the fueling station than to tie up along the river. He and Mario had slept on the boat to protect the supplies before piloting it upriver this morning.

Unfortunately, thievery was rampant along the river and he kept a shotgun and pistol on board for protection. He left as early as light permitted, knowing he had to get home as quickly as possible. There was so much to be done, and these monthly supply trips stole much of his time. It was dangerous traveling and he was glad to have Mario with him. He must have dozed off during the night long enough to have this dream. He hadn't had much time to dwell on it because of all he had to do. He had not even mentioned it to Sherry when he got home. He would be sure to discuss it with her over dinner, whenever that might be.

Dusk was approaching and this was the first quiet moment of his day. He stopped and sat on an old tree stump and gazed at the river. While there, he saw Edwardo standing with three other men on the jetty they had built two years ago. It managed to survive floods and storms, but looked like it was going to be strangled by river grass which seemed to have a penchant for surrounding the twenty foot long breakwater.

Daniel rose to his feet and continued his walk to the river. "What have you got there, Edwardo?" Daniel shouted. They were all at the end of the jetty, gesturing and arguing with excitement. Daniel put down the two buckets. With growing curiosity he walked out onto the jetty to see what was causing the commotion. When he got there, he could barely see a small basket tangled in the tall river grass, but there was no mistaking the wail of a baby coming from it.

Edwardo came up to him and said, "We have a problem. It's too far for us to snag with a pole, and our boat can't get in there. The reeds will clog the motor."

Daniel thought for a moment then said, "How about one of those flat bottom boats the children pole around in on the river's edge looking for bait? That might knock down the reeds and allow you to glide right over them?"

"It's worth a try." Edwardo answered, pointing a short way down the river. "There's one pulled up under that tree over there. Let's see if we can borrow it."

Edwardo and Philippe commandeered the small craft and they began working their way to the basket as the crying continued. If anything, it had increased in intensity. Their efforts seemed to be succeeding; they were drawing closer to the trapped basket. Finally, with a long reach, Edwardo managed to grab the basket and get it into the boat. He looked down at the small, naked child. It was a baby boy and looked to be no more than two or three months old. From the extent of soil inside of the basket he thought the baby might have been adrift around twenty-four hours. He resisted picking him up in case there was an injury. "Can we bring him up for Sherry to check out and see if he's hurt?" Edwardo asked.

"Good idea," said Daniel. "Just wait for me to fill my buckets." This trip he would be bringing more than water home to his waiting wife.

As Daniel and Edwardo entered the house, they could hear Sherry talking on the satellite phone in the other room, but the baby was crying so loudly they could not make out what she was saying. Daniel wondered who was calling. They only used the phone for emergencies, and to talk with family once a month. It was too early for that kind of call; they called at the end of the month and today it was only the sixth of June.

In the other room, Sherry was questioning whoever was on the phone, and in an excited voice said, "You mean you have all had similar dreams from God? That fact alone is almost too

63

much to take in. The fact that I have had a similar dream is mindboggling! I can't wait to hear what Daniel has to say about this. I think I hear him in the other room, but he has a crying baby with him. It sounds like there is an emergency of some kind. Let me call you back in a half hour or so. That will give me time to treat the emergency. Then I can tell Daniel about all the dreams."

A brief good-bye was said and Sherry went to check on all the commotion. What was happening with the baby? Whose was it and where did it come from Sherry wondered? Whatever the problem was, he certainly had a good set of lungs.

CHAPTER TWELVE

THE VILLAGE, PARAGUAY
JUNE 6

Sherry followed the commotion and found everyone in the kitchen. The baby was still in the basket. She turned to Daniel and Edwardo with a questioning look and said, "What's going on here, and where did you get this baby?" The intensity of the baby's crying was starting to diminish.

Sherry did a quick visual check on the baby before picking him up. He was very red, but that was most likely caused by his prolonged crying. He appeared to be moving his arms and legs without problems, and he was able to move his head from side to side. If the odor was any indication, his bowels were functioning, and a fine spray of urine arced over the basket attesting to his bladder function.

Sherry grabbed a towel and leaned over to pick him up out of the soiled basket. "Get that smelly thing out of here," she said. "We can find something better to lay him in after I've cleaned him off and examined him."

Edwardo went to grab the basket and Daniel stopped him. "Don't get rid of the basket just yet. Put it aside in the workshop. Maybe we'll find some clue as to where he came from. It appears that something bad may have happened given the way he arrived."

They both looked back to Sherry who was holding the crying baby. His sobs were subsiding and he appeared to be dropping off to sleep. "Let's let him sleep for a bit; he can be bathed later. A little dried poop never hurt anyone. My first order of business now is to get him some nourishment. Let me see if there are any nursing mothers around who might be willing to take him on." Sherry wrapped another towel around him and placed him in a small cradle that she kept in the kitchen for the babies of her local patients. She then walked out into the afternoon sunshine.

There were several tall trees in the compound. Benches had been built under them for people to sit on after they completed their chores, waited for checkups, or just visited and enjoyed the shade. Sherry enjoyed sharing her shade with the villagers. Sitting on one of the benches just happened to be Constanzia, Edwardo's wife. On her lap sat their six-month-old son Paulo noisily nursing. Three-year-old Maria, their pretty little daughter, sat next to her. "Just the person I need," Sherry thought. She walked over and sat down on the bench. "Connie, I need your help. I have a small baby of about two to three months who was found floating down the river in a basket. He appears to be healthy, but needs to have someone with plenty of milk to feed him, at least for a day or two until we see if we can find his parents. Would you be willing to take on the job, even if it's just temporary?"

Connie replied with eagerness, "Where is he? Can I see him? When do you want me to start? Paulo could use a little brother as long as Edwardo doesn't mind, and I have plenty of milk for both. Where is the poor niño from? Where are his parents?"

66

"He came from upriver. We don't know anything else about him. He appears to have been adrift in the river no more than two days, judging from the condition he is in and the mess in the basket. Come inside and I'll show him to you. Edwardo is in the kitchen already. He was one of the men who found him."

Sherry and Connie walked into the kitchen and Connie immediately began talking excitedly to Edwardo in their native language of Guarani. She was talking so fast Sherry had trouble following her, but she got the main idea. Edwardo walked over to his wife and hugged her. He bent down and kissed her forehead in a sweet show of affection. "This is a wonderful, unselfish woman God has given me. Her kindness and generosity grow day by day, and she never ceases to amaze me. She is willing to take on the care of this child. If there is a lack of parents, she wants to volunteer us. She says Paulo has plenty of room in his crib and one more baby won't be that much trouble. If you remember; her younger sister Lara lives with us and she can help. If neither of you have any objections, she'll take it from here."

Daniel and Sherry looked at each other and shrugged. Sherry said, "Problem solved. It will be a big burden off me. My only concern is that you not get attached too quickly; not until we know whether the parents are going to show up. I have some baby clothes and diapers if you need them. Let me know if there is anything else you might need. Bring him back tomorrow for me to give him a thorough checkup. He appears to be in good health if his lungs are any indication."

Connie glanced down at the sleeping baby and he began to stir. "No," she answered quietly, "I've got everything I need." With that, she gave Paulo to Edwardo and scooped the child up out of the cradle hugging him to her. Taking Paulo back, she walked out

67

of the kitchen with the two babies, one on each hip, and a smile on her face. "I'll feed him and bathe him when he wakes up," she said as she continued down the path toward her house with little Maria bringing up the rear.

CHAPTER THIRTEEN

THE VILLAGE, PARAGUAY
JUNE 6

The three of them stood there watching her go. Daniel opened his mouth to speak when Sherry remembered the phone call. "Oh my goodness; I forgot, I was supposed to call Joe back in a half hour and that was a while ago."

"Do you need me to leave?" Edwardo asked, as he sat drinking a cup of coffee from the bottomless pot that was always on the stove in the kitchen.

"No," answered Sherry. "I want you to hear about this dream that Joe and several other people had back home. The really strange thing is I had a similar dream also last night."

"What was this dream about?" quizzed Daniel, trying to keep a note of excitement out of his voice.

"Well, Joe said theirs was about a call from God, to help a native that was being assaulted by evil forces. My dream was similar. We didn't have time to say much because you came in with the baby."

Sherry was about to say more when Daniel interrupted her. "This is truly amazing; I had a similar dream last night also. This can't be a coincidence when so many people are having the same dream."

Edwardo broke into the conversation, "Well I hope there's room for one more, because the dream I had last night sounds similar. I was going to tell you about it when you returned from your supply trip, but finding the baby distracted me."

They looked at each other in utter amazement, wondering what this could possibly mean. Surely God had to be behind this and wanted to get them involved in His plan.

"I wonder if the baby has something to do with these dreams," Edwardo asked. "It's such an unusual thing to happen, and now we find out that we are not the only people having these dreams."

Sherry answered cautiously, "My dream was also about a tribe that had been attacked. It was a terrible dream and terrible things happened. I saw a massacre taking place in an outlying village. A large, barbaric tribe was attacking, and all the babies of the village were being sacrificed in a fire to an evil god. I was reminded of the scripture in Matthew 2:18 where Herod tried to kill the baby Jesus by massacring all the baby boys less than two years of age. Was that situation in your dreams also?"

Sherry looked over at Daniel and Edwardo and they both nodded. Daniel answered in a quiet voice, "It was a terrible dream, very graphic. It was as though I was watching a video of it actually taking place. I could hear the screams and almost smell the smoke."

Edwardo spoke up, "I saw the same thing. What's tragic is I have heard of this kind of thing happening in the remote northern villages. It is an abomination to God. We must find out why we have been shown this terrible sight. We need to call your brother back and find out what he knows about these dreams and what they mean."

"Alright, if you think so," Daniel said questioningly. "We can tell him about our dreams and see how they compare with their dreams."

He went to get the phone while Sherry poured them each a fresh cup of coffee. Daniel returned and said, "Before we call Joe back, let's just pray and ask for God's wisdom and guidance. We don't want any confusion or misunderstandings to create a problem."[33]

After praying, Daniel turned on the speaker phone and dialed the number Joe had called from. Daniel realized Joe wasn't calling from home by the call back number that was on the phone. It rang twice and a woman's voice answered, "Hello."

"Hello, this is Daniel Albright and I'm calling for my brother Joe. Is he there?"

"Yes, let me get him. We're going to put the call on speaker phone if that's all right with you?"

"No problem," Daniel said, "we have you on speaker phone also."

"Daniel, can you hear me?" Joe yelled into the phone with excitement.

Daniel replied, "Loud and clear. What's going on? Wait, before you say anything else, let me tell you that there are at least three of us here who have had similar dreams last night: myself, Sherry, and our young pastor, Edwardo."

The silence Daniel heard on the phone spoke volumes. Then Joe replied, "This is certainly extraordinary."

"Tell us what's happening up there," Daniel said. "With everything that's transpired down here, we haven't had much time to share our dreams with each other."

---

[33] James 1:15.

Joe answered, "Well let me start by telling you about our dream. We are all at my friend Bekah's house. There are seven of us up here who have had the dream thus far.

"Josh, the Mission's Director from a church in Oklahoma had the dream first. He was shown a vision of God in His temple, just like the vision Isaiah had. God told him there was a tribe of people calling out to Him for help. They were being attacked by a barbarous and evil tribe. It's hard to describe, but a powerful tribe of warriors was attacking a neighboring tribe and taking all their infant children and offering them as a burnt sacrifice to their evil gods. God said He was sending us to help them.

"Bekah, whose house we are at now, seems to be the connecting point of our dreams. We all dreamed of God calling us, and that we were to seek Bekah out. Everyone knew that an isolated tribe of people were being attacked by evil forces, but they didn't know where they were.

"In Roberta's dream, and mine, we were instructed to call you in Paraguay." Joe paused to let that sink in. "Josh had his dream on the first of June. God told him of a quest to fight against the forces of evil, but he had to search for Bekah from the limited information God gave him. He came to her house yesterday afternoon; right after Bekah had her dream.

"Next Renato had the dream. He works for Bekah in her apple orchard and has known her all her life. Also of interest is the fact that he was born in Paraguay. He immigrated to the U.S. when he was a teenager, around fifty years ago. He came from the area you are in now. He also speaks Guarani.

"The next one was Ted, Bekah's ex-husband. God asked him to fund the trip.

"That night, Roberta and I had the dream. Roberta works part time for Bekah in her needlework shop. Our dreams were a little different. As I said, we were told to contact you in Paraguay.

"One other person here had the dream, that was Sylvia, and she also works in the needlework shop, but she was told to stay and pray. She is going to be organizing a prayer group, to pray for us as we go and fight the battle. She will also be our stateside contact and supply coordinator."

Silence descended upon the room. There was not a sound coming from the phone. "Have we been disconnected?" asked Joe. "Check the connection."

"No," they heard Daniel say in a stunned voice, "we are just dumbfounded at the magnitude of what is occurring. We are almost speechless after listening to what has happened up there. We are not even sure what is happening down here. We all had our dreams last night and only just found out about them after your first call. I have been down river for supplies and just got back this afternoon. Then we had a Moses experience. We found a small baby in a reed basket stuck in the river weeds. We haven't had time to say more than 'I'm back' to each other before this phone call. "

"Well, do you want to go into that now or wait until we get down there?" Joe asked. "We all really feel that time is of the essence, and God is urging us to move quickly. Even though we haven't heard your dreams, after hearing ours, does it agree with yours?"

There was silence, and then Josh spoke up. "Daniel, this is Josh speaking. Do you think that the rescued baby may indeed be one that escaped the massacre? Take extra care with him. Keep him safe; Satan doesn't like to be cheated."

"I'm glad we all got to talk. Now we can think and pray on this situation having all the facts God intended us to have. I'm sure God still has some surprises in store, but He is working for us and not against us. We will deal with what we need to today and let tomorrow take care of itself."[34]

Daniel spoke in a voice full of excitement and anticipation. I'm so glad we are overcomers. We all need to be on our guard, and open to take input from each other. Remember the phrase 'divide and conquer'. Satan would like nothing better than to use that on us.

"By all means, come down. Well find room for everyone. How long do you think it will take you to get everything together and fly down, and how many will be coming?" Daniel had one hundred questions, but these two were a good start.

Joe answered with his best estimate, given the fact that they had done no real planning yet. "I'd say three or four of us will come down first. We're all going to have to work out the logistics before we go anywhere. We really haven't had any time to digest this. We're going to have to have one or two more meetings here to get a better picture of what we are doing, and what is involved. Also, Bekah buried her grandmother yesterday and she has some legal issues that must be handled before she leaves.

"While I'm thinking about it, what is your suggestion about supplies? Should we get them here and ship them, or purchase them there? This is something Sylvia can think about while all of us are putting our plans together."

Daniel came back on the line. "Our heads are probably all spinning right now given the enormity of the task before us. Why don't we answer those questions and any others you might have

---

[34] Matthew 6:34

74

tomorrow night after we have had a day to digest what's taken place. Before you hang up, let's pray over this situation. Would one of you want to pray?"

Another voice came over the speaker. "This is Josh. Since I'm the one who had the first dream, I kind of feel like a pastor or shepherd to this group. If nobody minds, I'd like to pray."

After waiting a moment to see if anybody spoke up Josh prayed, "Heavenly Father, we come before You tonight in the mighty name of Jesus.[35,36] We pray for Your wisdom and guidance. We come against any confusion and speak peace into each and every person who has been called to this quest. We speak protection for us against all the fiery darts of the enemy,[37] and loose ministering angels to go about on our behalf, fighting for us against the forces of darkness.[38] We thank You Father, for a successful outcome, and we give You all the praise and glory. Amen". Josh thought a moment and then said, "Well unless any of you have anything else to say, we'll say good night, and talk again tomorrow night."

For a moment it was quiet and then Daniel said, "No, we're good here. We'll talk with you tomorrow night. Can you call about five?"

"Sounds good," said a voice over the phone and the connection broke.

---

[35] Philippians 2:9-11
[36] John 14:13
[37] Ephesians 6:16
[38] Hebrews 1:14

CHAPTER FOURTEEN

THE VILLAGE, PARAGUAY
JUNE 6

Daniel, Sherry and Edwardo were staggered and sat quietly for a time, just trying to take in the extraordinary circumstances. They were all contemplating the upheaval they were going to experience in their lives because of the dream, and what they were being called to do in just a short time. Daniel finally said, "I know it's late, but I feel a real need for us to at least go over our dreams. We didn't have much of a chance when we were talking to Joe. Are they all the same, or do we also have some different tasks set out for us by God? If it's alright with both of you, I'll start.

"I had my dream last night on the boat. I woke up this morning recalling it, but because so much was happening, I had no time to discuss it with anyone. I was called to go on a quest also. I was told God was sending an army from the north to join us in battling the forces of darkness and to bring hope to a group of hopeless people crying out for help. I was to be part of that army."

Sherry started to speak, "I had my dream last night also. I was not called to go on a quest, but I was given a Scripture. Let me read it:

'Then what was said through the prophet Jeremiah was fulfilled:

A voice is heard in Ramah, weeping and great mourning,
Rachel weeping for her children and refusing to be comforted, because they are no more.'[39]

"This was quoted in the Bible after Herod killed all the male babies under two years old in Bethlehem. Satan was using him to try to kill the Messiah, Jesus. He did not succeed in his plans then, just as he will not succeed in whatever he is attempting to do now. God has bigger and better plans and we are His instrument to implement them. God saw to it that the rescue of a small baby was made today. I don't believe it was just a coincidence. I believe that the circumstances surrounding his appearance are connected with the quest we are called to. I believe he is from the village that was attacked, and somehow, God orchestrated his escape. " Sherry stopped and turned to Edwardo.

Edwardo began, "I also received a call. A quest may be involved, but first I must raise an army, and then outfit them with the weapons of warfare. I was given Scripture also. I have my Bible with me. Let me read it to you:

[10] Finally, be strong in the Lord and in his mighty power. [11] Put on the full armor of God, so that you can take your stand against the devil's schemes. [12] For our struggle is not against flesh and blood, but against the rulers, against the authorities,

[39] Matthew 2:17-18 New International Version

against the powers of this dark world and against the spiritual forces of evil in the heavenly realms. [13] Therefore put on the full armor of God, so that when the day of evil comes, you may be able to stand your ground, and after you have done everything, to stand. [14] Stand firm then, with the belt of truth buckled around your waist, with the breastplate of righteousness in place, [15] and with your feet fitted with the readiness that comes from the gospel of peace. [16] In addition to all this, take up the shield of faith, with which you can extinguish all the flaming arrows of the evil one. [17] Take the helmet of salvation and the sword of the Spirit, which is the word of God. [18] And pray in the Spirit on all occasions with all kinds of prayers and requests. With this in mind, be alert and always keep on praying for all the Lord's people.'[40]

"Knowing the importance of these dreams and the revelation from God, we need to understand that we are walking into uncharted territory," Daniel said. "We've been told there's an evil enemy, and that we must raise and train an army of God to fight the forces of darkness. We need to pray and seek God and ask Him for clarity, ask Him for further direction, and ask Him for strength. Edwardo, I'll see you tomorrow morning for breakfast as usual, and we can talk about this some more. I bet Connie has supper waiting for you now. It's been a long day."

Darkness descended and the pace of life slowed. The breeze picked up and in the distance thunder could be heard

---

[40] Ephesians 6:10-18 New International Version

rumbling across the valley. Lightning lit up the heavens like the flash of a camera and the smell of the coming rain was redolent in the heavy night air. The rain would be welcome tonight, discouraging the mosquitoes, but unfortunately, tomorrow the ground would be a quagmire.

Daniel lay in bed recalling the events of the day; about as strange a day as anyone could have. First he had his dream: then the discovery of the baby, then the phone call, then everyone's dream. Life was always a little chaotic on the mission field, but he had a feeling things were escalating. Everyone talked about time being short and Jesus coming back soon, but he felt as though they had just taken a giant step closer to His return.

Daniel glanced over at Sherry. She had fallen asleep almost immediately, but he had been awake for almost an hour. He kept thinking about all that had happened and all the extra work this would entail. Finally, he did what he always did when he was stressed. He prayed, "Lord I don't know what to do concerning everything that is happening, but You do. I know You'll tell me what I need to know and show me what I need to do. I put my trust in You."

Having said that, he rolled over and put his arm around his wife. She snuggled up next to him and made a contented little sound. He closed his eyes. When he opened them again it was daylight.

CHAPTER FIFTEEN

OGUNQUIT, MAINE
JUNE 6

After the phone call, everyone stayed and talked for an hour, discussing things that needed to be done before they embarked upon their quest. Everyone had loose ends they needed to tie up. Unfortunately, Bekah thought her list was rather lengthy given the fact that the rest of Nana's arrangements still needed to be completed.

Even though there was still some daylight, dusk was rapidly approaching. In these northern latitudes the night fell quickly. Exhausted mentally and physically with the strain of all the revelations that had taken place, everyone had gone home. This whole chain of events was miraculous, but dealing with miracles could tire you out. Bekah wondered how Jesus and his disciples had handled it.

In spite of the fact that she was exhausted, Bekah thought she ought to at least start to look through Nana's desk. Tomorrow she would give their lawyer a call and see if there was anything she needed to do. As she headed for the office the phone rang. Given the events of the day, she was a little gun shy of unexpected phone calls. "Hello," she answered cautiously.

"Hello Bekah," a familiar voice replied. She recognized the voice of Jim Pritchard. He was the family lawyer and a longtime friend. "Sorry to bother you. Do you have a moment to talk?"

"Sure," said Bekah, surprised that she had just been thinking of him.

"I have an envelope here in my office for you. Your grandmother gave it to me about a year ago and instructed me that upon her death I was to give it to you as soon as possible. Would you like to come by and get it tomorrow, or can I run it by The Eye and leave it there for you? How are you doing? I know you must miss her terribly." Jim said.

"I'm doing alright, and yes, you're right, I do miss her. This old house is still full of her though. Every room I walk into is crowded with memories and I expect her to be there. I'm sure that will pass with time, but it's disconcerting right now. Every time I hear the floor creak, and old houses creak a lot, I think it's Nana Sara coming into the room.

"Tomorrow, I have to stop at The Eye and check on some shipments I'm waiting for. I'll pick it up then. Thanks, I appreciate your concern. I wonder what she's up to now. Nana always had her secrets and her way of doing things. I hope this is not one of them. I need a little peace and quiet."

Bekah sighed and Jim went on, "Well you take it easy, I'll bring it by, and if there's anything else you need, just let me know. I'm more than happy to help."

"All right, thanks again," Bekah responded. She turned and looked at the old desk with all its secrets and thought, "I'll deal with you tomorrow. Right now, I think I need to go for a walk in the garden." She did an about face and walked outside into the gloaming. The sun had set, but there was still a glow to the western sky. She stood closer to night than day, and enjoyed the silence that the approaching darkness brought.

The heat of the day had carried over into the night. Even the breeze had disappeared. As she walked, Bekah glanced over at Renato's house across the orchard. Both Ted and Josh were staying with him now. That was a good choice for all of them. She knew that at times Renato got lonely. Ted already admitted his life was lonely, and the sooner Josh just got to know some of the people he would be involved with, the better.

The garden took on a look of stillness as it descended further into night. The birds had gone to bed and the crickets were tuning up for the tonight's symphony. The shadow of the two towering pine trees lay across the yard filtering the light coming from Renato's house through their myriad of branches. An owl hooted, and the sound of it matched Bekah's mood. She felt very melancholy and alone. Tears welled up in her eyes and overflowed down her face. She silently brushed them away.

Bekah looked around her. She loved this old house, the garden, and the orchard. She didn't want to leave. She didn't want to be a missionary or go fight the enemy. She was opposed to any kind of conflict. She wanted to stay where she was and sleep in her king size bed with its soft, pillow top mattress and down comforter. She liked hot and cold running water and indoor plumbing. She was very comfortable with the status quo, and was definitely unhappy about the fact that her life was being thrown into turmoil.

She did not like adventure, she did not like roughing it, and she did not like camping. She liked creature comforts, and was mourning their loss even before solid plans had been made. She knew they would have to go. God had clearly called all of them to some sort of quest. Just how it would be accomplished remained to be seen. She just hoped she would get to come back home.

Turning around, Bekah retraced her steps. Entering the darkened house she didn't even turn on the light. She climbed the familiar stairs and walked into her bedroom. She went to bed knowing that tomorrow would bring a new set of challenges and she would be expected to meet them.[41]

Laying her head on her pillow, she prayed a short prayer of thanks for all her many blessings, even though they felt pretty skimpy tonight. She asked God to help her keep a good attitude, and then she closed her eyes and went to sleep.

---

[41] Matthew 6:31-34

CHAPTER SIXTEEN

THE VILLAGE, PARAGUAY
JUNE 7

Sherry looked over at her husband. "Good morning." she said. "Did you sleep well?"

"Not at first," Daniel answered, "my mind was in a whirl. I finally did what I always do; I prayed and put my trust in God. Next thing I knew, it was morning."

"Well I slept like a rock." Sherry put her arms around him and gave him a quick hug and a kiss on the forehead, but looking at the clock she said, "We're a little late. I'll get up and start breakfast if you will go get water."

"Sounds like a plan. Make the coffee strong, I have a feeling we're going to need all the energy we can get." With that last remark, Daniel got dressed, shaved, brushed his teeth, and went out to greet the morning. He picked up the two empty water buckets and headed down to the river. He didn't meet anyone on the way down, but on the way back he saw Edwardo and Connie walking toward the house each carrying a baby, and little Maria, as always, trailed behind.

"Good morning," he called, "Just in time for breakfast. We're a little later than usual, we overslept, but I smell coffee and I can almost hear the potatoes frying."

Breakfast was a ritual they had started many years ago, and even with children tagging along, it was still a pleasant way to start the day. Everyone got to discuss what was going on and make plans for what needed to be done. Only today there was more going on than usual, and more plans that needed to be made.

Daniel poured the water into the water barrel, but left the buckets in the corner. He knew he would be making several more trips to the river before the day was done. He got out the cups and poured coffee for everyone.

"Well," he said to Connie, "Did Edwardo tell you about the phone call last night and all the dreams?"

"Yes he did, and I surprised him with my own dream. I also had a dream from God. He told me I am to enlist my prayer friends and form a prayer army. We are to stay here and fight the battle with our prayers. Just as Edwardo's dream said, we are not fighting a regular battle, although there may be that kind of fighting also. But we are fighting a spiritual battle to support the whole army that God is putting together. Since we're fighting a spiritual battle there may be more than just men involved."

Daniel and Sherry stood there surprised at the speech that Connie had given. Her English wasn't as fluent as Edwardo's, but in saying what she just did, she hadn't hesitated or faltered one bit. Maybe this was a gift of tongues in a way they had not seen before.[42]

Daniel questioned Connie, "How did you make out with the baby last night? Were you able to feed him? Did he sleep well or did he fuss a lot?"

"I had a little trouble feeding him at first; of course I was unfamiliar to him. My smell was different and my voice was different. It was helpful that he was very hungry. He just needed a

---

[42] Acts 2:4

little encouragement. Once he was clean and fed he was a happy baby.

One thing I noticed when bathing him was a mark on his bottom. It's not there now, it faded. He must have been laying on something while he was in that basket."

"Let's look at the basket while the girls finish making breakfast," Daniel said to Edwardo. They headed out the backdoor and into a building they used as a store room and work shop. The basket was lying on the table where they had left it surrounded by all kinds of clutter.

As Edwardo went to grab it, he noticed something sticking out from under the soiled boar skin the baby had been wrapped in. He picked it up for a better look and couldn't believe his eyes.

Resting in his hand, covered in filth, was a beautiful Conquistadorian crucifix. It was encrusted with what appeared to be several beautiful jewels. It also appeared to be solid gold. It measured approximately eight inches long and five inches across. He called Daniel over to see it. They stood there stunned, their minds filled up with questions, but no answers were forthcoming. "Let's take this in, show the girls, and get it cleaned off," Daniel said.

They walked back into the kitchen with the mysterious crucifix. Sherry and Connie were hard at work, frying potatoes, bacon and eggs.

"Breakfast will be ready in five minutes, I just have to put the eggs on," said Sherry.

"Hold off a minute and come look at what we found in the basket. Also could you bring a bowl of soapy water, it's pretty dirty. It's been sitting in baby poop for a while," Daniel replied.

Sherry got a bowl of hot water from the pot that sat on the stove simmering continuously, and put some dish detergent in it. She took the pan of potatoes off the fire, and walked over to the table where the men were standing and inquired, "What is so important that you postpone breakfast?"

Then she saw the crucifix in Edwardo's hands and stopped short. Connie was seeing to Maria's breakfast and hadn't come over yet, but she knew something was happening from the sound of the silence in the room. She finished quickly and hurried over to see. Her first reaction was also silence, and then she said "That is what put the mark on the baby's backside. Oh my goodness! Is it real?"

"We don't know for sure, but it appears to be. Let's get it cleaned up. Connie, you and Sherry finish getting breakfast ready while Daniel and I work on cleaning this thing up."

As they ate breakfast they kept passing the crucifix around the table. It was mesmerizing to look at. So many questions went through their minds: Where did it come from? Who put it in the basket? Did it have anything to do with the quest? What did it have to do with the baby?

Finally Sherry spoke up, "You would have a hard time convincing me that all of these things; the dreams, the baby, and the crucifix, are not interrelated. I'm just waiting to see what happens next. Let's finish breakfast, get the children settled, and start making plans. First of all, we are going to be having a bit of company. We need to figure out where to put them and how to feed them."

CHAPTER SEVENTEEN

OGUNQUIT, MAINE
JUNE 7

Morning brought a break in the weather. Clouds were hovering and there was thunder in the distance. The hot spell was over and it was sixty-eight degrees outside. The wind was blowing fiercely and the first drops of rain were pelting the windows of the old house, sounding like a rat a tat tat, rat a tat tat. Then Bekah looked more closely and realized it wasn't rain, but hail.

She ran to the television to get the weather report. Hopefully this would be short lived. Hail was the kiss of death to a garden. She tuned to the local station. They were saying mild and sunny. "Look out the window;" Bekah chastised them; "Someone's made a mistake."

It appeared as though the hail pellets were getting bigger. They were nickel size now; big enough to damage the garden, and even the apple trees were vulnerable. They were in the process of blooming, and the blossoms at this stage were very delicate. The leaves were not yet fully formed to protect them.

Bekah prayed for their safety. Many people depended on the produce from her garden. For others, jobs were on the line if the trees received too much damage. A few minutes went by and the storm appeared to be abating.

Bekah put on her work boots and ventured outside. From a distance the orchard didn't look too bad. There were some leaves and blossoms flying around, and some on the ground, but it didn't appear to be too serious. The garden, on the other hand looked battered and bruised. Stepping over row after row of torn lettuce and spinach, she was heartbroken over the loss. The tomatoes and squash seemed to fare somewhat better. They looked a little ragged around the edges, but since they were a later crop, most of their fruit was smaller and was protected by denser, sturdier foliage. She used the front of her shirt as a bowl and harvested as much of the lettuce and spinach as she could. It looked like it would be enough for a large salad for everyone's lunch today.

One of the things on her mind she needed to take care of immediately to prepare for this quest was to see if she could find someone to take care of the garden and bring the produce to The Eye. Bekah thought of giving Roberta's daughter a call. School was out and Bekah could afford to pay her a small salary. Maybe she could even help Sylvia at the shop. Perhaps things weren't so bad.

They were all getting together for a brunch today around eleven o'clock. It was time for her to get back in the house and start planning a menu. Bekah did what she always did when she was feeling stressed. She began to cook. Most everyone she knew just threw food in a pan and hoped that something tasty showed up. But to her, cooking was like art; it required thought and attention to detail.

Because of the need to use up some vegetables, she decided to do a salad buffet. She still had a few salads left over from the funeral brunch and she would add what she needed to round out the meal.

Bekah heard someone pulling in the yard and looked up to see Renato, Ted and Josh getting out of Renato's truck.

"Well responsibilities showed up, whether you wanted to face them or not. I can't stay in my own little world," she reflected. "If everyone felt the way I did, nothing would get done. I don't want to be a Jonah. I want to meet the day with a good attitude and conquer whatever enemy there is before me. Lord, forgive me for my pessimism and my grumbling. You won't hear it again. I will greet each morning thanking You for what You have done and for what You are going to do." With that said, she put a smile on her face and went out to greet her Three Musketeers.

The three men looked up as Bekah came out the door, smiled and said "Good Morning." You guys are starting to look and sound like the Three Musketeers. I'm glad you're my protection. You're too late for breakfast and too early for lunch; how about a cup of coffee and some banana bread?" They all smiled and nodded their heads.

"Renato," Bekah began, "How did the trees look, was there much damage from the hail?"

"No," he answered, "we lost some blossoms and leaves, but it's early enough in the season that it won't make a difference. It was an unusual storm though. We drove around a little before we came over, and we seemed to be the main farm that was hit, as though we were targeted. I'm just grateful to God for His protection; it could have been a lot worse. It appears the enemy is already trying to cause trouble."

As they turned to go inside Bekah said, "I have to go into town after the meeting. I have to check on some orders at The Eye, and Jim Pritchard called. He said Nana had left an envelope with him over a year ago, that he was to give to me when she died. I'm really curious about what's in it, but a little nervous also. You know how Nana could be. She had her secrets and she didn't share them with anyone. Would you all come over when I get back from town? I don't want to be alone when I open it. It may have nothing to do with what's going on now, but I want company, just in case."

Renato looked at her with concern on his face, "Bekah, we're a group now. Just like the musketeers you called us earlier. We're 'One for all and all for one'. God has joined us together. We may have different jobs to do, but we have the same goal. Anything we can do to help each other, we will."

"Thanks," Bekah said, touched by his support. Even Ted and Josh seemed to be in total agreement.

CHAPTER EIGHTEEN

OGUNQUIT, MAINE
JUNE 7

The gang was all present and accounted for. They had finished the brunch and it was all cleared away. Everyone had a cup of coffee and it was time to get down to business. Bekah asked Josh to open with a prayer.

After that she said, "We've all had a night to sleep on it. Does anybody have anything they want to say concerning our quest? I'm still trying to digest everything that has happened." She looked around the room, glancing questioningly at everyone.

Finally Sylvia raised her hand. "I don't know whether I've had a short dream, a vision or an impression last night, but it was definitely concerning our quest. I was told that I would have a counterpart down in Paraguay who would be praying for all who were involved down there. I was told we needed to keep in touch because sometimes I would have things she needed to hear and sometimes she would have things I needed to hear. Can you tell me about the communication system they have down there? I understand that it isn't a regular telephone."

"No," answered Joe, "It's a satellite system, and it's pretty expensive."

Ted broke in, "Don't worry about the cost of anything. I told you God asked me to fund the quest. I have more than enough to do the whole job."

"OK." Joe answered, "Checking out the logistics of the phone will be one of the first things we do."

Just then the phone rang. Bekah recognized the overseas number and put it on speaker as she handed the phone to Joe. "Hello," Joe said. "Is this Daniel?"

"Yes," Daniel answered. "I know I'm calling earlier than was agreed, but something came up we think you should know. We told you yesterday we found a baby in a basket yesterday. Well today we looked at the basket a little more thoroughly and found something very unusual in it. It looks to us like a golden, jeweled Conquistadorian crucifix. It's about five inches by eight inches and exquisitely beautiful. I don't know if the baby and the crucifix have anything to do with our quest, but it will sure be some coincidence if they don't. This whole scenario keeps getting stranger and stranger.

"We have one more piece of news. It seems Pastor Edwardo's wife, Connie, had a dream also. She is called to lead a team of prayer warriors against the forces of darkness, and to raise a Heavenly shield of protection for all of us. Didn't someone in your group have the same type of dream?"

"Yes she did," Joe answered, "Its Sylvia, and I'm glad you reminded me. We were going to discuss this when we called later, but this is a good time. We think Sylvia and Connie should have easy access to one another. Maybe we should get a second phone. We will bring it with us when we come, so if we are not in the village, there will still be a phone there. Don't worry, we have the funds. God has provided for everything we will need. So when you're making plans, don't count pennies, our needs are met. I don't think any of us can make it down there until around the fifteenth, but as time goes by, or circumstances change, we will firm up our plans. Also, did we decide to ship the supplies or purchase them there, and will we need tents or do you have places for us to stay?"

"We can put up some extra housing quickly. I have been buying wood supplies with any spare funds we have for building projects that come up. I would say this qualifies. Whatever we build, we will always find a use for it when this is all over. What you will need are cots, pillows and blankets to sleep with, also mosquito netting, lots of it. Be sure to buy quality material. That's one thing you don't want to skimp on. They're not that bad down here right now, but I still recommend it. Since funding isn't a problem, you can purchase everything in Asuncion when you get here. Anything you forget could probably be purchased in Puerto Bahia Negra before we head up river.

"We are still praying and asking God for further direction, but my feeling is that He will show us more when we act on what we know. This is certainly a faith project. We all know that faith comes by hearing His Word,[43] audibly, and spiritually. Is there anything else we need to talk about now? If not we'll call tomorrow evening," Daniel said.

"Are you going to have someone examine that crucifix to verify its authenticity? If it is real, it would be interesting to know how it got in the basket and where the basket came from," Joe asked.

"No," said Daniel, "I think we are going to keep this pretty close to the vest right now, but I have to tell you it looks authentic. I don't want word of it getting out and end up with a crowd of fortune hunters hanging around, especially with everything else that is going on. Well, if that's it, we will say good-

---

[43] Romans 10:17

bye until tomorrow evening. Can we do seven, instead of five? That gives the problems of the day time to resolve, and allows peace to settle as the day draws to a close."

Joe said, "No problem, I think that would work well for us also. It will give us a chance to get home from work and get through with dinner. We will say good-bye for today, unless you have anything else you want to discuss."

Daniel said, "Tomorrow would be soon enough. We'll say good bye then until tomorrow evening."

Josh turned to the group. "Well I think Daniel's right about the fact that we need to do something, not just have meetings. I realize we don't have much of an idea about what we are going to do when we get there, but we know we are going to Paraguay in the middle of June. We need to find out what the weather is going to be like and what kind of clothing to pack. If we have jobs, we need to make arrangements. We need to check on passports and immunizations. We need to check flight schedules and see what airlines service Paraguay. These are a few chores someone could take on."

Roberta volunteered, "I've already been doing some preliminary checking. The weather for June is cloudy with 30% to 40% chance of rain, temps in the 70's during the day and 50's at night. Besides mosquito netting, we will all need boots or rubber shoes of some kind, especially since we are going to be close to the river; though it doesn't look like we will need any sun screen. I'll make it my business to check out the logistics, and make a list of these items being mentioned and any others I can think of that we might need. If any of you think of something, make a list and give it to me. Sylvia and I can even do some research while we're at work at The Eye tomorrow."

Bekah spoke up, "Ok. Let's leave it for today. Tomorrow we'll deal with personal issue and meet again at seven to see where we stand. We'll have time to discuss any other issues that come up. Then we can call Daniel again."

Everyone agreed and left shortly after. Bekah reminded Renato that she would call him when she got back from town with Nana's envelope. She promised them a lite supper also, if they promised to do the dishes.

CHAPTER NINETEEN

OGUNQUIT, MAINE
JUNE 7

Bekah parked her car in front of her shop. She had just put up a catchy new sign last year and paused to admire it. "The Eye," it said; with a picture of an eye, "of the Needle," with a picture of a threaded needle. She was proud of her shop and was glad to see that it was open. With both Sylvia and Roberta at the meeting, there was no one to man the store, but it appeared they had made a beeline for it, and arrived before she did.

Bekah walked in and they were both there along with a few customers. One was a regular whom she saw from time to time. She waved a hello. The two others were probably vacationers. The store did a brisk business in season, and the season was just starting. "I wasn't sure anyone was going to be here, no less both of you."

Sylvia answered, "Well, we knew you had a lot on your plate. We thought we would check up on orders for you and put out any stock that was needed. A few customers came in when they saw the lights were on. Don't worry about the store; we've been here long enough we can do your job too. We just let you hang around for window dressing."

"I'll bet you can," Bekah said, "probably better. Alright, did Jim Prichard happen to drop off an envelope?"

"He dropped it through the slot in the door, and I put it on your desk," said Sylvia.

Bekah walked back to her desk. It was littered with copies of bills, invoices, and samples of yarn in assorted colors and textures. The new shipment of cross stitch kits had come in and they had left several samples on the desk for her to look at. They were arranged by difficulty, from easy to complex; yet even the easy ones appeared lovely from the pictures.

There was also a sample sweater made by a friend. Bekah would display it to show the attributes of that particular yarn. It was a beautiful azure blue, one of her favorite colors. Lying on the corner of the desk was a large, brown manila envelope. Bekah felt a sense of foreboding rise up in her heart. She picked up the envelope and could feel that it contained many papers and an unusually shaped object she couldn't identify. She tucked it under her arm, and went into the back room which doubled as a stock room, and food bank. The two tables of veggies were running low. It was still early in the season and she did not have much, but what was there could be given away. It would be one more thing she would have to add to her growing list of things to be done. She returned to the front of the store and said her good-byes.

Driving home, Bekah's mind went to Nana and she wondered again what secrets this envelope held. Nana knew everyone else's secrets, but she rarely shared her own. Well, she would find out soon enough. Bekah called Renato on her cell phone and told him she was almost home. When she turned down the drive, Renato, Josh and Ted were all waiting for her in the yard. "Come in and I'll put on coffee," Bekah said.

CHAPTER TWENTY

They all sat at the big round table staring at the envelope, wondering what the mystery would reveal. Some mysteries were exciting; others were horrific. Which would this one prove to be? Bekah said, "I can feel that it contains different kinds of papers, but there's also something solid in it and I can't tell by the feel of it what it is. It keeps moving around and changing shape." Taking a steadying breath she said, "I feel like I'm opening up Pandora's Box. That didn't turn out to be a good choice for Pandora. We'll find out in a moment what kind of a choice this will be for me."

Bekah slit open the envelope and the papers slid out onto the table. On top of them dropped what appeared to be a solid gold crucifix encrusted with an assortment of gems. Bekah looked at it and gasped, "I was right, this is Pandora's Box! I think this mystery has just taken a turn for the worse."

They all sat there staring at it. Finally, Josh reached over and picked up the crucifix. "Real or not, what do you think?" He looked around questioningly? "It sure looks real, and if it is, this has to be a key, or one of the keys to our quest." The crucifix was approximately two inches by three inches, and it was carried on a heavy rope chain that also appeared to be gold. The chain was approximately thirty inches long. By itself, the chain must have been very valuable judging from the weight of it. The crucifix was studded with what looked to be diamonds, rubies, sapphires, and some gems she was unfamiliar with. Thy lined every surface of the crucifix.

"What should we do now?" Bekah asked mystified. "One crucifix was enough, now we have two, and if the other is anything like this one, we have a monumental mystery on our hands. I'm just speechless; I don't know what to think. Maybe we should read the letters and see if they shine any light on the situation."

Bekah sorted through the letters. There were four. Three were from her father to Nana Sara, and the fourth was from Nana to her. Bekah picked up Nana's letter first and began to read it out loud.

Dear Bekah,

If you're reading this, then I know I have gone home to be with Jesus. Don't think sad thoughts, be happy for me, I am finally at peace. Don't grieve, or at least don't grieve too long. I'm free at last of all cares, burdens and secrets, especially secrets. I've kept so many; I don't know what it feels like to be free.

I know over the years you must have noticed my times of depression and secretiveness. Well now I can finally tell you why. Being dead gives you a freedom you didn't have in life.

Before you were born, and while your parents were still in Paraguay, God spoke to me in a dream. He revealed that your mother and father would be killed and that I was to take on the care of raising you. I was to live the life of a Christian before you and bring you up in the knowledge of Him and all His ways.[44] He said He had a plan and a purpose for your life[45] and that the fullness of time to accomplish His purpose would arrive when I was gone. Isn't it ironic that God had this plan in His mind from the beginning of time, and I've had to wait all these years and not even see it come to pass? Don't think that I'm not watching from heaven, because I still don't know the answers to all the questions yet.

When you were young, I used to get depressed thinking that I might die and you would be left all alone in this world; not that you could ever be alone when you were walking with God. I worried about how God would carry out His plan. Isn't that a foolish thing? I realize that now, but hindsight is always clearer than foresight. If God has a plan, He has a way to work it out. We need to remember that all God's plans are successful, even if they don't look that way to us.

I was also depressed, knowing that my only son and his wife, your mother and father, would die and leave you orphaned. That would leave both of us alone in the world except for each other.

Now Bekah, I have some things to tell you that may shock and disturb you.

Your Daddy was married twice. His first wife was your Mother. I know very little about the marriage only that it occurred about six months after he met her. His letter, telling me of it is enclosed. His next letter is telling me of your mother's death. She died in childbirth, giving

---

[44] Proverbs 22:6
[45] Jerimiah 29:11-13

birth to you. She made him promise that he would give you the crucifix when you grew up. She was the daughter of the chief and the crucifix was passed down to the chief's children.

Six months later your father married again. He wrote that he had remarried, and was bringing you home with his new wife. She was also a native, but could speak both English and Spanish.

He said no one could know of your birth. There were problems in Paraguay and he had been forced to leave quickly. He was very secretive about the problems, only stating that they had to do with his marriage.

Selfishly, I wanted him to be married here. He had only been married by the Shaman of the local village they were living in. What kind of example was that for a Christian missionary? I arranged for a close friend to watch you while they were here. They were married in the apple orchard, under the large, beautiful tree that I love so much. It was where you are supposed to bury me. I hope you followed through with my final wishes.

The first time I saw you, you were less than six months old, but a beautiful dark eyed child. I did not know your birth mother, your father's first wife, but I got to know your step mother while they stayed here, and I did not like her, or the influence she seemed to wield over your father. She was a very proud and beautiful woman. In talking with her, she let it slip that she had had child before she married your father. She did not mention whether or not she had a husband, but she admitted to leaving behind a little daughter so she could marry your father and come to America. She said the little girl was just your age. Her name was Luna. I asked her if your father knew and she said with a shake of her head, 'It wasn't any of his business."

Well you know how I am; I can't leave things alone, especially knowing she deceived your father into marrying her. She convinced him, a Christian missionary, that they be married by a tribal shaman. She seemed to manipulate people and I felt your father was under her spell.

One afternoon, Fuego heard your father and me discussing her. She came into the room yelling and screaming at me in what had to have been her native language. She was so violent I thought she was going to physically attack me. Your father did also, and he pulled her away and raised his voice to her, saying something that quieted her down.

He asked me if I had the crucifix. Fuego wanted to know where I was keeping it. I told him it was in a safe deposit box in the bank in Ogunquit.

He said he was taking you and his wife away, that you were all flying to California the next day. He had already purchased tickets and had a job lined up. He was very secretive about what kind of job it was. I never knew. When he got there, he said he would let me know his address and then I could send him the crucifix.

Well, you know the rest of the story. They were both killed less than two years later in a motor vehicle accident. I never saw either of them again, and I never saw you again until I went to pick you up in California *after the accident. I never sent the crucifix out to them, but kept it safe all these years. Even though it was a crucifix, I did not feel good about you having it in your possession; so I kept it a secret.*

Your father called once asking for it. I told him I would hold it for you until you were of age. I told him I didn't trust his wife, that she had deceived him in order to marry him, and maybe there were other things she had deceived him about.

I don't know if this crucifix and Paraguay have anything to do with God's plan for your life, but I'm guessing they might.

Please forgive me if I've hurt you by my secrecy, and don't be mad at Renato for keeping my secrets. I made him promise. If people in heaven can pray for those left behind, know that I will be praying for you.

I will love you always,

Nana

The sound of silence echoed around the table. Bekah looked up from the letter, tears streaming down her face. Three stunned faces stared back at her. No one said anything right away, they were all astounded.

Finally Josh, who was still holding the crucifix said, "I wonder what other secrets are out there we know nothing about. Renato, do you have anything else to add to this picture? It seems Nana trusted you enough to take you into her confidence. We don't want to be making plans with surprises like this waiting out there to rise up and bite us."

"I'm sorry Miss Bekah," Renato replied with a look of remorse on his face, "some of this is as much of a surprise to me as it was to you. I knew about you, but I thought that woman with your father was your mother. I assumed your father was just going through the marriage ceremony to satisfy Nana Sara. I didn't know this was his second wife, and I never knew about the crucifix.

Maybe we should call Daniel and see if he is aware of any circumstances surrounding your birth and your mother's death. Also maybe he knows something about your step-mother. Do you know where in Paraguay your father's mission was? Maybe he can make some inquiries. It was quite a while ago, but someone may remember. Do we know their names? Maybe you should check your father's letters."

"That's a good idea," Ted spoke up excitedly. "Also, maybe one or two of us should go down and try to tie up loose ends. These are some pretty big ends to be loose, but maybe being down there we can get to the bottom of this rather than trying to do it by phone."

Josh spoke up again, "I think that's a good idea Ted, but before we start making any moves we need to pray and ask God's wisdom and guidance. This thing is growing, more people are getting involved, and we need God's help to keep up with everything. Also we need to know who to send down there.[46] As long as God is in charge, we know no matter what happens He's with us."

Bekah spoke up, "I've looked at my father's letters. They are very short and to the point, but they do give his wives names. He said his first wife's name was Gabriella. His second wife was called Fuego. They had no last names. Does anyone know what Fuego means?"

---

[46] Acts 13:1-3

"Yes," answered Renato, "it means fire."

Bekah sighed, "I can't think about this anymore. Let's pray and be done."

When they had finished praying Josh said, "I really feel like Renato and Ted need to be our advance team; Renato, because he speaks the language and was born in Paraguay, and Ted because he can get loose without too much difficulty. Also, we should let the others know what is going on.

"Renato," Josh questioned, "Do you have a passport? Ted, do you have yours with you?" They both answered in the affirmative.

Then Josh questioned, "Is there somewhere in town where we can all get together for a cup of coffee and a quick meeting? This way everyone doesn't have to drive all the way back out here."

Bekah thought a moment then answered, "Yes, there's a small restaurant just down the block from The Eye. They have a couple of small rooms in the back they rent out for small parties and luncheons. I know they won't mind if we bring our coffee back there. Let me call everyone and ask them to meet us there in half an hour."

CHAPTER TWENTY-ONE

OGUNQUIT, MAINE
JUNE 7

Bekah and her Three Musketeers walked into The Lobster Pot, a quaint little restaurant like so many others along the Maine coast. It had lobster traps hanging from the ceiling and pictures of lobster boats all over the walls. There was a large tank containing an assortment of lobsters of varying sizes waiting to be picked for someone's special dinner. Joe, Roberta and Sylvia were sitting there waiting.

Roberta said, "I already talked with Jean, and she said no problem. In fact she said she would bring us back our own pot and a tray of cookies."

"Well you can't ask for better service than that," Ted replied. He had a sweet tooth and liked to have that itch scratched on every possible occasion. In fact, you could usually count on him to have a pocketful of whatever was his candy of the month. This month it was Almond Joy, and he probably had several miniatures in his pocket.

They all followed Roberta into the back room. There were three round tables with six chairs around each, and as promised, a tray with all the accoutrements needed along with a large plate of cookies.

Josh said, "Joe, would you pull one of those chairs from the other table over so we can all sit together? We're not eating a meal; being a little cramped shouldn't pose a problem.

"Sorry to drag you out again, but some new information has been added to what we had. It appears Nana Sara had some foreknowledge of what was going to happen, but she had her dream before Bekah was born. Bekah, why don't you read them Nana's letter."

Bekah read the letter through, then took the crucifix out of her pocket and put it on the table. There was a hush as everyone stared at it. Finally Joe asked, "May I pick it up?"

"Yes," Bekah answered, "You can pass it around for everyone to see. That is the main reason we called this meeting. We want to keep everyone in the loop. We're reasonably sure this is probably a smaller version of the crucifix that Daniel has. It seems like too much of a coincidence for it not to be."

Josh stood up and added, "We prayed about this at the house and feel like God is directing us to send two people down quickly to get the lay of the land. There seems to be more of an urgency to get things moving, and maybe see if we can find out some more information about who Bekah's mother was and what happened to her. Gabriella was Bekah's mother's name, and Fuego was her step-mother's name. There are no last names.

"We wanted to meet with everyone to make sure we are all in agreement. Then, if everyone agrees, Renato and Ted will fly down as soon as they can pack and we can get tickets."

"I think it's a good idea," said Joe, "sending both Renato and Ted. Jesus sent the disciples out by two's[47]. Even Paul and Silas were sent out together."[48]

Before anyone could say anything else, Ted interrupted. "We don't need to get tickets, my plane is here and Renato and I can fly down there with our luggage and some of our supplies. I may be slower than a jet, but I can get us into some of the smaller, more rural airports closer to our destination, and cut back on boat or truck rides through the jungle. I can fit quite a bit of equipment in that plane. If we scramble, getting the information and supplies we need and putting together a flight plan, I think we should be able to leave day after tomorrow."

"Hold on a minute," said Sylvia. "It's almost five thousand miles to Asuncion from Portland. I already started getting some facts. It would take several days to fly a small plane down there. American Airlines flies out of Boston on Monday, Wednesday and Friday. The flight, including layovers, takes less than twenty-four hours. We appreciate the offer of your plane Ted, but logistically speaking, a commercial airline would be so much better timewise. We can get you both into Paraguay on commercial flights and then you can look into renting a smaller plane to get into Puerto Bahia Negra. From there the boat ride back up river can take two or three days depending on the river."

Ted looked disappointed, but agreed, "You're right, it would take too long. I'll have to be satisfied buying the tickets. Can you print out some maps tomorrow to see where we are going? I'm also going to get everyone a thousand dollar debit card to purchase whatever they are going to need for this trip, and get

---

[47] Luke 10:1-2
[48] Acts 15:40

another thousand in cash to cover any other expenses," he said, looking at Bekah.

"I'm working some things out." said Bekah. "I think Sylvia may be able to get me some help for the garden and the store. Maybe Roberta's daughter, who is home from college, will be looking for a job. I'll make the arrangements tomorrow."

Bekah inquired, "What does everyone think about Josh and me flying down to Washington D. C., to the Smithsonian, or New York to the Metropolitan Museum of Art, to have them look at this crucifix and see if they can tell us something about it? We could probably do it in one day taking the shuttle from Boston if we got an early enough fight."

"I think that's a great idea," Ted said as he was texting on his cell phone, "just give me a few minutes before you make final plans. I have a friend in New York who is a jeweler and works with antique jewelry and other works of art. He may not have experience with sixteenth century pieces, but he will be able to authenticate the crucifix for us. We don't want to expose this piece to too many people until we find out where it came from and how it got here. It seems we may have to go to Paraguay to find that out. Meanwhile, we need to keep a low profile here."

Joe was shaking his head in agreement. "You are so right. Daniel said the same thing, we don't want treasure hunters hanging around and getting in the way. Does your friend know how to keep quiet?"

"Yes," Ted answered, "we go way back. We were in flight school together. I trust him completely. On top of that, he's one of the few people I know who says he's a Christian. He will be so glad when I tell him I finally got off the fence and landed on the right side. I haven't seen him in several years, but I know he will be glad to hear from me."

"OK, he just texted me back. He'll be in his office tomorrow after ten. Perfect. You both can take the shuttle down and meet him, and be back the same day. I'll give you his name, address, and phone number. You can call him when you get there. Let me just text him back and tell him you're coming. I'm glad we are doing something, and tomorrow night, when we talk to Daniel and Sherry, we should have some news for them.

"Also," Ted continued, "is there somewhere in town where I can pick up those debit cards?"

"Tomorrow you can go to one of the banks," Bekah answered. "I don't think Walmart would do ones that big. Josh and I aren't going to need them tomorrow. We won't be dining at any five star restaurants. There are plenty of wonderful and inexpensive places to eat. We won't starve in New York City, that's for sure."

Bekah asked, "Is everyone clear on what's happening? Let's go over our plan. Josh and I are going to New York tomorrow, June eighth. Renato and Ted are going to Paraguay on the tenth. Joe and Roberta, can you work on supplies, what we'll need and where to get it?

"Sylvia, I don't want you to think that what you are doing is unimportant. It's probably the most important job. Please call your friends and organize our prayer army. All of you will be doing a lot of the fighting. Also," Bekah asked, "could you firm up the help for the garden, the food bank and the shop? That will take a big burden off me."

"I'm already on it." Sylvia said, "When you get back from the city, everything will be finalized. And I already told you I will do anything I can to help out. Don't be apologizing to me anymore."

"You're right. Thanks for all you do. I just don't want you to feel like I'm taking you for granted. Your help and friendship mean so much to me."

Sylvia responded with affection and a hug, "I'll let you know if I need reassurance. Until then, if I feel needy, I'll come give you a hug. Now, if everyone has their game plan, let's go home, get a good night's rest, and start in early tomorrow. Also Bekah, I think the shuttles to the city run about every hour from Boston. If you take the nine o'clock flight, you should arrive at La Guardia around ten. Then you can rent a car and drive into the city, or take a limo and have them drop you off where you need to go."

"Sounds good," said Bekah, "We'll leave here at seven and drive down to Boston. Can we take your car, Josh?"

"Only if you have coffee ready before we go."

"Sounds like a plan," Bekah replied with a smile. "Let's meet back here tomorrow night at six to discuss our day. Josh and I may be late, so you may have to fill us in when we get here. Hopefully we'll make it back before the phone call to Paraguay. We'll tell them we will send down pictures of the crucifix with both of you when you go. Can anyone think of anything else? If not, I guess that about wraps it up. Josh and I will see you when we get back tomorrow evening."

CHAPTER TWENTY-TWO

THE VILLAGE, PARAGUAY
JUNE 7

After finishing breakfast Sherry began to share her thoughts. "I know God is amazing. I know we don't always understand what He is doing, and I know we are not to question God. His word says that we are to trust Him and He will work everything out for the best, but there sure is a lot happening that I don't understand.[49]

"We have a baby being found, which also means that someone has lost a baby. So far, we have eleven people having interrelated dreams. We have what looks to be a five hundred year old, jewel encrusted crucifix down here, and a smaller one in Maine, and I also believe we're going to have some company shortly; not the whole group, but two or three. We need to start planning where we are going to house them and how we are going to get them here."

"You're right Sherry," Daniel said. "Since we still have some time this afternoon, I'm going to visit the chief to see if he will let us hire a few men to build two sleeping areas and another outhouse. We'll barter some chickens for the work we need done. While I'm gone, why don't you make up a list of supplies we'll need. I can pick them up when I go to get our visitors. I better order some extra chickens also. I think we only have about

---

[49] Romans 8:28

twenty-five or so left and we may need them to pay the help. In addition, the chicken coop really needs to be cleaned out. Maybe I can get some of the older children of the village to do it."

"I think that will work," Sherry agreed.

She sat down at the table and started writing everything down. "Do you think when they get here I should ask some of the younger women if they would bring in some bananas and other assorted fruit? Maybe the men would trap some small game for meat, and catch some fish for us. We're going to have a lot of extra people to feed."

"Yes," said Daniel, "I think that's a great idea. I'm going to look for Edwardo and see if he'll come with me to talk with the chief. I'll check with you when I get back."

Daniel walked over and gave Sherry a brief kiss and a hug, and turned to leave. As he was going out the door, Edwardo rushed in. Panting, and soaked in sweat, he gasped out, "I just ran up from the river. They are carrying up the chief's wife Noemi. She's bleeding badly and in terrible pain. She appears to be in labor. They'll be here anytime."

"Daniel, will you first put on another large pot of water to boil," Sherry said, "then go look for the chief."

As she was talking, the men walked in carrying the writhing woman. Actually, she was really a girl, probably no more than fifteen, but marriage and motherhood started at a young age in the jungle. "Some of these girls just aren't ready to be mothers so young," Sherry thought. "Their bodies aren't fully mature, and it makes giving birth very difficult, if not impossible."

She looked down at the young girl as they carried her back into the clinic and could tell that was one of the problems in this situation. The young woman was barely five feet tall and very

114

thin. As she started her examination she could see her large belly was stretched tight and she was straining against a contraction. By all appearances, she was hemorrhaging heavily.

Sherry had seen the girl last week and was quite worried. After the exam, Sherry had told her she needed to rest, and to stay off her feet. She asked about her diet because the young woman was so very thin. Though the local people were poor in our way of thinking, because of the lush jungle, their extensive gardens, and a rich game supply, hunger was not usually an issue. The young woman said her mother-in-law told her she needed to stay thin so that when the baby was born her husband would still want her.

Sherry had tried to tell Noemi that being this thin was unhealthy for her and the baby, but Noemi was convinced her mother-in-law was right. Now, it looked as though she was reaping the consequences of her decisions.

Just as another contraction hit, Daniel and Manu came rushing in followed by several other men from the tribe.

Manu, the chief of the village, had given them permission to build their compound next to his tribal village when they came up the river more than four years ago. He had come to see the clinic when it was finished, but had little to do with Sherry or Daniel since. Even though he did not attend their small church, he did not discourage others in the village from attending. Sherry recognized the men with him now; they were Manu's counselors and headmen of the village. She did not know them personally; they had not been to any of their church services either.

Church services were held twice a week, a Sunday morning service and a Thursday morning Bible Study. They had a very small congregation, only fifteen or so people, but Daniel was always optimistic, and Edwardo, their young pastor, and his family were so very faithful. Sherry was convinced that a breakthrough was coming.

The chief came up to the table and grabbed Sherry by the arm. He shouted at her in fear and frustration, "Pray for her! You are always saying your God hears your prayers. Show me! Pray now!"

Just at that moment, the young woman began to strain. Sherry prayed out loud. "O Lord, God of Heaven and Earth, I ask that You show Yourself strong in the midst of this situation as a witness to this chief and the village of Your power and Your grace. Strengthen this young woman and show me what needs to be done. I pray this in the mighty name of Jesus."

Just at that moment, Noemi pushed, and Sherry could see the top of the baby's head crowning. "Come on little momma," Sherry said under her breath. She pushed again and the baby slid out. The hemorrhaging continued unabated. The baby started to cry immediately and Sherry wrapped it in a towel and called to Daniel, "Come here, take the baby and cut the cord."

Sherry gave her full attention to the mother, concerned about the substantial loss of blood. Sherry administered a drug to help the uterus contract, but the hemorrhaging continued. "O Lord," she whispered, "Please don't let this little girl die. She's a momma now and her baby needs her. Let her life be a witness to Your power."

If she had been in a city, in a hospital, with all the equipment she needed available to her, and with a few pints of blood to replace what had been lost, Noemi might have had a fighting chance. But here in the jungle, God was her only hope, and Sherry was counting on Him to come through. Adrenalin pumped through Sherry as she used every option available to her to stop the flow, but it appeared to be a losing battle. As she sat by the young girl and held her hand, Noemi began to die. Her color was fading and her respirations were decreasing, leaving Sherry thinking that each breath would be her last. Her life's blood was slowly seeping out of her, and Sherry could only sit and watch.

Sherry prayed again, "Lord I know that for each of us it is appointed a time to live and a time to die;[50] but in your goodness and mercy, I ask that this be the time for life, not only for this baby, but also for Noemi his mother." Sherry closed her eyes and continued holding the girls hand.

Minutes went by with no change. Suddenly, she felt her hand being squeezed. She looked down at the young girl, surprised she was still breathing. Sherry went to take her blood pressure, wondering if she would even get a reading. To her amazement it read 80/50. Low, but living.

The placenta had delivered with just a small amount of blood. Of course, with the blood loss the young girl had experienced thus far, there couldn't be much left.

The baby was crying loudly and the girl's eyes fluttered. Something began to change. God was stepping in and throwing off the spirit of death. Blood began to flow again, this time inside her body. Her color came back and her respirations began to improve. Sherry took the baby from Daniel and put it to the mother's breast. A suckling child stimulates the uterus to contract, and helps stop the bleeding. Noemi opened her eyes and looked up at Sherry. "Is it a boy?" she whispered.

---

[50] Ecclesiastes 3:1-8

Sherry nodded yes, unable to speak. "I have witnessed a miracle," she thought. "This girl should be dead considering the loss of blood she has experienced." Sherry turned to Manu, the chief, and said with a smile, "See; my God does answer prayers."

"Yes," the chief said. "He has done this wonderful thing for me. What can I do to pay Him back? He must truly be a powerful God to overcome the god of death. I have a prize bull in my herd. The neighboring tribes bring all their cows to my bull because he is big and strong and makes good calves. I will sacrifice him to your God as an offering for my wife and son."[51]

"No," Sherry replied, "God doesn't want you to sacrifice your bull. He doesn't need your bull; He owns the cattle on a thousand hills. [52] He just wants you. He wants you to serve Him and Him alone. He wants you to reject all your other gods. Have they ever done something like this for you? Your wife was literally brought back from the dead. Only my God can do something like that. He wants to be your God also.

"Thousands of years ago people sacrificed bulls, sheep, and goats to God so that their sins would be covered with the blood of their sacrifice. That blood didn't change anything. People kept on sinning, and more and more animals died.[53] Then God sent a better sacrifice, His own Son, Jesus. He was sacrificed for our sins, and just like your wife, God raised Him from the dead.[54]

"The blood of Jesus does not just cover our sins; His blood washes our sins away. If we turn our lives to God, and Jesus His Son, and are truly sorry, our sins are not only forgiven, but they

---

[51] 1 Samuel 15:22-23
[52] Psalm 50:10
[53] Isaiah 1:11-18
[54] Hebrews 9:24-26

are forgotten.[55] Also, something changes inside us and we don't want to sin anymore.[56] God changes our heart of stone to one that is tender.[57] Would you like to know this God and His Son Jesus?"

Manu stood there for a moment looking at Sherry. He had just been through a traumatic experience with the birth of his son and near death of his wife, and he had seen God answer prayer and escort Nomi back from the brink of death.

Manu looked at Sherry, and then he looked at the men he had brought with him. A small voice inside his head whispered, "If you pray with that woman you will look weak and foolish before your men. You need to stay strong." With regret, Sherry watched as he turned and walked away.

Sherry watched as the joy and wonder faded from Manu's face, to be replaced by pride and cynicism. She wanted to call him back but she knew she couldn't. He had to make the choice himself; she couldn't do it for him.

Sherry turned back to Noemi, his wife, and the baby. She put a smile on her face to hide her distress at the choice the chief had made. She prayed that he would have another opportunity. Today a seed of hope and truth had been planted, and Sherry was determined that it would grow to be harvested another day.

Sherry looked down at Noemi and saw she had been listening. Noemi looked up with wonder and said softly to Sherry, "I would like to know about your God and His Son Jesus. The gods our people serve are cruel."

---

[55] Ezekiel 18:21-22
[56] Romans 7:14-25
[57] Ezekiel 36:26

Sherry told Noemi, "Do you know that when we choose to serve God, He does not think of us as servants or slaves, but instead, He loves us as sons and daughters?[58] When we ask to serve Him, He comes and lives in our hearts in a special way that God designed when He made us.[59] This way He can always be with us."

"Will I still be able to do what I want?" Noemi asked looking worried.

"Of course," replied Sherry, "God has given us all a free will to do whatever we want. It's just that now you will want to do what is good and right. God is a good God, and you will want to please Him.

"Noemi, do you know what sin is?"

"Yes. It's doing a bad thing or hurting someone. It makes God angry."

"That's right," replied Sherry, "God will show you what is right and wrong, just like a father would, because He cares about you. He will speak to you very softly in here." And she placed her hand over her heart. "We all sin sometimes, but if we are sorry and ask God, He will forgive our sins and wipe them all away.[60]

"Noemi, why don't you rest for a while and we'll talk again later. Let me take the baby and clean him up, then we'll let him rest too. I'll lay him in the cradle, and put it alongside your bed."

Noemi closed her eyes. Then she opened them and tried to sit up. "Please, thank your God for saving the life of my baby and me. I'm so grateful we are alive. Would you tell him for me?"

---

[58] Romans 8:15
[59] Galatians 4:6
[60] 1 John 1:9

"I'll tell Him," Sherry said softly. "After we talk, you can tell Him yourself."

CHAPTER TWENTY-THREE

THE VILLAGE, PARAGUAY
JUNE 7

Sherry didn't remember when she had sat down last, she thought maybe breakfast. She had not had lunch, and dinner was only a figment of her imagination. She was sure there must be food around somewhere, but she was just too tired to make the effort. She heard someone coming and looked up.

Daniel was carrying a large pot from which enticing smells were emanating. Her stomach recognized the smell and started to reassert itself. Daniel was followed by Edwardo carrying Paulo, Connie carrying the new baby, and Maria was holding on to Connie's skirt.

Connie said, "We've come to share. I figured with everything that has gone on, you would not have had time to prepare a meal. I just used more vegetables to stretch the soup."

"Is that guiso popo I smell, and do I smell bread also?" Sherry asked. "I'm salivating like a dog. I don't know when I have ever been so hungry, and so very, very tired. You are a Godsend."

"Well," said Connie, as she pushed her hair out of her eyes and shifted the baby to the other hip, "we are celebrating an adoption. We have named the baby Emilio, and are formally adopting him. We talked with Manu, and he said it was good. He also said he would find a way to thank you and your God for saving Noemi and his son. Noemi was his second wife. His first wife and child died five years ago in childbirth."

Edwardo spoke up, "Manu is a quiet man, but one of strength and integrity. He is relatively young to be a chief, around thirty-five years of age. He is very self-conscious about this fact, which is why he surrounds himself with people who support him."

As she listened to what Edwardo had to say, Sherry placed bowls on the table and they all sat down to share the meal. Sherry put away her worries and concerns for the moment and focused on the food and fellowship. "I don't know what Daniel and I would do without you both," she said to Connie and Edwardo. "You are such a blessing to us. Sometimes it's hard for us, living here so far from family, and so near the jungle. But both of you are our family now, and this place is our home."

Connie came over and hugged her. "Well, we consider you both as family also. Now come and sit down, and let's eat."

Edwardo prayed and blessed the food. Dinner was delicious; hunger being a great seasoning. There was little talk and everyone concentrated on the meal. Even little Maria finished all her soup.

Finally Sherry got up and said, "I'm going to take some of this soup back to Noemi and see if she will eat. She needs to, in order to get her strength back. Connie, why don't you come back with me? The babies are getting restless and probably need feeding. You can feed them and we can visit. We will let the men go down to the river for water, and then, maybe they will clean up for us."

Daniel picked up the buckets from the corner and said, "Edwardo, let's stop by your home and get your buckets. It's a never ending chore and we might as well make the most of our time. We'll take Maria with us."

"Come on sweet girl," said Edwardo, "let's go get some water."

Maria liked going down to the river. There were always other children there and boats. She loved boats. Sometimes Edwardo would take her for a ride in one of the flat bottom boats. They were very stable. Her face lit up with excitement as she wondered if she would get a ride today.

They picked up Edwardo's buckets and followed the path down to the river. The night insects were beginning to sing their songs and the pace of life slowed down. Edwardo kept Maria very close. There was word of a wild boar in the area that was terrorizing people who ventured out into the jungle.

The village was not actually in the jungle, but it was close enough they could spit in it if they wanted to. Edwardo let Maria go and play with some other small children who were at the river. He told her to stay away from the water and stay close by.

As they were watching, Edwardo told Daniel, "I spoke with Manu about the shelters and the new outhouse you needed; that we wanted to hire some of the men to help build them, do some hunting, and gather food from the jungle. Usually the women go into the jungle to harvest its bounty, but with talk of the wild boar, the women are staying clear of the jungle. Manu was much more cooperative than usual. He even offered to have the men do it for free."

"Wow! That's great," said Daniel, "especially since he usually gets a portion of what we pay them. I wonder if what happened with his wife, and new son softened his heart. When Sherry told him about God, I thought for a moment that he would answer yes to the call of God. I just wish that his counselors had not been there with him. He was watching their reaction to what was happening and not listening to his own heart. We have to believe that seed was planted, and another opportunity will present itself for us to share the gospel."[61]

It was almost full dark and they needed to get back to the compound. Edwardo called to Maria and she came scampering over with a big grin on her face. In her arms was a small wriggling puppy.

There had been a litter of puppies born recently. Edwardo assumed they had been brought down to the river to give them away or to drown. That was usually the fate of unwanted animals.

Edwardo looked at the smile on his daughter's face, something he didn't see very often. She was a very serious child. She was almost four and he thought the puppy would be something to entertain her. How much trouble could a little puppy be? Edwardo squatted down and said to Maria, "You are almost four years old. Do you think that is old enough to have a puppy? They are a lot of work."

Maria's smile broadened. "Oh yes, Papa" she said. "I'm getting bigger every day. I'll work very hard for my puppy. Please Papa, may I keep it?"

Edwardo took the puppy from her and it squirmed in his hands trying to chew his fingers with its sharp little teeth. He looked down and saw it was a male. At least that meant no puppies. "Alright," he said, "but you clean up any messes. Your mother does not have time to deal with all of us and a puppy too."

---

[61] Matthew 13:18-23

If possible, Maria's grin got broader. "Oh thank you," she said as she wrapped her small arms around his legs.

He looked up at Daniel and shrugged. "Well, I guess we have a puppy."

"Better you than me. From the looks of those paws, he is going to be a big one."

They all walked companionably back to Edwardo's house to drop off his water and then on to the compound. They could hear Maria talking nonstop to the puppy. Maybe this puppy had some unforeseen advantages. It might bring Maria out of her shell and get her to talking, instead of silently watching everything that happened.

By the time they got back to the compound, Maria was asleep in one of Edwardo's arms, and the puppy was asleep in the other. It was quiet, and Edwardo and Daniel both walked through the house and back into the clinic. All three babies were asleep, Noemi was asleep, and Connie and Sherry were enjoying a peaceful cup of tea. Connie took one look at Edwardo carrying the puppy and said, "What did you get yourself into? This could not have been your idea."

"Well no, but the idea kind of grew on me as I saw Maria responding to the puppy. Don't worry; you won't have to take care of him."

"Well don't put anyone down. They are all asleep and I want them to stay that way. Head on home, I will follow with the two babies when I finish my tea. Daniel can accompany me so I will not be walking alone."

"Sure, no problem; whenever you are ready," Daniel answered.

Edwardo left after a short goodbye to everyone.

Daniel looked over at Connie and said, "I think when you see the puppy and Maria interact tomorrow, you will think it's a good idea. Before she fell asleep, Maria spent several minutes in deep conversation with that puppy, not baby talk, but an honest to goodness discussion. I'll take your cup if you're done with your tea. It's been a long day."

"Yes, come on, I'll have to feed these two gentlemen once more for the night." Connie turned back to Sherry to say goodnight, but Sherry was sitting there with her head on her chest, sound asleep. "Well let's go. Tomorrow won't wait, whether we're ready or not."

Daniel got back to the compound after walking Connie home. He heard talking coming from the clinic. Sherry was awake, and had just finished checking Noemi. She walked into their bedroom with a satisfied look on her face. "Everything looks good," she said. Sherry was not in the least bit surprised. God did not do partial miracles. He finished the job.

CHAPTER TWENTY-FOUR

OGUNQUIT, MAINE
JUNE 8

Bekah just finished brushing her hair when she heard a knock. Walking down the stairs, she went through the kitchen and opened the back door. Josh stood there wearing dark gray Dockers, a white shirt, and a black cardigan sweater. Bekah stared at him for a moment, then stood back and let him in. He also took in her appearance. Her hair was loose and curling. She was wearing a white shirt, black pants and black sweater, and she had a pretty green scarf tied in some kind of intricate knot around her neck. "Good morning," they said to each other.

Bekah led him into the kitchen and handed him a "to go" cup. "We'd better get going. Its rush hour and I didn't take that into consideration. It can take us two hours or more to get there if we hit any traffic. How do you take your coffee, with cream and sugar?"

"No," said Josh, "black is fine."

She picked up her purse, which was a little heavier than usual because of the weight of the crucifix, and her "to go" cup. Hers was also black, the same way Nana had always drank hers. They walked out the door into the bright sunshine. It was a beautiful day, and it would be a nice ride into Boston.

The drive into Boston went smoothly. It took less than ninety minutes, so they had time to stop at the airport and get more coffee and a muffin. They really hadn't talked much about what was happening. It was almost like they were avoiding the subject, but it had to be discussed, and it needed to be sooner, rather than later.

Bekah decided to take the plunge and broached the subject. "If everything goes as smoothly as it did this morning, maybe we will get back in time for the phone call tonight. It would be nice to tell Sherry and Daniel something about the crucifix. Plus, we're going to tell them that Renato and Ted will be coming down to Paraguay the day after tomorrow. Also, I want to hear what is happening on their end. They may have as much to tell us as we do them."

Josh listened, and then said, "It's going to be a big surprise for them to find out that they are going to have company shortly. If Renato and Ted leave the day after tomorrow, they won't get to Asuncion until the following morning. It will take Daniel a day to get to Puerto Bahia Negra and then shop for his supplies. Ted and Renato will also have to shop in Asuncion and then they will have to charter a flight up to Puerto Bahia Negra, load up, and take the boat or boats back upriver. Things are going to be very busy for everyone from now on."

"I think you're right," Bekah replied. "We better take advantage of our downtime in the city. Let's plan on having a really good lunch. I like cooking for everyone; but now and then I love eating out. Do you know if that address Ted gave you is near Time Square? I know there are several great pizza places there. We can stop and have a wonderful lunch. There is absolutely no pizza as good as a New York pizza."

"Sounds great," said Josh. "I haven't had a piece of good pizza in quite a while. Real New York pizza doesn't make it down to Oklahoma very often. I remember as a kid hearing my mom complain because she couldn't get the right kind of cheese to make her lasagna. My mom is Italian and those things were important to her. Great food is part of an Italian heritage. Things are somewhat better these days, but not much."

As they were approaching the airport, Josh said, "There's the airport entrance, start looking for a parking lot." After the car was parked, they made their way to the terminal. They already had e-tickets on their phone and they carried no luggage, so they went right to their gate.

Their flight was called and they got in line to board. The line moved slowly as people tried to put their carry-ons in the overhead space. There was no assigned seating so they took the first two seats they found together and settled back for the short flight.

Bekah was surprised when Josh shook her shoulder. She had actually fallen asleep. They were already pulling up to the gate. After exiting the secure area, they went into the terminal area where they were to pick up their ride.

They saw a man holding a sign with Bekah's name on it and they made their way through the crowd toward him. The driver already had the name and address of where they were going, so Bekah and Josh could just sit back and relax.

It was a quick ride into the city. Josh called the number Ted had given him, and said they would probably be there by eleven-thirty. The day was beautiful and it felt good to be alive. Bekah enjoyed Josh's company. She hadn't had very many relationships with men since her divorce. She sensed Josh's glance and decided that it felt good to be appreciated. She decided to take a chance with her next question. "Josh, you've heard some of my background and my story, can you tell me some of yours?"

"Sure," he replied, "I was wondering when someone was going to ask me. I had a normal childhood into my teenage years. My parents are both still alive, and they will tell you it's a miracle they didn't shoot me. I got wild in my teens. I had a close friend and we both hung around with the wrong crowd. We drank, smoked pot, and even wrecked a car or two. Thank God the youth pastor of our church took a special interest in us. We were his pet project, and he was our thorn in the flesh. He just wouldn't leave us alone. I think finally he just wore us down.

"He had been badgering us to come to youth camp for three years. It was our last year to qualify. He knew it, and we knew it. One day he caught us in a weak moment and we told him we would go, just to get him off our backs. Unbeknownst to us, he had everyone praying for us even before we arrived. We didn't stand a chance. If God was ever guilty of cheating, this was the case. God had an unfair advantage, and made full use of it.

"There were several beautiful teenage girls there from surrounding churches, and from the moment we saw them, we were sunk. We spent all our time together, going to Bible studies, church services, swimming or playing games. I guess it all worked. The prayers and the Bible studies finally got down into our hearts and took root. We both surrendered to God."

"All the swimming must have acted like a cold shower. We both watched our manners for the whole two weeks. I still get Christmas cards from Marilyn, she was my favorite. She's married now and lives in Oregon. She's got five kids.

"After graduating high school, my friend and I went to Oral Roberts University for six years and both got Master's Degrees. Then I enlisted in the Marines. I still thought I was a tough guy and wanted to prove it. I stayed in for fifteen years. I had a tour in Kuwait and later in Iraq.

"When I got out, I went back to school on the GI Bill to finish my doctorate. I lived at home and supported myself with several part time jobs. I must have delivered a million pizzas. I kept going to church and kept my faith in God. I became Mission's Director at my church, and here I am today. That's it, because here we are and I've talked enough."

CHAPTER TWENTY-FIVE

NEW YORK CITY
JUNE 8

They made arrangements with the limo driver to be picked up at one-thirty in front of the store. Their appointment was for twelve o'clock. It was now eleven forty-five. They were fifteen minutes early, but that was better than being fifteen minutes late. They walked into the jewelry store where a few customers were browsing at the counters, probably the lunch crowd window shopping.

The man at the desk behind the counter looked up when Josh and Bekah entered. He came around from behind the counter, and walked towards them. He held out his hand to Josh. "Hello," he said, "I'm Haydon Carlton."

Josh shook his hand and replied, "Joshua Randall, and this is Bekah Ryan. Thank you for taking the time to see us."

"No problem," Haydon replied with genuine enthusiasm. "Ted and I go way back, and I have to admit, I was curious. He didn't tell me much, but the little he did sparked my interest. Let's go in the back. I have an office where we can talk privately."

He opened the door to a lavishly decorated office. A beautiful old mahogany desk and two chairs filled one side of the room, the warm mahogany glowing in the diffused light. In front of it were two equally elegant chairs. Across the room was a leather loveseat and matching chair. The room was dimly lit by what appeared to be an exquisite Tiffany lamp. Clearly, Haydon Carlton enjoyed his creature comforts. He said, "Let me get some better lighting in here so we can get a good look at the piece you've brought me, and please call me Haydon." He proceeded to press several wall switches and a bank of recessed lighting illuminated the room.

Despite his apparent friendliness, and willingness to help, Bekah began to feel a sense of caution rise up inside her.

Haydon led them to the loveseat and he sat in the chair. "Now," he said, "let's see the piece that has provoked such curiosity and interest."

Bekah reached into her purse and took out the crucifix. She had wrapped it in a soft towel to protect it. She handed him the bundle. He opened the towel and drew in a hissing breath of astonishment. "Well," he replied with eagerness, "This is certainly an extraordinary piece of jewelry. Ted didn't say much, so I wasn't sure what to expect. This far exceeds my expectations." He looked up at Bekah and asked with excitement, "Do you have any idea what this is?"

Bekah answered, "We think it's a fifteenth or sixteenth century Spanish piece. My grandmother left it to me when she died. That's all we know. As Ted told you, it's a mystery."

Josh looked over at her questioningly, but she shook her head, no.

Haydon had his jeweler's loupe out and was examining the piece closely. Bekah could see the excitement building in him. He looked up, and she had a sinking feeling. The expression on his face made her uncomfortable, and confirmed her sense of caution. She saw something in his eyes that spoke of more than interest; it spoke of avarice. He wanted the crucifix. Bekah was sure of it.

"I know several people who would be extremely interested in a piece such as this," Haydon said excitedly, "No questions asked. I could sell it for you easily, and since it's for a friend I'd only charge five percent commission. This appears to be authentic, and from the short time I've had to look at it, the stones appear to be genuine also and top quality. This could be worth more than a small fortune. Why don't you leave it with me and I'll do some more research and make a few phone calls to some prospective buyers?"

Bekah said, "Thank you, but no. We'll take it with us. I don't want to sell it; I just wanted to find out if it was genuine. It's a family heirloom. But thank you for your time, and for seeing us on such short notice." She rose to go and Josh got up with her.

As they headed for the door, Haydon made one more try. "If you don't want to sell it, you should consider putting it in a museum, so everyone would be able to appreciate it. I could work that out for you also."

"No," Bekah shook her head. "I don't even care how much it's worth. I just wanted to know if it was genuine. Thanks again for your time." They shook hands and left. As they walked out the office, and into the store, Bekah didn't say a word.

When they left the store, Bekah turned to Josh and said, "I don't like him. He gave me a bad feeling. He wanted the crucifix for himself. I'm sure of it. I hope we don't have any trouble because of him."

Josh took her arm and they began to merge with the throng of people walking by. They had almost an hour to wait before the limo returned. They wanted lunch and spotted a great looking pizza place across the street. "Come on; let's get away from the store."

After ordering two slices of pizza each, they took their plates and drinks and sat towards the back of the room. "I think you are right about the guy," Josh agreed. "He was looking out for number one, and certainly not trying to help a friend. Maybe his original intentions were good, but once he saw the crucifix, greed kicked in and he was hooked."

Bekah drank her Coke and nibbled at her pizza; she wondered what kind of repercussions this situation was going to cause. Just then, her phone began to ring. It was Ted. Maybe she was about to find out. She answered warily, "Hello."

"Hello Bekah," Ted replied, "I just got a call from Haydon and he's worried about you. He told me he offered to help you find out more about the crucifix and how much it's worth; he even said he would sell it for you and you turned him down and left. Now he's worried about you walking around the city with something so valuable. He wants to provide you with protection. He says has an escort service that assists people carrying valuable purchases so they make it home safely. That sounds very thoughtful of him. Why don't you tell me where you are so I can have him send someone over?"

Bekah replied guardedly, "We came down without any problems and we'll make it home safely. Besides, I have Josh with me. He's my escort service. You didn't give Haydon my address, did you? I really don't feel comfortable with him."

"I didn't give the exact address. He asked how far you had to travel today and I said just to Ogunquit. I didn't see a problem at the time," Ted replied, a hint of unease in his voice. "Should I be concerned?"

"We'll talk about it more when Josh and I get back," Bekah answered, trying to keep annoyance out of her voice. "See you later."

"Do you think we really have a problem," Josh said, "or are we just misreading this and being overcautious?"

Bekah looked up with flashing eyes, "I think we have a big problem. Haydon wanted to know where we were so he could send an escort service to protect us, and get us home safely. What does that sound like to you, a nice person showing genuine concern, or a fortune hunter, who is trying to get his hands on the goods? Am I reading too much into this?"

"No," answered Josh, "unfortunately, I think you're right. He was real genuine until he saw the crucifix, and then his motives seemed to change. I don't know if he would actually do anything to hurt us, but he definitely wants to keep tabs on that crucifix."

CHAPTER TWENTY-SIX

NEW YORK CITY
JUNE 8

"Come on, its one twenty, that limo should be here momentarily. Let's go outside and watch for it." As Josh and Bekah were crossing the street they saw the limo pull up in front of the jewelry store. Haydon Carlton came out of the store. He walked up to the limo and spoke to the driver. He took out his billfold and gave the driver some money, then turned and walked back into the store. The limo pulled away; it left without them.

Haydon Carlton smiled. Josh and Bekah had told him they were expecting a limo at one o'clock. He had been watching for it. He had seen Josh and Bekah crossing the street and hoped he had enough time to get rid of the driver. Luckily, the driver wasn't too picky about how he earned extra money, and left with very little encouragement, other than five hundred dollars.

Haydon now turned to another member of his staff. He was employed as a sales person, but earned extra money doing odd jobs, and he wasn't afraid to get his hands dirty. In fact he enjoyed what Haydon liked to call sticky situations.

His name was Carlos Rampone. He was an attractive man of about forty, and just six foot tall. He had dark hair, which he kept that way with help. He wasn't quite a body builder, but he worked out enough to enhance his already muscular build.

"I've got a job for you." Haydon announced. "Come over here." He looked through the window and watched Josh and Bekah stand for a moment in shock, and then they turned to each other to discuss their alternatives. Haydon pointed them out to his employee. "Follow them. They'll probably head for the subway. See if you can get them separated in the crowd and then take the crucifix from her. She should be easy enough for you to overcome. Try not to attract too much attention. I don't want the police involved. Come back here when you're done. Use the back entrance. Be careful with the big guy. He looks like he could handle himself in a fight. Concentrate on the girl."

Bekah grabbed Josh's arm, squeezing it and hissing in his ear, "Oh my gosh! Look what he has done. He sent the limo driver away. Now we know he's not out to help us. What are we going to do? How will we get home?"

Josh grabbed Bekah's hand and pulled her down the street. "The first thing we are going to do is calm down; then we are going to get out of this area. Let's go find a subway station and see if we can get to the airport that way. If he has people out looking for us, we can get lost in the crowd."

They walked up to Forty-Second Street, unaware that they were already being followed. There was a subway entrance on the corner. They went down the stairs, and found a cashier booth with someone in it selling tokens. Walking up to the booth, Josh asked, "We're trying to get to La Guardia Airport, can you tell us how to get there from here?"

"Sure I can; no problem. Take the E train uptown, get off at Jackson Heights, and then look for the Q bus to the airport. Got that?"

"Thanks," said Josh and purchased two tokens. They continued on, going down the stairs to the subway level. It was extremely crowded and they worked their way through the throng of people to the front of the platform.

Meanwhile, Carlos was watching from a short distance away. He could get close, because they hadn't seen him before. After assessing the situation, he decided to work his way over to them, and at the right moment give the big guy a shove off the platform. In the subsequent confusion, he would grab the girls backpack and make for the stairs. She would be too worried about the big guy to try to follow him.

Several trains thundered into the station and Carlos still couldn't make his move. Bekah was clinging to Josh like glue. Then their train arrived. The doors opened and it seemed as though a deluge of bodies exited the train, everyone bumping and shoving. As the doors to the train began to close, Bekah squeezed into the subway car. Here was his opportunity. He pushed between them, elbowed the big guy aside, and shoved his way onto the train.

Bekah turned to look for Josh just as the doors closed. Josh was still on the platform. "Don't worry, I'll get the next one," he yelled. "Wait for me at the bus stop." He was unaware that he had been outmaneuvered, and that Bekah was in serious danger.

Trying not to panic, Josh prayed, "Lord, send angels to protect Bekah and keep her safe." Josh waited, and continued to pray. Ten minutes later the next E train showed up. While boarding, and during the short ride, he kept thanking God for protection for both himself and Bekah.[62] The train pulled into the station, the doors opened, and there stood a worried looking Bekah; worried but safe.

---

[62] 1 Thessalonians 5:18

"Thank God," she said as she grabbed Josh's arm. "I'm not letting go of you until we're on that plane. All I could think of was that something terrible could happen, but I kept praying God would keep us safe, and He did. I already purchased two bus tickets to the airport. The bus runs every fifteen minutes. Let's get on line."

The bus was right there waiting for them. They boarded, and took seats in the middle of the bus. They couldn't talk about what had transpired, because of all the people. The three o'clock shuttle to Boston got them in shortly after four.

They were unaware, that sitting behind them was Carlos Rampone. He had a pad out and was writing down anything he heard that would be of interest to his boss. Carlos had called him to let him know there had been no opportunity to take the backpack from the woman.

A tall stranger had engaged her in conversation, and stayed by her side the whole ride. There was something about his appearance that disturbed Carlos. The man was very big and his face had a strange quality about it. He could not describe it but it disquieted him. He thought the man might be a problem.[63]

Haydon told him to follow them. They were taking the Boston Shuttle and driving toward Ogunquit, Maine. He was to find out where she lived and anything else that might be of value.

After landing, it did not take long for them to find Josh's car in the parking lot. They settled in for the ninety minute ride to Ogunquit. It was quiet for a few minutes and then Josh broke the silence. "I think we'll be home in time for the meeting at the Lobster Pot. Didn't some of them say they were going early to eat dinner and relax before the phone call? We should make it in

---

[63] Hebrews 13:2

141

plenty of time. We have a lot of information to give everyone, and we need to talk with Ted."

Bekah answered, "I can't believe that Ted betrayed us all, if that's what you think. He was sincere when I talked to him that first day he showed up. I think he got taken in by Haydon. Ted put a lot of store in Haydon saying he was a Christian. Anyone can say that, but Ted doesn't realize that right now. He's a gullible baby Christian, and he needs to understand that it's not just saying you're a Christian, but acting like you're a Christian that shows your true nature.[64, 65]I'm sure when Ted finds out what happened he will be as upset as we are, if not more, because he will feel responsible, and he will also feel betrayed."

"I'm tempted to call Ted and tell him what happened," said Josh, "but I don't want to do it while I'm driving, and I want to wait until everyone has arrived so there will be no confusion. We should be home soon."

As Josh parked the car in front of the Lobster Pot, Bekah recognized two of the cars already there. They walked into the restaurant and went right to the back room. Everyone had just finished ordering their dinner, and they were all talking excitedly when Josh and Bekah entered the room.

Ted came hurrying over with a look of concern and grabbed Bekah's arm. "What happened to both of you, why didn't you take the limo? Haydon called. He didn't know what happened to you. He wanted me to call him when you both got home."

"Don't even think about it," Bekah stated in an angry voice. "We were across the street when the limo driver showed up. He was a few minutes early. As we started crossing the street,

---

[64] Matthew 7:15-20
[65] James 2:14-20

Haydon came out of his store, walked over, and talked with the driver. It looked like he gave him some money, and the driver took off. I'd like to know what he said to that driver, and how much he paid him to make him leave us stranded."

"I talked to Haydon," Ted said, "He told me you both didn't show up for the limo."

"Well we did," huffed Bekah, "and no thanks to him, we made it home safe. I don't think there should be anymore conversations with Haydon Carlton. I don't trust him. He was more interested in obtaining the crucifix than anything else. I wonder if he might even want it for himself. His office was filled with amazing artifacts from all over the world. Well that's enough about this for a while. Tell us, how did things go here today?" Looking at Ted, and Renato she said, "Have the two of you finished getting organized for your trip? You still have all day tomorrow to get ready."

"Yes," they answered.

"Take a seat and order dinner," Ted said. "We all voted that food and fellowship were important. We'll have enough time to eat dinner and relax over coffee. Then we can call Paraguay."

When the meal was finished and everyone had a second cup of coffee, Joe got out his phone and dialed. "I'm putting it on speaker phone." Joe said.

Meanwhile, Carlos was cruising down the main street of Ogunquit, looking for Josh's car. He had followed them to the parking lot to find out what kind of car they were driving. He wrote down the make, model, and license number. He knew he would not be able to rent a car in time to follow them, but was confident he knew where they were going, and hoped to spot the car by the Lobster Pot. By sitting behind them in the plane, he had gleaned a few pieces of information that were proving helpful to him. He parked two cars down and watched the door, waiting for them to come out. When they did, he would follow them, and make new plans. He called Haydon.

CHAPTER TWENTY-SEVEN

THE VILLAGE, PARAGUAY
JUNE 8

Morning always seems to come early when you are tired and have what appear to be too many tasks for the time allotted. It seemed to Sherry as though she had just closed her eyes, and here it was daylight. Unfortunately, during the night, she had to get up three times for Noemi and the baby.

Being so thin and undernourished, Sherry wasn't sure Noemi could produce milk. She had Noemi put her child to her breast for a time, but he was hungry and the well was dry. She had to go boil some water with a little sugar and powdered milk, just to tide him over. If Noemi did not start producing milk on her own, Sherry would be looking for another nursing mother.

Sherry immediately started to bring to mind all the women she had recently delivered. Through process of elimination, she came up with the name of Erecia. She was a young girl herself, not much older than Noemi, but this recent child had been her second. The first had died of dysentery, a common ailment in the back jungles, due to poor sanitation and lack of refrigeration.

Small children, infants, and the elderly were very susceptible to prolonged bouts of diarrhea, and there were many other things that could cause this problem. Being in the jungle, she had limited resources, and infant mortality was high, though the rate in the area she served was significantly lower than other places. Sherry attributed that fact, in a slight measure, to her skills. Mostly, she believed it was due to the prayers they sent up to heaven and a loving, caring God who responded in kind.

After quickly washing and dressing, Sherry took time to brush her teeth. It was important to take care of yourself also, as well as all who were placed in your care. Other than herself, it was an eight to ten hour boat ride to a doctor, and she had no idea where the nearest dentist was located. She had pulled several teeth for various members of the tribe since she had been here. She did not want to have to pull one of her own.

Sherry made up a bottle for the baby in case it was needed and brought Noemi cornbread and honey with hot tea to drink. Noemi needed to drink as much fluid as she could tolerate, to offset the drastic blood loss from the near fatal hemorrhage. Sherry was convinced Noemi's recovery was a miracle, but as God had done His part, it was important that she do hers.

She walked back into the clinic and saw that Noemi was sitting up attempting to nurse the baby. There must be something there because he was sucking for all he was worth and seemed to be satisfied. "Don't let him suck too long on one breast or it will get sore. Switch him to the other. Did you get up and get him yourself?"

Noemi smiled and nodded. "I was a little wobbly, but I was careful. He is a good, strong baby. He will be like his father. Manu came to see me last night. He did not want to disturb you. Both you and Daniel were sleeping."

Sherry stood there a moment, surprised at that comment, and then replied, "I'm going to make breakfast; I'll be back with some shortly. Meanwhile, this should hold you over."

146

Sherry found Daniel in the bedroom getting dressed. "Noemi told me Manu had come to see her last night while we were sleeping. He's never been in this house before yesterday, and now, late last night, he comes through uninvited and unannounced while we were sleeping. I know it's a special circumstance, but I feel uncomfortable about this. Up until now, everyone has always respected our privacy. Maybe I'm making too much of this, and maybe all the recent happenings have put me on edge."

"I understand your concern. Let's pray a hedge of protection around the whole compound.[66] It could have been his concern for Noemi and the baby that overrode his manners. We'll ask that angels guard the perimeter and repel all the fiery darts of the enemy."[67] As Daniel finished praying, noises were coming from the kitchen. He took Sherry in his arms and gave her a squeeze and a kiss on her forehead. "That will have to hold you till later," he said with tenderness. "I think Edwardo is here with his growing family for breakfast. I'm going to say hello."

"Alright," Sherry said. "You get coffee going while I get Noemi something to drink that will help stimulate her milk supply." Sherry walked back to the clinic and found Noemi up and wrapping her baby in a blanket. "What are you doing, and where do you think you are going? I'm getting you breakfast, and here is something for you to drink to help your milk production. You need a few more days rest to get your strength back."

"No, Manu told me he would come for me this morning. He said he will get someone to help me for a while. He wants me home." Noemi smiled a shy smile. "He said that he misses me."

---

[66] Job 1:10
[67] Ephesians 6:16

"Well rest until he comes. I'll talk to him and explain that you are weak and need to rest for several days. I'll bring you breakfast as soon as it's ready, some nice fruit, rice, and hot tea."

Sherry walked back into the kitchen, and said hello to everyone. Their small kitchen was getting considerably crowded with four adults, two babies and one little girl. She also noticed an addition; a small, squirming puppy that Maria was holding tight to her chest.

Sherry thought back to the times when it was just her and Daniel. That seemed a lifetime ago. She hadn't told Daniel yet, but if she was correct, in seven months it would be even more crowded. She thought this was as good a time as any.

As she opened her mouth to make the announcement both babies began to cry, the puppy started barking, and Manu walked in. He was alone this time, not being followed by his usual entourage.

CHAPTER TWENTY-EIGHT

THE VILLAGE, PARAGUAY
JUNE 8

As Manu walked into the kitchen, he took note of the crowded conditions. "We must make you a bigger kitchen. There are too many people in here. I will send more helpers today to do the kitchen, the other sleep places, and the outside bathhouse. When does the company come?"

"They leave tomorrow," Daniel answered. "It may be three or four days until they make it up the river. We'll know more after we talk to them tonight."

"Good, that will give us time to finish. Also, I have a gift for Doctor Sherry. She gave me back my wife and child. I have already lost one wife and baby in childbirth because no one prayed. She changed that."

Sherry stopped him, "I didn't do much more than pray. God gave you back your wife and child."

"Yes," said Manu, I know He did, but you helped also, and you said God didn't want a sacrifice or present, so I'll give it to you."

With that said, Manu unwrapped the package he was holding. Inside was a gold crucifix encrusted with gem stones and threaded on a long, heavy gold chain. Daniel and Sherry stared, mouth agape and speechless. Connie and Edwardo also looked on, at a loss for words.

Manu said, "This has been passed down from the chief to his children for a very long time. If it wasn't for you I wouldn't have a son to pass it on to. This is part of the tribe's wealth, but it is the chief's to give, and I want to give it to you." He held it out to Sherry.

Sherry was awestruck. She held out her hand to take it, and then quickly pulled it back. "Manu," she said, "I can't begin to tell you how much I appreciate this gift, and I hope you realize that whether I take it or not, just the fact that you offered it to me is such an honor. I have never been offered a gift of this importance or value, except the gift of salvation that God gave to me when I asked Jesus to be my Savior and come into my heart.[68] The only way I will take this is if I can give it back to your son. Something like this should not be lost from your tribe and your history. If you feel you must give me something, give me your friendship."

Manu looked at Sherry for a long moment, and then replied seriously, "I want that very much. I also want to find out more about your God; Noemi and I both do. We talked last night while you were sleeping, and we decided that serving your God was better than serving our gods. Our gods do not seem to care; they do not appear to love their people, they only takes from them. They do not answer prayers, they only want sacrifices. Your God has done me a great service and I must find out what I can do for Him."

"That's such a good thing Manu. It will be good for you, for your family, and for your village. When the leader follows God, the people usually follow. Let us make a time to get together so

---

[68] Acts 4:12

you can learn more about God. For now, go back and see Noemi and you can tell her. I will bring you both back some breakfast."

Manu walked back into the clinic and Noemi was sitting up, holding her baby. "Manu, come look; he is awake. Isn't he a beautiful baby?"

Manu smiled affectionately at his young wife. He looked down at the sleeping child and took him from her arms. He held him tenderly and responded, "Yes, he is. We will call him Juan, after my father. My father was a brave and wise chief. Juan will be one also."

As Manu left the kitchen, Sherry turned and looked at everyone. "All of you heard what Manu said. All of you saw the crucifix. It was smaller than the other, but very similar. Now there are three. I just don't know what to say," Sherry continued. "This mystery is taking so many twists and turns I can't keep up. I can't imagine what everyone in Maine is going to say. Maybe we will have some additional information by the time we call them. Also, Manu and Noemi want to know more about God. Manu said that since God has done so much for him, he wants to do something for God."

Sherri walked across the room to get a tray, filled it with fruit, mbeju, a pancake like bread made with a yucca starch and cheese, and a local herbal tea called mata cocido which everyone drank.

Sherry walked back through the clinic to bring Manu and Noemi the tray of food. They were bent over the baby, admiring his good looks. Manu looked up and questioned Sherry, "Do you think I should let Noemi and the baby stay here? This way I could come over and you could tell us about your God."

"I think that would be a wonderful idea," Sherry said, thinking that this would solve a few problems. "This way she can be resting and you can come over when you want."

Just then Manu's four counselors ran into the room. They all began talking excitedly to him. Sherry listened closely and gathered that there had been another injury. Two women had ventured into the jungle looking for fruit and root vegetables. A wild boar that had been roaming the area attacked them, injuring them badly. They were both being brought up to the clinic.

Sherry left Noemi and Manu to their breakfast and walked back into the kitchen. "Did you hear what happened?" she asked.

Daniel and Edwardo both nodded. Daniel asked, "What can we do?"

"Daniel, please set up two tables on the far side of the room, away from Noemi and the baby. In fact, if she is up to it, she can come into the kitchen and sit with Connie and the children while you and Edwardo are back there helping me. Connie, would you mind?"

"No." Connie said. "I was looking forward to getting to know Noemi better. Also, I can start answering any questions she might have about Jesus. Maybe she will pray with me and ask Jesus into her heart."

"I've got some boxes in the back we can put blankets in for extra cradles." Sherry said. "I think Manu is right. We do need more room. We need a bigger kitchen, another room in the clinic, and another bedroom."

As Daniel walked back into the room he listened to the end of the conversation. "I understand the need for the enlarged kitchen. We can have meetings and guests without crowding, and the extra clinic room, one for emergencies and one for recovering patients, but I really don't see a need for an extra bedroom. We are already building two sleeping areas for our guests coming down from Maine. That should be more than adequate."

"Well," replied Sherry with a sheepish look on her face, "we won't need it right away, but we will in six or seven months." She looked over at Daniel with a Mona Lisa smile on her face and he stopped what he was doing to come over and give her a long, quiet hug. Words weren't necessary.

Finally, he whispered, "I can't tell you how happy I am. I don't have the words." To Edwardo and Connie he said, "If ever things calm down, we will have a celebration."

CHAPTER TWENTY-NINE

THE VILLAGE, PARAGUAY
JUNE 8

Right at that moment, the two injured women were carried into the kitchen by several tribesmen. Sherry led them back to the clinic and had the women put on the tables that had been set up. She did a short triage on them to determine the seriousness of their injuries and what needed to be addressed first.

The first thing she noticed was that there was a lot of blood, and that neither woman was making a sound. They both appeared to be unconscious. She asked one of the tribesmen if they were married, and if so, would they go get their husbands. It turned out they were both married.

They both appeared to be in their late twenties or early thirties. It was sometimes hard to tell because of the hard life these women led. Usually by this age they already had several children; some living, and some dead. Sometimes they were even grandmothers.

It was obvious that one woman was already dead. Sherry covered her with a sheet and turned her attention to the other.

The woman's left arm had a deep gash that went from the elbow to the shoulder, but upon examination, she knew the artery had not been compromised. The bleeding was minimal to that injury. Sherry wrapped a quick bandage around it to apply pressure until she could get back to it. The woman had numerous scratches all over her body, and her clothes were torn to shreds. But the injury that worried Sherry most was a wound to the inside of her upper thigh. She was pretty sure the femoral artery had been affected. It was pulsing blood with regularity.

Sherry applied a tourniquet to stop the bleeding, enabling her to see the extent of the injury. It was a deep gash, about nine inches long. "Daniel, do you have that water boiled?" she asked.

"Yes. What else can I get you?" he answered.

"I'm going to need my suture kit, a dozen clean towels, a large pot of boiled water, several bowls, and I need you to boil several scalpels, needles, and scissors. I'll also need several pairs of sterile gloves, a gown, some disinfectant, and the large syringes I sometimes use for irrigation. That's all I can think of at the moment. I'll also need you to assist me." Upon thinking some more she said, "I'm also going to need four men to assist me in holding her down in case she wakes up. I don't want to give her any sedative, because the loss of blood has weakened her already. I'll also need an IV set up to start when I get to it."

As Sherry went about preparing for what needed to be done, she thought again of all the things that were unavailable to her. Number one was an autoclave to sterilize all her instruments. It would save so much time having that done, rather than having to wait while everything was boiled.

Daniel went about following her instructions. He called over to Sherry, "I'm going to get Edwardo to ask some of the men if they will help hold the woman down."

"I've got so much on my mind," Sherry said, "but I want God's hand upon me and this woman as I attempt to repair this artery and close this wound on her leg, and on her arm. Before we

155

do anything else, would you please pray and ask God's blessing, mercy and grace on this poor woman and upon me as I attempt to deal with her wounds?"

Daniel immediately went over and placed his one hand on Sherry and his other on the woman. "Dear God," he prayed, "we come in the mighty Name of Jesus and lift this woman up to You. She needs a miracle. Thank You for working in her life, and in the lives of this whole village, for showing Yourself strong on their behalf. We thank You for this miracle, that it be a testimony to the village of the mighty works of a caring God. I also pray for Sherry, that You give her skill beyond any that she has had thus far, and strength to complete the task. I pray that You are her hands and her eyes. Be with her from start to finish. Amen."

Manu stood there with uncertainty, "I will send some of the young men down to fill the water barrels. How are the two women doing?"

"I'm sorry, this woman is dead, and the other is seriously injured." Sherry continued her preparations as she talked to him. "Can you have some of your men find the dead woman's husband and tell him what has happened? Will you ask them to take her body to her home and ask some of her neighbors and friends to see to her?"

"This other woman is the wife one of Leonardo, one of my counselors. Her name is Ciba," Manu stated as he pointed to the woman Sherry was preparing to work on. He walked over and raised the sheet to look at the dead woman. "This one was called Mara. I will send for her husband. Could you not save this woman?" Manu asked, gesturing to the dead woman.

"She was already dead when they got here. I will do my best with Ciba," Sherry said.

"Can you not pray to your God and ask His help?" Manu requested. "He helped Noemi and my son."

"Daniel and I have already prayed," responded Sherry. "I've also asked four of your men to help hold the woman in case she wakes up while I'm trying to sew up her wounds. Daniel will assist me. If you would ask everyone else to leave the room that would be a great help."

Sherry heard Daniel's voice behind her. "Sherry, I've got several forceps and clamps, and hemostats boiled also. There's a sterile gown, mask and gloves on the table. We have sterile gauze bandages and dressings. I also put out several packages of assorted needle sizes, the pre-threaded ones. There are some betadine swabs, large syringes and a bowl of betadine mixture to irrigate the wound. While you are washing over at the table, I'll start preparing the patient. I've already washed the area with antiseptic soap. I'm going to scrub and gown up and then use the betadine swabs to sterilize the surgical field."

Sherry turned around and bumped into Manu. He was still standing there. "Is there something else you needed?" Sherry asked impatiently.

"I want to stay and watch. I have never seen anything such as this before."

"That's great," said Sherry. "You can stand behind me and hold the light. If you think you are going to be sick to your stomach or pass out, call someone over and give them the light, don't drop it"

Manu replied indignantly, "I would do no such thing. Do you think I am a weakling?"

Sherry gave him a brief smile. "No," she answered, "I just wanted to be sure."

157

Sherry turned back to her preparations. As she worked, she thought what a good team she and Daniel made. They had worked together before and he knew what was needed. He just filled in what she had left out. Sherry had her gown, gloves, and mask on and turned around to go to the table.

Sherry took one last look at the preparations. She called out to those in the kitchen, "Send Edwardo back in. He can get anything else we may require, and I need one more person to hold the other light." With that, she began the procedure. First she had to flush out the wound with a mixture of betadine and boiled water. She took a large syringe and squirted the wound to wash out any debris left in it. She repeated the procedure several times until she was satisfied with the results. Then she turned her attention to the artery. She had Daniel tighten the tourniquet she had applied. The artery was not completely severed, but the ends were jagged. Sherry felt it would be better to cut off a small portion of each end and have even edges to sew together. Next, she used her smallest needle and thinnest suture material to join the edges. She made the smallest stitches she could, and kept them as close together as possible. When she was through, she asked Daniel to loosen the tourniquet and held her breath. She watched a moment, looking for leaks. There was some bleeding, but not from the artery.

Sherry said a silent prayer thanking God for His help. Then she asked Manu to get a towel to wipe her face. The lamps were hot, the air in the room was hot, and she was soaked right down to her underwear. She reminded Manu not to touch anything but her face with the towel. She observed Manu as he approached her. His eyes were big, but that was understandable. He was seeing things he had never seen before. Thankfully, he did not appear nauseous or light headed.

Then Sherry turned her concentration back to the patient. She squirted the betadine solution over the wound and began to trim the jagged tissue in and around the wound. Having a clean edge would facilitate the suturing of the wound. Jagged tissue was difficult to suture and left large, unsightly scars. This injury was definitely going to leave a large scar, because of the size of the wound. She did not want to add to it by doing sloppy stitching. She had to ask Manu several times to hold the lantern higher so she could get a clearer view of the wound.

Finally she began to close the wound, suturing first the muscles, then the flesh. She left a small drain in it to eliminate any fluid that might accumulate from inflammation or bleeding. Applying a bandage, Sherry took a breath, and then moved to the wound on the woman's upper arm.

"Thank God it hadn't damaged the artery also," Sherry thought. She didn't know if she had the stamina to go through all that a second time. After cleaning the wound, squirting the betadine solution, debriding and suturing the muscle and flesh she finally applied a bandage, took off her gloves and mask, and sat on the floor.

Tired beyond measure, Sherry just sat there and let her head drop to her chest. Daniel didn't see her sit down. He was taking the woman's vital signs, but Manu was standing right there and bent down in concern. "It's OK," she said, "I'm just so tired I didn't know if I could stand anymore."

Manu took Sherry's arm and carefully helped her up. "It looks like your God worked hard today, Ciba is still alive."

"What are her vital signs Daniel?" Sherry asked.

159

"Eighty-two over fifty-eight pulse of One hundred and forty and respirations twelve," Daniel replied.

"Let's put something under her feet to raise them and get her blood flowing better." Sherry looked at Ciba's color and felt her skin. She seems to be stable considering the amount of blood she lost. "Edwardo, would you get a bed ready for her? Also, would someone get me a cup of tea? How long did the surgery take?"

"As far as I can tell, it lasted close to two and a half hours," said Daniel.

"Well it feels like ten," answered Sherry as she walked over to her drug cabinet and took out some antibiotics and a syringe. After injecting them into Ciba's good arm Sherry questioned, "How is everyone in the kitchen? Noemi has been up a long time."

"It's OK," answered Edwardo, "Connie took everyone home to our house and they had some cake and tea. They're all napping last I heard. Lara came and helped Noemi walk. Noemi is much stronger than I expected her to be."

"That's what I need," said Sherry, "a cup of tea, a piece of bread, and a short nap. I am beyond exhausted; but I need someone to sit with that woman. What's her name?"

"Her name is Ciba, and her husband Leonardo is waiting to see you. Leonardo is one of Manu counselors. The other woman's husband is there also. His name is Riki."

"Would you find someone to sit with Ciba for a few hours? Where are Leonardo and Riki?" Sherry asked.

"They are waiting for you in the kitchen," replied Edwardo.

"I want to thank all of you for your help", Sherry said to Edwardo. "Without it, I don't know if that woman would be alive.

She still has to fight off infection. Thank God, His grace is sufficient."

As Sherry walked out of the clinic with Manu, she heard Daniel ask Edwardo to wait a few minutes while he went and found someone to sit with Ciba. Sherry stopped and called back, "What happened to the other lady's body? Who took it?"

Edwardo said, "Her husband, Riki, came for it while you were still working on Ciba. It is at their house being prepared for burial."

CHAPTER THIRTY

THE VILLAGE, PARAGUAY
JUNE 8

Sherry nodded and went into the kitchen with Manu. Riki and Leonardo were waiting for her. She stopped and got four cups out and asked the men, "Coffee or tea?"

They all replied "Tea."

Sherry put a spoonful of loose tea in each cup and poured hot water from their never ending supply over the tea. She put the cups on a tray, along with a loaf of chipa, bread made from yucca starch, cheese, eggs, milk and aniseed. She put the tray on the table and sat down. The men grunted their thanks.

Manu told Sherry, "These are Mara and Ciba's husbands, Riki and Leonardo. They have questions they want to ask."

"Of course," replied Sherry, groaning inwardly. She didn't know if she had the answers.

Leonardo spoke first. "I want to thank you for all you did for my wife and for praying to your God for her. Manu told me of the miracle that happened when you prayed to your God for his wife. I want to find out more about this God also."

As Leonardo took a breath to go on, Riki interrupted angrily. "I want to know why your God didn't help my wife. She didn't deserve to die. She has left me with six small children. How am I to take care of them? Will your God help me?"

Sherry sat there stunned at the anger and antagonism she observed coming from this man. She took a moment to think, and then responded with as much understanding and compassion as she could muster. "Riki, I'm very sorry that Mara died, she was already dead when they brought her into the clinic. There was nothing I could do for her. All I know to do now is pray and ask God to comfort you in your grief."

Riki pushed his chair back from the table, upsetting all the cups and spilling the tea. In a fit of rage, he grabbed his cup and threw it at Sherry. She put her arms up to deflect it, but it hit her cheekbone below her left eye. Losing her balance, she fell off her chair.

Manu rushed over to Sherry just as Riki turned back for a moment and bared his teeth. He muttered something under his breath and then said, "I will get even with you and your God. Now I will pray to my god and we will see what he can do. I will show you who the most powerful god is. You will be sorry you ever came to this place. My god will triumph and drive you away. If it had been my decision, you would have never been allowed to stay in the first place. We already have our gods and don't need yours."

Hearing the commotion, Daniel came running in from the clinic and saw Sherry sitting on the floor. Mario and Leonardo had run out to follow Riki, but turned back when Manu called to them. "What's happening?" Daniel asked. "I heard the yelling from inside the clinic." Looking at his wife he asked worriedly, "Sherry, are you alright?"

"Yes, I think so, but I think I'm going to have a black eye in the morning," she moaned.

Manu sat down next to her. He took Sherry's hand and held it. "I have never seen anyone who cared so much, and worked so hard for my people. What made you do it?"

Sherry looked at Manu and said, "It's not just me, but my God in me Who loves all of you so much. He helps me to love you and your people, even those I don't know."

Manu took Sherry's arm and carefully helped her up. "It looks like your God worked hard today, Ciba is still alive."

Daniel came over and ran his fingers gently over the already bruising eye. Sherry winced. She turned back to Manu and Leonardo and explained, "I did what I thought was right. To have spent time with Mara, who was already dead, might have cost the life of Ciba. Manu, as chief, I want to ask your permission to pray for Riki and his family."

Manu asked gravely, "Will you put a curse on him also for what he did?"

"No," said Sherry. "I want to pray for peace for him and his family, and that God will heal the hurt in his heart, and help to provide for them."[69]

Manu and Leonardo nodded yes, with a confused look on their face. They had assumed curses would be called out because of the attack, and to counter Riki's curse.

Daniel and Sherry joined hands. They closed their eyes and lifted their faces up to God. "Heavenly Father," Sherry prayed, "we ask for Your grace and mercy to be upon Riki and his family. We ask that the Holy Spirit, the Comforter, be with them in this time of trouble. Please, heal the hurt in Riki's heart and help him to be aware of Your love and kindness. Also, we break the power of the curse that he pronounced. Your Word promises that no

---

[69] Matthew 5:44

weapon formed against us shall prosper.[70] In Jesus' name we pray. Amen."

Manu and Leonardo stood there stunned. They had never heard this kind of prayer. They did not know of a loving or kind god. One thing they did know, this was a powerful God and they wanted to know more about Him and His Son Jesus. They spoke as one, "I want you to tell us of your God so we may serve Him, but first I must take some men and hunt down the wild boar that attacked these women.

---

[70] Isaiah 54:17

CHAPTER THIRTY-ONE

THE JUNGLE, PARAGUAY
JUNE 8

Manu left the village to kill the wild boar. He took four other men with him, two were the best trackers in the village, and two were the best hunters. They all carried large machetes, bows and arrows, and special spears about eight feet long with a small cross piece about three feet from the point, to stop the spear from penetrating too deeply, so the speed and power of the wild boar would not push all the way up the spear and injure the hunter.

They also had two large dogs with them trained specifically for hunting wild boar. These dogs were trained to bait and worry the boar, distracting it so the hunters could get in close. They kept the dogs near as they walked to the spot where the women had been attacked; approximately ten minutes north the village.

When they arrived at the spot, they checked for wind direction to appraise which way their scent would carry. They walked around the area until the trackers found the boar's trail. Then they set off. They were downwind of the direction the tracks were heading, but there was no guarantee the boar would continue on that same course.

The dogs were very obedient and stayed close, but it was apparent they were excited. They knew what their job was and they were anxious to get to it. After following the trail for less than twenty minutes, the dogs began to growl and their hackles rose. The trackers signaled them to go and they took off barking loudly.

Manu and the others began to run along the trail. They were following animal tracks that led through the jungle. As the barking got louder, they saw the dogs circling the boar in a small clearing. He was a large one. He was four to five feet long and appeared to weigh about four or five hundred pounds. His tusks were about five inches long. He was a formidable opponent.

They let the dogs worry him for a while and then began to move in. Two of the men notched their arrows and began to shoot at him. It was a big male. Because the hide of a boar is so thick, it's difficult to penetrate with arrows. After several attempts, two of the arrows penetrated. The two dogs, showing courage, attacked and one of them got the boar by the nose. The boar stopped and swung his head from side to side, finally dislodging the dog, but not before one of the hunters was able to spear it in its side.

The boar was bleeding from his nose and a large stream of blood was running from its side. The dogs started in again, circling and lunging at the boar. He stopped and squealed, which only drove the dogs to a greater intensity. One of the dogs grabbed his nose again and the boar paused and tried to trample the dog. One of the hunters got another spear in the boar's chest. As he tried to back out of the way, he stumbled and the boar was after him with his head down. The hunter screamed as the thrashing tusk ripped into his leg. The dogs charged again, this time attacking the softer underbelly. This distracted the boar long enough for the wounded hunter to start to move. The boar had only grazed him with his tusk, but it left a ten inch gash on his leg.

The fight continued. They had been fighting this boar for an hour and everyone was tired including the boar. They knew they had to finish the fight or the boar would escape. Manu stood still for a moment and then said, "God, you helped Sherry do what she needed to do to save Ciba. You gave her the strength to finish the job. Please help us do what needs to be done to kill this wild boar that has been menacing our village."

That said; Manu hefted his spear. He turned to the three other hunters and said, "Let's attack him all at once. I prayed and asked Daniel and Sherry's God to help us." They all looked at each other and then nodded yes.

With the dogs at the boar's head, trying to get his snout again, the hunters were left with the rest of the body. Two of their spears impaled his chest and one his underbelly. They backed away quickly and called the dogs off, watching for any sign of weakness. The boar was bleeding profusely from the spears to the underbelly. One appeared to have ripped it open and entrails were protruding. He stood still for a moment appearing to be confused. The hunters used that moment to launch the last of their spears. All of them penetrated the boar and he dropped to his knees. One of the hunters rushed forward with his machete and slit its throat. With a loud bellow it fell to its side and lay still, his blood staining the ground.

Everyone stood unmoving for a moment and then slowly sank to the ground. It had been a difficult fight. They were all covered with the boar's blood, but only one of them had been wounded. He had managed to wrap banana leaves around the wound to staunch the bleeding. Manu asked two men to stay with the boar to keep any animals from taking any of it. Then Manu

168

started back to the village. He and the other hunter assisted the injured man.

It was a long walk back supporting the wounded hunter. Everyone was exhausted from the fight. Finally the village came into view and Manu call out for help. Several men came forward and lifted the hunter. Manu instructed them to take him to the clinic, and for six men to go and help butcher and carry back the meat from the wild boar. He felt a satisfaction in knowing that no more of his people would be injured by that boar, and that there would be food for many days from its meat.

Manu walked into the clinic not realizing that he was covered with blood. As he walked into the clinic he called out, "Doctor Sherry, are you still here? I have an injured man who needs attention. Can you help him?"

CHAPTER THIRTY-TWO

THE VILLAGE, PARAGUAY
JUNE 8

Sherry had been sleeping in her bedroom when she was awakened by Manu's call. She hurried into the clinic and three men were waiting. All were wearing blood soaked clothes, but one had a bandage on his leg. "How many injuries do we have here?" Sherry questioned.

"Only one," answered Manu. "The blood you see on us is the wild boar's blood. The boar gored Juan's leg during the fight. We could not stop to help him because of the intensity of the battle. He was able to crawl away and bind the wound with banana leaves. We have not removed them because we did not want the bleeding to begin again. We tried to protect the leg in transporting him back to the village, but the bleeding has started again, although it doesn't appear quite as much as originally."

Sherry looked at the clock on the wall in the clinic. It was the only clock in the village. Time was a measured commodity here. It wasn't measured by minutes and hours, but by daylight. When the sun came up work began, and when it set, work ceased. Very little took place in the way of overtime. Some emergencies required a monumental effort to bring light to a situation or project that demanded attention, but for the most part, things waited until the next day.

Fortunately for Sherry and the village, she had the means to extend the day if required. She had kerosene lamps that threw enough light on a situation to at least serve the minimum requirements.

Sherry heard Daniel and Edwardo in the kitchen stoking the fire in the stove and putting additional water on. She had Manu put Juan up on the table while she gathered the surgical supplies she would need and brought them out to Daniel to be boiled.

"Well, we're operating on second shift, but there is no shift to replace us. It's almost four thirty and I'm tired. I had a short nap, but I don't feel capable of repeating the surgery I did this morning. While those instruments are boiling I'm going to check on Ciba. When they are ready, bring them in and I will remove the makeshift bandage and we will see what we have. It's not bleeding profusely and the man is conscious. I'm believing it won't be another two or three hour surgery. When the instruments are done boiling, bring them in. Also bring in two lamps, and we'll get ready to deal with round two.

Sherry grabbed two basins and poured hot water into them. She brought them back into the clinic and grabbed some towels. She told Manu that he and Ernesto were welcome to use them to wash off some of the blood on their face and arms. Then she went over to examine Ciba.

Ciba was breathing well and her color, though a little pale was not abnormal, given the circumstances. Her skin was not hot and dry. There was no fever. The wound had no unusual swelling and there were no signs of bleeding. Sherry again thanked God for His mercy and grace to Ciba, but also to herself. He gave her the grace and the ability to complete the surgery successfully.

Sherry started assembling the supplies she would need to complete this procedure. She went over to talk with Juan and realized that he was one of the members of their small congregation. She spoke softly to him in Guarani. She told him when Daniel and Edward came in they would all pray for his recovery and her strength and skill.

Sherry proceeded to take Juan's vital signs. They were fairly strong, which encouraged Sherry. If there had been a significant loss of blood, they would have been depressed. Sherry opened the cabinet containing her small amount of drugs and observed the vacant spaces on the shelves. She would have to send out an order for more antibiotics and more pain medication. Thankfully, she had a doctor back in Boston whom she had worked with before coming to Paraguay. She didn't have a complete pharmacy here, but she had some basics available for situations like this. Sherry drew up the antibiotic, and some Demerol to ease his pain and relax him so he would be able to lie still during the procedure.

"Daniel," Sherry called, "are you almost done there? I can't start without you."

As Sherry turned back to Juan, she put on a pair of latex gloves and began cutting away the banana leaves and some kind of moss Juan had used to stop the bleeding. The natives used lots of local remedies to treat their illnesses and injuries. Some Sherry had found useful, but other appeared to be no more than superstition. She had some dressing ready in case the leg started bleeding heavily.

She pulled off all the plant material and got her first look at the wound. There was minimal bleeding from a ten inch gore to his left calf. It began just above the ankle on the inside of the left leg, and ran up to curve just behind the knee. Thankfully, except for the very center of the wound, most of the damage was superficial.

Daniel and Edwardo walked in and brought all the supplies over to the work table that was next to Sherry. Then they gathered around Juan and began to pray. When Manu saw and heard what they were doing he called to them. "Wait, I want to pray with you. I now believe in your God. Will he listen to my prayer?"

"Of course He will," Daniel responded. "He hears everyone's prayers."

Manu quickly hurried over and called to Ernesto, "Come quick so you can pray also."

Ernesto held back, "I don't serve your God. Why would I want to pray to Him? He does not know me."

"I will tell you about Him when I know more. He does not know me very well, but He hears me. He healed Noemi and Ciba. He will heal Juan." Manu did not know how to pray, but he listened to the prayer of Daniel, Sherry and Edwardo and thanked God with them.

After Sherry scrubbed and donned her surgical mask, gown and gloves, she cleaned the wound. Thankfully, it was not a ragged tear, but a clean slice. After injecting lidocaine to numb the area, she trimmed a few jagged pieces along the edge to facilitate a clean scar. She sewed the muscle first and then she sewed the edges. Again she left a small drain in the wound as she had with Ciba's, to reduce swelling. She bandaged the leg and looked at the clock. It was not quite five thirty. She was done in less than an hour. They moved Juan over to a cot by Ciba.

Edwardo volunteered to sit with Juan for a short time to keep an eye on both him and Ciba.

Sherry removed her gown and mask, thankful they were disposable and did not have to be laundered. She already created a mountain of laundry without adding gowns and masks to the pile. She employed one of the women from the village to do her laundry. There were just not enough hours in the day to do everything that was required, especially when emergencies such as these occurred. She paid the woman one chicken a week. The woman now had her own chicken coop and more chickens than Sherry. She was now able to pay other women to do laundry. She took care of the chickens. It appeared capitalism had spread to the village. Sherry smiled at the thought.

CHAPTER THIRTY-THREE

THE VILLAGE, PARAGUAY
JUNE 8

Manu and Leonardo were waiting in the kitchen for them. Manu's clothes were still blood spattered. He and Leonardo were both tired from dealing with the events of the day, but they wanted to find out more about God and would not be put off. As tired as Daniel and Sherry were after all the surgeries of the day, they recognized the importance of Manu and Leonardo's request. They prayed for strength and clarity of mind and invited them to sit at the table with some tea and bread and began to share the Gospel, the "Good News".

- They told of how God sent His Son Jesus to die for the sins of all of mankind, those who lived long ago, those living now, and those yet to be born.[71]
- They told of His miraculous birth announced by angels,[72] and of the attack by God's enemy Satan, trying to kill the Child Jesus by killing all the baby boys in Jerusalem under the age of two.[73]
- They told of all Jesus' mighty miracles.[74]

---

[71] John 3:16
[72] Luke 2:8-14
[73] Matthew 2:16-18
[74] John 21:25

- They told of His death on a cross,[75] and that it had been foretold over a thousand years before.[76]
- They told of His resurrection,[77] of defeating Satan by saving all those who will call to God and serve Him.[78]
- They told of his ascension into Heaven,[79] where He rules and reigns at the right hand of His Father God.[80]
- They told of His promise to come back again to take us to heaven to be with Him always. [81]

Manu and Leonardo sat there in awe, listening to the Good News that was being shared with them. They understood what a sacrifice for sin was. They had made many such sacrifices, and they had to keep making them. But now there was a God who gave His Son as a sacrifice for them, and forgave their sins. It was hard to imagine anyone willingly giving their child to die for someone else.[82] They had heard of tribes who still sacrificed babies, whether for sin or some other reason, and it terrified them. But God was not asking this of them. He had already done it Himself. At that moment a seed of faith was planted in their hearts.[83] They had heard all they needed to hear. They looked at each other and nodded. "We want to serve your God!" they replied. "We want Him to be our God."

---

[75] John 19
[76] Psalms 22
[77] Matthew 28:1-10
[78] 1John 3:8
[79] Acts 1:9-11
[80] Ephesians 1:19-21
[81] John 14:3
[82] John 3:16
[83] Ephesians 2:8

Daniel and Sherry took their hands and asked them to repeat this prayer. "Dear Heavenly Father, I am sorry for all my sins. I believe that You sent Your Son Jesus to die for my sins, that you raised him from the dead, that He ascended into Heaven, and that He will come back again. I don't want to sin anymore. Please send Your Holy Spirit to come live in my heart and make me a new person.[84] Help me to love and serve You with all my heart. Amen."

Daniel spoke to them. "Now as you know, there are still evil forces in the world today. They are trying to oppose the plan of God, and destroy His people.[85] It's our job to fight them. We can do that two ways, with swords and spears and arrows, or with prayer and using His weapon, the Word of God, to attack the enemy and defend God's people.[86] Tomorrow morning would you both come back, and bring anyone else who wants to know about our God? We will tell you more about Him and how much He loves and cares for you."

Both Manu and Leonardo agreed to come after breakfast. They talked excitedly to each other as they went back to the clinic to see Leonardo's wife Ciba and Juan one more time. Then they were going to check on Riki before going home.

Sherry went back to their bedroom to rest for a short while. Daniel followed her. He put his arms around her and whispered a blessing over her. "Father, thank You for being with Sherry. Give her peace for her soul and rest for her body. Let angels be a guard around her and keep her safe. Thank You for all You did today, and the breakthrough in the lives of Manu and

---

[84] 2 Corinthians 5:17
[85] 1 Peter 5:8-9
[86] Hebrews 4:12

Leonardo. We give You all the praise and all the glory in Jesus' name. Amen."

Daniel and Sherry stood there in awe of what God was doing. Just as He has always done, God was able to take circumstances the enemy, Satan, had meant for harm and turn them to good.[87] Excitement and expectancy bloomed in both Daniel and Sherry's hearts. They had recently been brooding over the fact that they did not seem to be having much success in spreading the Gospel, but they had believed for a breakthrough. Well it appeared that the breakthrough had arrived, and they thanked God for it.

---

[87] Genesis 50:20

CHAPTER THIRTY-FOUR

THE VILLAGE, PARAGUAY
JUNE 8

Daniel walked into the bedroom with a tray of soup, a cup of hot tea, and some flat bread. Sherry was still sound asleep. She had slept only two hours, but it was almost time for their phone call to Maine. She needed to be awake for that.

Daniel sat on the bed beside her and gently touched her arm. She jerked awake and almost upset the tray of food. "Relax honey, everything is OK. It's almost time for our phone call and I knew you would want to be awake for that. Here," Daniel handed her the tray, "have something to eat and drink, and then we'll go inside. Connie and Edwardo are already here; and before you ask, Ciba and Juan are resting comfortably. They both woke up briefly and I gave them some tea, and took their vital signs. Ciba's looked better than they were before, and Juan's were normal, so that's good."

"How long have I slept?" Sherry asked. "However long it was, I needed it. I was exhausted. Have Leonardo and Manu been back? Has anyone heard how Noemi and the baby are doing?"

"Leonardo and Manu went back to check on Ciba and Juan one more time," Daniel replied, "and also to check on Riki."

"I hope Riki is alright," Sherry said "He was so upset at the death of his wife."

"I don't know," responded Daniel. "From what you told me, he seemed more upset about who was going to take care of his children. And even if he was upset, that's no reason to attack you. Your cheek and eye are already bruising. Let's pray right now about this," and he grabbed Sherry's hand.

"Heavenly Father, I pray a hedge of protection over Sherry and all who come in and out of our home and the clinic. I commission angels to guard the north, south, east and west sides of the compound, even the top and bottom, that they might quench all the fiery darts of the enemy.[88] Though the Devil is out there like a roaring lion, we're under the protection of the Lord God Almighty and His Heavenly Host.[89]We thank You for Your continuing help in completing the quest You have called us to. Thank You for strength, guidance and wisdom in all we do, in Jesus' Name we pray. Amen."

Sherry and Daniel sat on the edge of the bed while Sherry finished eating. "Are you ready?" Daniel questioned. Sherry nodded, as she put down her tea cup and picked up the empty tray. Together they walked into the kitchen.

Edwardo and Connie were sitting at the table. Connie said, "I left the children at home under the care of my sister Lara. Manu came by and brought Noemi and the baby back to his home. His step mother Chabuto is there to help with their care. Everything is quite calm at my house, as opposed to what has been happening here. Edwardo told me what happened with Riki. Let me see your eye."

Connie took Sherry's face in her hands and shook her head. "Riki should be punished for this. Unfortunately, it is not the

---

[88] Hebrews 1:14
[89] 1 Peter 5:8-9

first time he has injured a woman. His wife had frequent marks upon her skin that all know came from him. He has been a troublemaker in the village as long as I can remember. They have not been able to find him yet. Maybe he left the village and is not coming back. Good riddance if that is the case. His children will be better off without him; they suffered at his hands also."

"You may be right about that," Daniel agreed, "But we all need to stay alert and be prepared. Riki is out there and he has threatened us.

"One thing that happened you don't know about Edwardo," Daniel said with a grin on his face, "is that Manu and Leonardo both made a commitment to Jesus."

"They are coming tomorrow, with anyone else who is interested," Connie interrupted, "to learn more about Jesus. I also think this is a significant breakthrough for the Kingdom of God. I believe many people will follow Manu's example and come with him and Leonardo. I found this out because Manu's was just at our house. He brought Noemi home when she woke up from her nap. She is doing well and wants to come tomorrow also. He and Leonardo could not stop talking about all the wonderful things that God had done for them."

"The rest of the elders were all there listening to what Manu had to say about our God, and about what happened with Riki. They knew Manu would come to get Noemi and were waiting to talk with him. They were also worried that Riki might be dangerous. He has been known to delve into the black arts, and use their spells against those who angered or opposed him."

As Sherry was about to respond, the phone rang. "I'm putting it on speaker," Daniel said excitedly. I can't wait to tell everyone all the events of the day. Daniel answered the phone, "Hello, this is Daniel."

"Hello from Maine, this is Josh. How are things down there? It's been a crazy day for us up here. Sorry our call is late."

"Well I bet we can match you point for point because it's been mind-boggling since we last spoke," Daniel said. "You go first and we'll listen."

"First off, to give you a heads up: Renato and Ted are heading down the day after tomorrow, Saturday, the tenth," Josh related. "The whole flight, including layovers takes about twenty-four hours. They should get to Asuncion on Sunday morning, the eleventh. With so much happening, we thought it would be a good idea to send down an advance group to survey the situation and just be more boots on the ground in case there is trouble. Let us know if there are additional supplies we need to bring. We know we have an enemy out there and he can't be happy about what is going on.

"We had some trouble here this morning," Josh continued, "Bekah and I flew to New York to see a jeweler who was an old friend of Ted's. We wanted him to look at the crucifix and verify its authenticity. He appeared very helpful and sincere until he saw it. All he wanted after that was get his hands on it.

"When we left his store, he called Ted and asked where we were. He wanted to send a guard with us to see we got home safely. It sounds innocent enough, but you didn't see his eyes when he looked at that crucifix. It was almost as if a spell had come over him.

"Ted told us he claimed to be a Christian, but there was no evidence of that this morning."

Josh related what had occurred that morning with the limo driver, and about having to take the subway and bus back to the airport. "We managed, but it was a nerve-wracking experience."

"Wow!" Daniel said, "It sounds like you have opposition up there. Since all this happened this afternoon, I assume you don't have any idea yet whether he will pursue the crucifix or let the matter go?"

"No, we don't. We're going to keep watch and make sure everyone stays safe. I haven't said anything yet, but I am going to suggest that Bekah and the crucifix spend the night elsewhere."

"Sounds like a good idea. Better to play it safe. Well, we have some news too," said Daniel. "Is everyone sitting down? There's another crucifix and chain. It appears to be very similar to the one Bekah described to us. We don't have it. It's the chief's, but he wanted to give it to Sherry for saving his wife and newborn son's life.

"He has a very young wife who was having a very difficult delivery with tremendous blood loss. It appeared she was dying. Because of a lack of facilities and blood to transfuse, there was little Sherry could do. We were standing there, myself, Sherry and the chief, helpless, watching the life bleed out of her. Sherry prayed desperately, and asked God to intervene, to show Himself strong, and He did.

"Miraculously, the bleeding stopped and she regained consciousness. Her vital signs began to improve. She is now awake, alert and eating and drinking. God surely performed a miracle.

"After that, we had a wild boar attack, with one woman dead. The other woman, God had to have had His hand upon. She was gravely injured, but Sherry prayed again, and worked on her for over two hours. She is recovering.

"Then Sherry was attacked by the dead woman's husband. He didn't put his hands on her, but shouted violently and threw a cup at her. She was struck in the face and knocked off her chair. Tomorrow, she is going to have a very colorful eye. Thankfully, no real damage was done, but it also appears as if this man was pronouncing some kind of curse on her and a challenge to God. I'm glad we serve the all-powerful God.

"Lastly, but probably most important, the chief and the man whose wife was injured gave their lives to the Lord."

"Wow! You have had quite a day. It seems as though the heat is being turned up." remarked Josh. "God is moving and the devil doesn't like it. We'll make sure we have our prayer warriors in place so they can be praying now, even before we leave the country.

"We are going to send down some extra supplies with Renato and Ted. We also wanted to bring down gifts for the chief and the people. How big is the village, and what would you suggest?"

Daniel looked to Edwardo and questioned, "How many do you think Edwardo? I'll defer these questions to you."

Edwardo spoke up. "We don't take a regular census, because people move about. Some come for a visit and stay. Some go for a season, and then come back. But a rough estimate would be fifty family units, between one hundred and seventy-five to two hundred men, women and children."

"As far as gifts go," he said, "they would appreciate knives or hatchets, any simple farming tool, good rope, shovels, wheelbarrows, hammers, hand saws and fish hooks of assorted sizes with plenty of fishing line and fish nets. They need virtually anything a person can use to live in the wild. The women would appreciate cloth, needles and thread, small knives for foraging, bowls and soap. The young girls would love combs, hair clips and ribbons; maybe some soccer balls, or plastic cars and trucks for the boys. They might all like crayons and coloring books. I don't know if they have ever seen them, but maybe you can find some Christian ones, and we can tie it in with the Bible studies we will be doing. The children make their own entertainment. They also love sweets. Everyone does, and they get so little of it. Anything anyone else can think of?"

"Not necessarily for the locals, but for yourself," said Daniel, "bring plenty of toilet paper, your own soap and shampoo, think about any medications you might need and be sure to bring enough. You can bring cots if you want, but we can provide hammocks, and they're pretty comfortable. Be discreet about cameras, they don't like having their pictures taken. Bring packaged snacks of all kinds, for yourself and as small gifts. Bring extra socks, and rubber boots. It's very wet around here; beach or water shoes would be good if you have them. Cheap flip flops work great around the village. I'm sure there are fifty other items that need to come with you, but off hand, that's all I can think of.

"I would love to suggest Bibles, unfortunately, very few can read. We have a terrible need for a school. But that's another issue, and we have more than enough to deal with right now. I also think that since the chief and one of his counselors became a Christian, many more will follow."

Ted said, "I think we can round up some of these things before we leave. We have all day tomorrow to prepare. The rest we can send when the second group goes down. How many counselors does the chief have? I'd like to bring down their gifts on this trip. What about a special knife or machete for the chief and smaller knives for the counselors?"

Edwardo answered, "That's a great idea. The chief has four counselors, and as we said, one is now a Christian."

"One thing I would love to have," said Sherry, "is a small generator, big enough to run some big lights when needed. The last surgery I did, I had to do with the light of a kerosene lamp. The generator could be purchased in Asuncion along with the lights, and brought when you come out to the village. That seems like a tall order, but God can do anything."

Sherry looked around the room and saw the water buckets in the corner. "Lord," she thought, "running water would be great. I don't see how it could be done, but if You think we need it, Lord, I know You could work it out."

Daniel added, "I'm sure we told you to bring lots of mosquito netting. Mosquito repellent would not be a bad idea, and anything you feel you must have to eat.

"We eat very basic here, mostly small game and fish, and an occasional wild boar. We have also brought in some goats and chickens. The natives do farm and the women scour the jungle areas for roots and fruit and vegetables. Most of them now have chickens, because we trade them for food, and sometimes for small jobs.

"Our starches consist of a few roots they grind into flour and some corn, also a traditional dish called mandioca or cassava root which is served with most meals. It's not bad, but kind of bland. It's simple, but nourishing. The plants are high quality due to the richness of the soil."

"Connie, do you have anything you want to add?"

Connie thought for a moment, "I'm sure we will all think of more things. We'll make a list."

Josh asked, "How long a trip from Asuncion to Puerto Bahia Negra?"

"It's around three hundred fifty miles," Daniel answered, "but there's no straight shot. You might have to hire a charter, depending on when you get there and how much cargo you will have."

"That's no problem," Daniel heard Ted answer, "but how do we get from Puerto Bahia Negra to where you are?"

"That's going to be the challenge. We are going to have to hire a few boats to transport you and all you are bringing up the river to where we are. It's about forty miles. It usually takes eight to ten hours to come down and twelve to fourteen hours to come back up river. But sometimes it can take as many as twenty, depending on the river, weather, and any unforeseen circumstance that just happens to pop up. Just let us know when you will get there and we will start out the day before. We will spend the night in Puerto Bahia Negra in order to do our shopping and be there when you arrive."

"That sounds like a plan." said Ted, "We'll call you again tomorrow night and before we leave to make sure we have all our i's dotted and t's crossed. Call us if you have any other questions or think of anything else we need to bring. Otherwise we will be on our way Saturday night and get there Sunday morning. We'll call when we arrive in-country."

"Sounds like a plan," Daniel replied. "Goodnight for now."

CHAPTER THIRTY-FIVE

OGUNQUIT, MAINE
JUNE 9

Bekah woke up, her head throbbing to the sound of a drumbeat that was reverberating inside her. She had dreamed she was in a jungle and being hunted. There was fire and smoke in the air and she was running. Her heart was pounding and she was wearing a sheen of sweat. Her mouth was dry and her throat was scratchy, almost as if she had actually been breathing the smoke and living the dream.

Bekah slowly got out of bed, trying to shake it off. Because it had been so real and so vivid, she was still haunted by the drumbeats. "Well, this won't do," she thought. "I've got too much to do today to start off this way. I'll just have to do what God's Word says and think on things that are good and pure and lovely. I'll thank Him for all He's done for me, and He'll give me peace.[90] Thank You Father for everything.[91] Thank You for peace in the midst of the storm. Thank You for this day and all that will be accomplished."

Freshly showered and dressed, she walked down the stairs and then remembered that Ted was sleeping on the sofa. Bekah refused to stay at Renato's, but she thought it best to leave the crucifix with him. Ted volunteered to spend the night on the sofa

---

[90] Philippians 4:6-8
[91] 1 Thessalonians 5:18

as a deterrent. Thankfully, it appeared as though none was needed. She looked in and the sofa was empty and the blanket folded.

Bekah walked into the kitchen, and there sat the three musketeers, all looking up at her with large grins on their faces. They looked like the proverbial cat that had swallowed the canary. They all rose and escorted her to the table, pulled out her chair, and seated her. Then Renato said, "We are making breakfast for you today. Coffee is ready, muffins are in the oven, and bacon is sizzling in the pan. We even cut up some fruit. We want you to just sit and relax."

"After the dream I had," said Bekah, "this is a welcome luxury."

"You didn't have another dream, did you?" questioned Josh in a concerned voice.

"I had a dream about Paraguay, but I think it must have been more of a stress dream than a dream from God. I dreamt I was being hunted in a burning jungle. There were terrible drums beating a frenzied rhythm, and the smell of smoke in the air. I woke up in a panic, but I've calmed down now; at least my heart isn't racing anymore. I prayed and God helped me overcome the fear and emotional impact of that dream."

Bekah looked up at the three of them. Their smiles had disappeared and their faces had sobered. "Let me pour coffee for everyone and we'll talk while the muffins finish baking. All of you are looking troubled. Don't tell me you have had similar dreams. I thought that the dream issue was over."

"All of us had a similar dream," Ted said, "fire, smoke, and drums. We were all looking for you. We were discussing it before you came down and wondering whether we should tell you or not; we didn't want to worry you."

"Oh my," said Bekah, "does this mean that something like this is going to happen to me? I know I told God I want to help. I know I told God to send me, but this is getting very scary. I've never been hunted or pursued by dangerous people. Should we call the others and see if they have had similar dreams also? Should we ask Daniel and Sherry? The Bible says if we lack wisdom we should ask.[92]I want to know what it says about fear and courage."[93]

Josh answered, "It says to be strong and have courage because we can only see with our eyes. If we could see with His eyes, we would see the mighty multitude that is fighting on our side.[94] It also says that perfect love casts out fear."[95]

"Why don't we all join hands and pray?" Bekah asked. With looks of concern on their faces, they all joined hands. "Lord, You said if any of us lack wisdom we should ask, so we are asking.[96] We don't want to go down to Paraguay ill- advised, ill-prepared, or uninformed. We have done what we know to do, and trust that You will show us anything else that needs doing. We thank You that You will keep us safe from the enemy and all those serving him. We stand with, and for You Lord, and in the power of Your might. No weapon formed against us shall prosper.[97] We pray for unity of mind and purpose, and that we all

---

[92] James 1:5
[93] Joshua 1:8-9
[94] 2 Chronicles 32:7
[95] 1 John 4:18
[96] James 1:5
[97] Isaiah 54:17

walk in love with one another. We give You all the praise and glory in Jesus' name. Amen."

Everyone remained standing there, quietly letting His peace envelop them. Finally Ted looked up and said, "What about breakfast? I'm really hungry. What about the rest of you? Those muffins aren't burning, are they?"

As Ted rambled on Josh announced, "Those muffins should be ready and I can tell by the smell the bacon needs to come out of the pan. I've cut up a few tomatoes and some of the fruit I saw in the refrigerator. We'll have a regular brunch, and we can say we all helped."

"Are you responsible for the feast Josh?" asked Bekah.

"Well, I fried the bacon and made the coffee, but Renato made the muffins. They smell pretty good too."

Renato spoke up, "I learned how to make these from Nana Sara when I was a young man. I was a teenager when we moved here from Paraguay, and started working part time in the apple orchard while I was still in school. Nana Sara took me under her wing. These are apple cinnamon muffins, with a secret ingredient that no one knows now but me. I'll reveal it to you Miss Bekah, in my will."

He smiled smugly as he took the tray of steaming muffins out of the oven; just looking at them made their mouths water. Smelling them brought it to another level. There was an unfamiliar aroma in the air that everyone was sniffing questioningly. Renato smiled like a Cheshire cat as he turned them out onto a tray and put them on the table. He set out the butter dish, a crock of honey and some apple butter and said, "Breakfast is on the table. Come and get it."

They all sat down to a lighthearted breakfast, teasing Renato about the recipe, and enjoying the good food and each other's company. For a time, they pushed the dreams aside and let the food and fellowship refresh them. Worrying never accomplished anything. Hopefully, they would be able to hold on to this frame of mind throughout the day.

Josh spoke up as they were finishing the dishes and said, "Do you need to go to The Eye? We can drop you off and go do some of our chores. You can give us a call when you're through and we'll swing by and pick you up. Maybe later we can pick up a few lobsters and throw them on a grill. I assume you have a grill somewhere Bekah. When you're in Maine, you are supposed to eat lobster at least once a day, and I've fallen behind my quota. I haven't had a one since I've been here." They all laughed, enjoying the camaraderie they had been sharing. A bond was forming between the four of them and it needed to be strong, because it was going to be tested in the coming days. God's Word said that He would not allow us to be tested beyond what we could handle, and that scripture was going to be questioned by all those involved in the quest in the days to follow.[98]

Josh brought up one more subject before they got up to leave. "I want to ask you something and see if you feel as I do?"

"Go ahead," said Ted. "I don't think there is too much out there that would surprise us anymore."

"I wouldn't be too sure of that, but hopefully this won't throw you too far. I have been feeling that we should all leave tomorrow. Think about it and pray about it today. When we have our meeting tonight, we can discuss it."

---

[98] 1 Corinthians 10:13

"The only people we have to discuss it with are Roberta and Joe," said Bekah. "If I can get all my ducks lined up, I'm all for going tomorrow. I still have all day today and tomorrow morning to get done what I need to do. It shouldn't be too much of a problem. I'll talk to Roberta when I get to the shop and see how she feels about it."

Bekah decided to take her own car to town, and the three musketeers followed her. They were determined to keep her safe. They did not want to let her out of their sight.

CHAPTER THIRTY-SIX

OGUNQUIT, MAINE

JUNE 9

Bekah glanced at her watch as she walked into The Eye, taking note that it was almost lunch time. They had frittered away the morning, but she felt rested and refreshed as a result, in spite of the distressing dream they had all experienced.

Bekah had a flashback. She remembered when she had opened the shop almost ten years ago. It was right after her divorce from Ted, and she desperately needed something to distract her from the hurt she had felt from his rejection. It had started out as just a twelve by fifteen store front with a small stockroom and office area in the back of the store. As time went by and business grew, she purchased the space on both sides of her as they became available. Now she had a room for needlework, such as cross stitch and crewel, with all its threads, fabrics, and books, and she had a room for knitting and crocheting with all its yarns, needles and hooks. Her last room was for catalogs and books of designs for thousands of projects that might involve needlework of any kind. There was a table for assembling projects and also a small area for framing. In the back was a small room for her office, a much larger area for a stockroom and her food bank.

Immediately, she noticed that something was wrong. Roberta and Sylvia were there, along with three other women she knew from church. They were at the corner table, speaking to each other in hushed tones.

Sylvia motioned Bekah over. Bekah recognized Sandy, Kay and Shirley. They were part of a large prayer group that met every Thursday morning. Bekah wondered if Sylvia had recruited them to form her prayer army. Bekah walked back to the table and said, "Good morning," and she greeted everyone with a smile." Turning to Roberta and Sylvia she said, "Sorry I'm late. Renato, Josh and Ted made breakfast for me. It was nice to take some time and relax. How are all of you doing?"

Sylvia spoke up, "I've asked Sandy, Kay and Shirley to be our partners in prayer, and they have agreed. I have told them some of the story, so they know what's going on. I wonder if they should be with us when we have our phone calls to Paraguay, to keep them up to date. We were just discussing another dream that some of us have had.

Bekah felt the blood drain from her face. "Oh no," she thought, "Not everyone again."

"Sit down Bekah," Roberta said worriedly, noting her pallor. "Let us tell you what happened. Sylvia called Joe and me early this morning. It seems at least the three of us have had another dream."

As Roberta paused to take a breath, Bekah held up her hands and said, "Stop! I can't believe this is happening again. I dreamt I was in a burning jungle. Fire was raging and I was being hunted by someone. I woke up this morning in a cold sweat, with my heart pounding as loud as the rhythm of the drums in my dream. Then I found out Renato, Josh and Ted had the same dream also and if possible, I felt worse. Now, are you are telling me the rest of you had this same dream?"

Sylvia walked around the table and put her arm around Bekah. She squeezed her shoulder and said, "Don't worry honey; it will be alright, God's on your side.[99] Remember fear has torment, and God's perfect love overpowers fear.[100]

"We have been talking here all morning, and have decided that we will pray all day as the Holy Spirit leads us, but we will come together every morning at ten o'clock and pray together for at least an hour, maybe two if we feel the need. We will also get together here at seven in the evening and call down to Paraguay, as we have been doing. They can keep us abreast as to what is happening down there. They can also let me know if they need anything shipped down there, or if they need me to do any research for them."

Then Roberta spoke up, "I hope this isn't going to upset you, but I'm not so sure I should be going with you. I don't know what expertise I could add to the group. I know we all said, 'Here am I, send me.' I just assumed I was going with Joe. The more I think and pray about it, the more I feel that I am supposed to remain here to pray, and help on this end wherever I can. In fact, if I can speak for Joe, he feels that he should stay back also. Maybe Edwardo and Connie are taking our place. Maybe we were involved as a link between Maine and Paraguay.

"Another thing is that Joe is concerned for the safety of the people left here, especially after what happened to you and Josh in New York. Bekah, pray about this and see if you are in agreement. If you are adamant about us going, we will, but we just don't feel right about it."

---

[99] Romans 8:31
[100] 1 John 4:18

"Has Joe mentioned this to Josh, Renato and Ted?" Bekah asked.

"No," Roberta replied. "He was meeting them for lunch this afternoon and was going to tell them when they were all together."

"There was another thing the four of us discussed this morning before coming into town. We all feel the need to get to Paraguay as quickly as possible. All that's necessary to do to is purchase two additional tickets for Josh and me, and to pack whatever we can quickly.

Just then the telephone rang. Roberta walked over and answered it. "Good morning, this is The Eye of the Needle, how can I help you?"

"Good morning," said a pleasant voice, "may I speak with Bekah Ryan?"

"Hold on, she's right here." Roberta handed the phone to Bekah.

"Hello. This is Bekah Ryan. How can I help you?" Silence greeted her. "Hello," Bekah repeated again. "That's strange, no one is there. Maybe we were cut off. If it was important, I'm sure they will call back."

CHAPTER THIRTY-SEVEN

NEW YORK CITY
JUNE 9

On the other end of the dead phone line Haydon Carlton sat musing over a picture he had of his crucifix. He had the picture blown up from a security camera in the office. He already considered the crucifix his, and was willing to go to any extreme to gain possession of it. It had become a fixation for him. He was not concerned. He had had these fixations before, and they only acted as an incentive for him to get what he wanted. Haydon allowed nothing to get in his way.

He picked up the phone and dialed. All he said was, "OK, she's not home. Get over there and find it and anything that pertains to it. I want as much information as possible. The more you get me, the more you will be paid. Call me when you're through."

Hanging up the phone, Haydon sat back in his chair and thought about the crucifix. He was mesmerized by it. It almost seemed to have him under a spell. He had coveted many things in his life, but nothing like this crucifix. It seemed to be calling him and he had to possess it, no matter what the cost. He gave no thought to Josh and Bekah. They were just obstacles, set in place to obstruct his plans. Given enough force, any obstruction could be broken down, gone around, or obliterated. He did not have any scruples to hold him back. Haydon Carlton would do whatever it took to gain possession of his prize.

On his desk lay a book on sixteenth century artifacts. It was opened to a page of jeweled crucifixes. One of them was circled. It had a remarkable resemblance to the crucifix that Josh and Bekah had brought to him yesterday. He looked at the book, and then looked back at the photo he had printed of his crucifix. The caption on the picture stated that this crucifix was believed to have been part of a shipment of golden artifacts recovered from a shipwreck in 1599 off the coast of Uruguay. It had been transported from up river in Paraguay. He shook his head. What was the matter with him? There were other works of art that people were willing to sell, or that he could obtain more easily. Why was this one so important? He didn't know. In the past, he had broken a few laws and pulled a few shady deals, but today, he was prepared to do anything to possess that crucifix. Try as he might, he felt compelled to continue on with his quest.

Haydon had few friends, and no family. His collection was his life. He spent hours, sometimes days brooding over each new procurement. This next acquisition would be his crowning achievement.

He had a small, hidden room behind his office, where he kept part of his collection. The pieces he displayed there were the pieces he had acquired illegally. He removed a jewel encrusted, golden dagger that had been found in the Amazonian forest of western Brazil, and dusted the shelf it had rested on. It was the place of honor. Now a new piece would reside there. He thought it interesting that both pieces came from the same area and the same era.

No one knew of this collection, or of the room that contained it. The room had a false wall behind a bookcase. His grandfather had built it over sixty years ago as a type of bomb shelter back in the fifties, during the cold war. His father had started the secret collection, and Haydon followed in his footsteps. So many laws had been broken and so many people wounded by his deceptions and outright thefts that guilt no longer plagued him. His conscience had been seared by his repeated offences.[101]

Haydon sat down, in the midst of his treasures, to wait for the phone call. He knew the crucifix was his. It was just a matter of time.

Carlos Rampone checked out of the motel. He had spent the morning scouting the area, and making a trial run to the apple orchard. It was twenty miles outside of town, and on a good road. It took him thirty minutes to get there. Now all he was waiting for was a phone call from Haydon Carlton. He had decided to wait on a nearby road to give him all the time he might need. He figured he would have a few hours to make the search.

After receiving Haydon's phone call, it only took him five minutes to get to the orchard.

He drove up to the house and noted there were no cars in the yard. As a precaution, he went up and rang the bell. If someone came to the door, he would pretend to be lost. But no one answered the door. He took out a pair of latex gloves, put them on, broke the window, and unlocked the door.

He walked into the house, and proceeded to walk through every room to get an idea of the area he had to search, and the

---

[101] 1 Timothy 4:1-2

contents of each room. He came back to the office and looked at the imposing desk. "You," he said to the desk, "Are the first thing I will investigate. You look like you have the potential for a great many secrets." He went back out to his car and brought in a sledge hammer and a crow bar. He proceeded to pry open the cover of the desk. He had several large black trash bags with him to put the contents in. Each drawer was locked, and had to be broken into. By the time he was done with the desk, it was shattered into pieces, and nothing appeared to have escaped his notice. He made note of the fact that one drawer was empty. Perhaps the new owner had decided to go through it drawer by drawer. He wondered where its contents had been stored. "If it's in the house," he thought, "I will certainly find it."

Carlos went through every room, tore apart every piece of furniture, emptied every closet and searched all the clothes. He looked for hidden doors and drawers in all the furniture, walls and floors. When he was through, the contents were nothing more than a trash heap. In fact, he thought of lighting a match to it, but if there had been a possibility of him missing something, he did not want it destroyed in the conflagration. He pocketed some jewelry he had found through his searching. One was an old fashioned diamond ring. It looked to be around one carat, and a quality stone. There were some gold chains and earrings, and assorted other pieces of gold jewelry that he would take to melt down. The price of gold made it well worth his time and effort.

He left the door open. "No reason to close it now," and laughed out loud at the thought. He enjoyed his work. He enjoyed thinking of the anguish this would cause the young woman and her friends and chuckled again. He lit himself a celebratory cigar and thought, "Boy, is she in for a surprise when she comes home."

CHAPTER THIRTY-EIGHT

OGUNQUIT, MAINE
JUNE 9

Bekah looked at the five women who were staring at her and said, "I need to go to the bank this morning. When I get back, why don't all of you go to lunch? I need some down time. I don't want to think about any of this right now. I brought some of Nana's papers to go through. I'll just sit at this back table with them in case we get any customers."

That sounded like a good idea to everyone, so Bekah picked up her purse and walked out the door. The little bell above the door gave a bright jingle when the door opened and closed. Bekah remembered when she found the bell about five years ago in an antique junk store. She loved the sound it made and thought it added a quaint touch to the shop. It always lifted her spirit when she heard it jingle.

The day was beautiful, and she decided to walk the three blocks to the bank. Some of the stores had window boxes and the colors and varieties of flowers were as varied and vivid as an artist's palette. There was a hint of a breeze, and everything seemed right with the world, that is until she allowed her mind to wander to the crucifix she carried in her purse. She was taking it down to the bank to put in her safe deposit box.

Coming back into the shop, she felt a burden lift, knowing that the crucifix was safe. Bekah noticed there were two customers in the shop. She shooed her friends out with an admonition to take a long, leisurely lunch, and she put her purse back in her office. After taking a moment to ask each of the customers if they needed help, Bekah then went back and retrieved Nana's papers. She proceeded to spread them out, and sat down at the work table.

She had opened the top drawer of Nana's desk this morning, and taken the contents to town with her. She wasn't sure what Nana had kept in her desk. It was one of the mysteries that surrounded her. The desk was locked at all times, and Nana had the only key. Bekah had known where she kept it, but had always honored Nana's privacy.

The customers had browsed around for a few more minutes and left together. Bekah was alone. It felt good. She was not used to being encumbered by so many people, and the crowd of people surrounding her lately, as well meaning as they were, was getting on her nerves. Bekah sat down and browsed through the papers, separating them into piles according to their subject. For the first few minutes it appeared to be copies of bills and receipts. Then she came upon a small tablet that was filled with names, dates, and amounts of money.

Bekah didn't recognize any of the names. She did not know what the book was; she had never seen it before. She put it in her purse to show Renato tonight when they had dinner. The rest of the papers seemed to deal with repairs on the house, equipment, and the orchard. She gathered up the papers and put them back in her purse, just as the ladies all came back from lunch.

Roberta came up to Bekah as soon a she walked in the door. "I don't want you to be angry with me for not going to

Paraguay, but the more I think about it, the more I know I am doing the right thing. In fact, we were talking at lunch and I decided Joe and I should be the ones to stay at your place and work the garden and the food bank. I may need help now and then, but I love gardening, and Joe and I were out of town when it was planting time in Maine. Remember, we were gone for almost a month and didn't get back until the end of May. I probably could have still planted, but the ground wasn't ready, I hadn't purchased plants or seeds, and I was just plain lazy. Well, I'm motivated now. I can handle this and I've got a few people who can give me a hand if I need it. Also, my daughter is home from school, so our house won't be empty."

Roberta put her arms around Bekah and gave her a strong hug. "I really feel that I am doing what God wants me to do. We can all pray about it if you think that's necessary."

"No, I don't think that's necessary," Bekah said, "I know that you listen when God speaks to you. I'm not upset at all. Maybe that in itself is a confirmation that you should stay. We all need to be in agreement with what we are doing. Remember Jesus said, 'A house divided against itself cannot stand.'[102]

"Maybe we can meet a little early at The Lobster Pot tonight to introduce everyone and have short time of prayer before the phone call. Bekah turned to Sandy, Kay and Shirley, "You're still coming, aren't you?"

All three nodded, yes.

"Would one of you make sure everyone knows to be there a few minutes early?"

Shirley told Bekah she would make sure everyone knew.

---

[102] Mark 3:24-26

That settled, Bekah said "Good, then I'll say Good-bye for now. I've still got shopping to do and people to see. Looks like it will be another long day. I also need to go get four lobsters for dinner tonight. Josh said he hasn't had any lobster since he's been in Maine, so Renato, Ted, Josh and I are going to grill some lobsters tonight for dinner. It will be late when we're done with the phone call, but it shouldn't take long to grill them. I'm going to cheat and buy some of Martha's homemade potato salad at the deli. It's really good and I'm just too tired to do much more than make a salad. I keep thinking of that poem that ends,

'The woods are lovely, dark and deep, and I have promises to keep

And miles to go before I sleep, and miles to go before I sleep.'[103]

"I don't know about miles," Bekah thought, "If I was writing it, it would probably say," 'and hours to go before I sleep and hours to go before I sleep.'"

It was almost six o'clock by the time Bekah finished her errands. She could hear the lobsters scratching on the sides of the Styrofoam cooler. It was a tight fit for four, but with banded claws, they couldn't do each other, or the cooler, much damage. She had even squeezed in the quart of potato salad to keep it cool.

Bekah had really wanted to make a quick trip back home and check on the garden. There hadn't been any rain for a few days and the garden needed to be watered, but it would just have to be done tonight. It was too far to travel with the time she had left. Bekah decided to go to the restaurant and have some coffee

---

[103] Stopping by Wood on a Snowy Evening, Robert Frost

and cookies. Breakfast had been a long time ago, and dinner was still a few hours away.

CHAPTER THIRTY-NINE

THE VILLAGE, PARAGUAY
JUNE 9

A loud noise jarred Sherry awake. "What was that?" she wondered. There it was again, sharp staccato sounds that reverberated through the house. She rolled over to poke Daniel and discovered that his side of the bed was empty. She quickly got dressed and followed the noise. It seemed to be coming from the general direction of the kitchen. When she walked through the door she was greeted with bright sunlight. The whole side wall of the kitchen was missing.

True to his word, Manu had ten other men from the village there helping him and Leonardo extend the kitchen, add another treatment room, and add another bedroom. She stood there, momentarily speechless as she watched. There was a beehive of activity going on. She realized it was late, and she must have slept soundly indeed to not have heard the construction noise.

Daniel and Edwardo were speaking with Manu. There was a lot of gesturing going on. Daniel looked up and saw Sherry and motioned her over. "Good morning sleepyhead" he said, "I'm glad you're finally awake. We need your input on some of the dimensions for the rooms. We're going to just double the size of the kitchen, but wondered what you wanted for the extra bedroom."

Sherry looked at them and said, "Good morning to all of you. I haven't given it that much thought because I didn't realize we were going to start the project so quickly. Doubling the kitchen sounds good. We can use one side of it for office space. As far as the bedroom goes, is it that much harder to build a big room rather than a small one?"

Edwardo answered, because he was the man in charge. He had built their original house and clinic, and so he had some experience in planning, and executing a plan. He answered, "It's not that much harder, it just takes more materials. Since everything we use is local except for the wood, and manpower is free, it's not an important factor in deciding. Daniel already has an impressive amount of 2x6's and 2x4's set aside for just this thing. Every time we go to Puerto Bahia Negra, he fills any empty space in the boat with building materials. You just think about the need and let that make the decision for you."

"Well if that's the case, let's double it," said Sherry. "I'm going to walk down to Connie's and see if she has anything for breakfast, but first I'll check on Ciba."

Sherry walked back through the kitchen, or what remained of it, and into the clinic. There, sitting up and eating breakfast was Ciba. Connie was sitting on a chair across from her. Maria was on her lap and the two babies on a blanket on the floor sleeping. Sherry was so surprised at the sight that she just stood and stared.

Connie had always been quiet and shy. Sherry could never remember her taking the initiative in anything. Now, since the call they had received in their dreams, and the advent of the baby in the basket, Connie was exhibiting more self confidence in what she said and what she did than ever before.

Connie stopped talking with Ciba and motioned Sherry to come over. "Get another chair," she said, "and have some breakfast with us. There's more than enough. I also made hot tea, and brought an extra cup in case you came in. Remember Sherry, you can't skip meals like you usually do; you have to think of your baby. I shouldn't need to remind you that the little one inside you needs extra nourishment to grow and be healthy. With so much happening, maybe you should think of asking one of the young women to help you cook and do some chores. You have more than enough to do, and you need to take care of yourself."

Sherry pulled over one of the chairs, but said, "Before I sit down Ciba, would you let me examine your arm and leg?" Ciba nodded and Connie went over to the counter along the wall, poured some disinfectant on her hands, and put on a pair of gloves. She filled a pan with a disinfectant solution and walked back over to Ciba.

Sherry looked at Ciba's leg first. She had thirty-two stitches on the inside of her left thigh. She examined the wound. The stitches were slightly inflamed; but there was minimal drainage. The skin was slightly pink, but the area was cool to the touch. "So far so good," Sherry thought as she re-bandaged the leg.

Next, she looked at the right shoulder. It only had eighteen stitches, and there had been no major damage to an artery such as her leg had sustained. Again, the wound looked normal, maybe a slight swelling at the base. She decided to give Ciba some more antibiotics, to ward off any infection that might be trying to flare up. When she was finished she washed up again, and then sat down to a late breakfast.

While Sherry ate her breakfast, she discussed the upcoming Bible study and asked when would be a good time to have it. Ciba and Connie left it up to her. She decided to go ask the men what they thought. But first, she went to check on Juan who was also sitting up and eating breakfast. If appetite was a good measure of health, Juan was 'in the pink'. Lastly, Sherry went over and knelt down by the two babies. She ran her hand over their soft, curling hair. With a tender sigh, she stood up and said, "December seems a long time away, but it looks as though I'll be kept busy. I think you're right about getting some help. I already have some days where I would pay a million dollars just to take a nap, and I think today is going to be one of them."

Out in the yard, Sherry cornered Daniel and Edwardo and asked them, "Ciba and Connie don't care what time the Bible study is, do you? Remember, we have the phone call at seven o'clock."

Edwardo said, "Let me check with Manu and Leonardo. I'll be right back."

Daniel said, "I'm coming with you, I have a question for Manu about the layout of the kitchen."

Sherry wandered over to a bench on the side of the yard and sat down in the shade. She looked around at the compound, and remembered what it looked like when they first came, four years ago. There was nothing here but the village, about thirty houses and a gathering place. There had been the skeleton of an old building they discovered had been a church that had been abandoned over thirty years ago. Then there were maybe one hundred people, including children; and they didn't have any animals, now they had chickens and goats, a few cows, and Manu's prize bull. Goat milk, goat cheese, eggs and the occasional chicken went a long way to add protein to their diet. Farming had increased, and every year their corn crop seemed to increase with it. God was blessing this village.

They now had another small meeting area where Edwardo and Connie had been allowed to hold church services. They had optimistically fifteen, maybe twenty people attending, mostly women and children. With Manu and Leonardo becoming Christians, she wondered if more people would follow their lead, especially some of the men. Manu had done nothing to discourage Christianity, but he had certainly not promoted it. Now, he and Leonardo appeared to have had a change of heart. Even their countenances were brighter. There was a joy inside them that hadn't been there before. They were both excited about their new found faith, and looked for opportunities to share it with anyone who would listen.

As Sherry sat there, a soft breeze began to blow softly over her. She leaned back against the large shade tree, and her head began to nod. Back in the bushes surrounding the house a dark figure squatted in the shadows and his menacing eyes stared at her with malice. Sherry stirred, as if she were aware of the malevolence of that dark gaze. Riki looked and saw there was no one near. He crept out of the shadows.

In one hand he carried a dead black bird. He had removed its long tail feathers, and had wrung its neck. It was still bleeding. In his other hand he carried some of Sherry's hair. With all of the commotion about, he had sneaked into Sherry's bedroom and took the hair from her brush. He wrapped the feathers together with the strands of Sherry's hair and laid the feathers on her head. He made a mark on her forehead with blood from the bird and placed the dead carcass in her lap, chanting under his breath. Then he heard voices; someone was coming. He quickly ran back into the bushes and watched from a distance, continuing to mutter under his breath, finishing the curse.

Daniel and Edwardo walked around the house and saw Sherry asleep on the bench. Daniel smiled, but then took in the whole picture. "Do you see what's in Sherry's lap?" he said to Edwardo in a worried voice.

"Come on," said Edwardo. They ran up to Sherry and Daniel picked up the dead bird. He lifted his arm to throw it into the woods when Edwardo stopped him. "We must burn it," he said as he took it from Daniel. Just then Sherry woke up and raised her head. They saw the blood on her forehead, and the bunch of black feathers fell off of her head and on to the ground. Edwardo stooped and picked them up also.

"What's going on?" asked Sherry. "What are you doing with a dead bird and those feathers?" She went to brush some hair out of her eye and felt the dampness on her forehead. "What is this?" she asked as she examined the blood on her hands. She looked at the feathers in Edwardo's hand and said, "Where did all this come from?"

"If I were to guess, I would say Riki. No one has seen him," said Edwardo, "but I would suspect that he is still in the area. This is about what I would have expected of him. He's definitely not a Christian, and there are still some who believe in the old ways and sacrifice to the dark gods. It was rumored that he was one of them."

Daniel grabbed Sherry's hand. "Come on honey, let's get you cleaned off. Edwardo, what are you going to do with the dead bird and feathers?"

"I'm going to take them out and burn them. They are part of a curse, and we don't want any part of that left behind. Go ahead inside. I'll take care of this, and then I want to have a little look around. Before I do that though, I also want to show this to Manu. He needs to know what's happening. He won't be happy about this either."

Sherry took Daniel's arm and walked with him. Somehow, she felt protected when he was near. He wasn't tall or muscular, but she knew that the life and power of God flowed through him.[104] She knew that if necessary, he would sacrifice himself for her.

Sherry went with him into the kitchen. The stove was still burning, and as usual, a pot of water was heating on it. Daniel ladled some into a bowl, got some soap and a cloth and sat Sherry down. He carefully washed the dried blood off her forehead. He pushed her hair back from her forehead and gave it a tender kiss. Then he hugged her to him. They had avoided a confrontation such as this thus far, and he was not willing to allow this attack put them in fear. He quoted one of his favorite Scriptures.

> Humble yourselves, therefore, under God's mighty hand, that he may lift you up in due time. Cast all your anxiety on him because he cares for you. Be alert and of sober mind. Your enemy the devil prowls around like a roaring lion looking for someone to devour. Resist him, standing firm in the faith, because you know that the family of believers throughout the world is undergoing the same kind of sufferings.[105]

---

[104] Romans 8:11
[105] 1 Peter 5:6-9 New International Version

He went to the door and threw the water into their small vegetable garden, and then went back inside. He proceeded to brew a pot of tea for himself, Sherry, and anyone else who happened by. As they were waiting for the tea to brew, Lara, Connie's younger sister walked in with a tray of fruit, and mbeju, a flat cake made with mandioca, a local starch, eggs and cheese. It was one of Sherry's favorite breads. At precisely that moment, Sherry's stomach gave a loud growl and everyone laughed. Then they sat down to enjoy the meal.

Sherry hadn't talked to Lara in a while and asked how she was doing. She was twenty-two years old and had the typical olive skin, long black hair and dark eyes, but God had graced her with unusual beauty. She was tall for a Guarani, around five and a half feet, and had a very slender build. In spite of all these exceptional attributes, she was very shy. Edwardo had already been approached by several young men interested in marrying her, but she had refused them all. She told Edwardo she did not want to be married. Sherry asked how her days were going.

As they began to eat, Lara said, "My days are filled with smiling babies, a playful puppy, and a happy little girl. What more could I ask for. I am content. I love my sister, and Edwardo is very kind to me. At night, after the children are sleeping, he and Connie read and study the Bible, and I listen to Bible stories. I enjoy listening to them. They are very interesting."

Sherry listened to the young woman talk, and then she said, "I hope you realize that these are not just stories, but are accounts of real people and what really happened many thousands of years ago. Some parts of the Bible were written over three thousand years ago, and yet it still has relevance to us and our lives today. Do you remember the story of David and Goliath?"

Lara nodded, "Oh yes, that's one of my favorite stories. I especially like the part where he uses little stones to kill the big giant."

"Yes," Connie said, "But it wasn't just a story. It really happened. If you look in history books you will see that David was a king of Israel, and that the Philistines were Israel's enemy. God inspired the writers of the Bible, telling them what to write, not only to keep a record of what had happened, but also to help us learn from it over three thousand years later.

"In the story, David used a small stone to knock the giant over. Then he used the giant's own sword to kill him. From that, we learn that we can kill our giants with the skills we have if we listen to God. Sometimes we even use our enemy's own weapons against him.[106]

"The Bible helps me to live my life in a way that is pleasing to God. It also guides me when I don't know what to do. When I have a problem, I can pray to God and He will answer me, sometimes by showing me something in the Bible that will help me, sometimes by speaking to me in my heart, or by using a friend to encourage me. When God leads and guides me, I know that even though I may have problems, He is with me and leads me through every situation. I don't have to be afraid.[107] He gives me strength and courage to fight my enemies. His enemy, the devil, is my enemy, and my enemies are His enemies.

"You know about the devil; even your beliefs have a devil. But does your god help you to fight him? Is he with you when you

---

[106] 1 Samuel 17
[107] Psalm 23

are hurt and suffering? Does He love you so much He sent His Son to die for you? No! Think about what I have said; ask God to show you the truth."[108]

Lara looked up. There was a glimmer of hope in her eyes. She was in some sort of battle. Sherry could tell. Sherry believed God had given her the words to say to help the young woman. She would water them with love and acceptance and trust God to give her, or someone else another opportunity to talk with Lara again. Then Sherry remembered the Bible study they were going to be having and she mentioned it to Lara.[109] "We're having a Bible study with Manu and Leonardo, their wives, and anyone else who is interested. Find out from Edwardo or Daniel what time it's going to be, and maybe you can come. If you have any questions, you may be able to get some answers then."

"Oh, that would be wonderful. I'll talk to Connie and see if I can go." Lara picked up the empty tray and waved as she went out the door.

---

[108] John 8:32
[109] 1 Corinthians 3:6-9

CHAPTER FORTY

Edwardo and Daniel found Manu and Leonardo discussing the building project with several men. Edwardo was still carrying the dead bird and the bunch of feathers. Manu looked up when he heard them approaching. His eyes widened in surprise when he saw what Edwardo was carrying. "Where did you get that?" he asked in agitation.

Daniel answered, "Sherry had fallen asleep on the bench outside the clinic. Someone left this in her lap, and put these feathers on her head, along with a smudge of blood on her forehead."

Manu looked at Edwardo with a worried frown. They both knew the significance of these things. "I'm sure it had to be Riki," Manu said, "I was hoping he would just leave, but apparently, he's still hanging around. He hasn't been back to see his family or care for them in any way. I have assigned someone to furnish them with food, water and wood, and to watch for Riki. He is to tell me if he sees Riki, or hears anything about him.

"You and Daniel stay here and work with these men; they need your guidance and expertise. I need to go and question Doctor Sherry further to see if she remembers anything else that happened this afternoon or when Mara died. Maybe she might think of something that pertains to this curse, because that is what it is. Riki has put a curse on Doctor Sherry, and I need to find out everything I can to break it."

"You can go talk to Sherry if you want to," Daniel said, "but understand God has ways of protecting us we are not aware of. He can even send angels to guard her and keep her safe.[110] Sherry and I prayed earlier that nothing the enemy tries to do will harm her. We put our trust in God."

"I am glad He protects her, but I'm going to help Him," Manu said with determination, and he turned and headed back to the house.

Suddenly feeling completely depleted of strength, Sherry went into the bedroom to lie down. She knew the early stages of pregnancy caused sleepiness and decided not to fight it. She gave in to the urge. The last few days had been very stressful, and this morning's activity just added to the intensity.

She and Daniel had discussed having children, and she had stopped taking birth control over a year ago. "Why now?" she thought. "God, I know you have a plan, but this seems like a very inconvenient time to be pregnant." She lay down and pulled a light blanket up over herself. Because of the shade trees, her house was cool, even during most of the summer. Sherry closed her eyes and let sleep take her.

Five minutes passed and there was a rustling sound from the closet. The door opened slowly and a dark head emerged, his face painted in black. Riki looked around and listened carefully. He reached back into the closet and brought out his club. It was made of a heavy, dense wood, weighing around twenty pounds. It was carved with dark and mysterious symbols. He hefted it up onto his shoulder and walked silently over to the bed. He began a

---

[110] Hebrews 1:13-14

quiet chant while standing there, as if in an attitude of prayer. The question then being, who was he praying to? When finished, he lifted the club from his shoulder and tightly grasped it with both hands. As he began to swing it, there was a loud shout, causing him to lose his balance. A large knife went flying across the room and embedded itself in Riki's back. He immediately dropped the club and crumpled to the ground.

Manu stood there for a moment and then ran over to the bed. Riki laid still, blood flowing from the wound and onto the floor. Sherry sat up in bed, awakened by the noise, and saw Manu standing there. "What are you doing here?" she asked. Manu did not reply, but pointed to the floor. When Sherry saw the body, recognized Riki, and realized what had happened, she groaned in distress. She got out of bed and reached down to check the body. Manu stopped her.

"Doctor Sherry, you must not touch him. He is dead, and his body must be burned to dispel the curse he put on you. He called up the spirit of death. I heard Riki chanting to him." Manu turned and looked at Sherry. "Are you well, did he hurt you?"

Sherry shook her head. "I'm not hurt, just overwhelmed by what has happened here. I need to pray and ask God to help us deal with this terrible circumstance." Sherry prayed, "Oh dear God, thank You for protecting me. Thank You for sending Manu to save me. This event has traumatized my feelings and emotions. God I pray for Your peace to come, not just to me, but to Manu also. I ask You to take away the pain and guilt involved with taking another person's life, even though it was to save mine. I ask You to help us think on good things and block out the thoughts the enemy might try to inflict upon us.[111]

"Manu, God sent you here to save me. Now you have given me back my life." Sherry looked down at Riki's body, and panic tried to take control, but a still small voice whispered to her, "Be still and know that I am God."[112] She felt the presence of God and felt His peace. She looked up at Manu and realized God was ministering to him also. She waited.

Manu took a deep breath and stared at Sherry, grateful her life had been spared. "I am glad to give you back your life," Manu said to her gently, "Now with the help of your God; you can go and save others."

"He is my God," Sherry said, "but remember, Manu, now He is your God also."

Manu stood still for a moment and then agreed, "You are right Doctor Sherry, He is my God and I helped Him save you. I hope He will let me help Him all the time."

After Sherry had recovered sufficiently, Manu took her by the hand and said, "Come, you can't stay here with Riki's body and blood on the ground in your house. Come to my house, Noemi will be happy to see you and I will see that this is cleaned up. Then I will find Daniel, Edwardo and Leonardo and tell them what has happened. We will all take rest at my house tonight and we will share last meal. Maybe we can speak more of God while you are there with us."

As they walked outside, they saw Daniel and Edwardo talking with Leonardo. Tears started to stream down Sherry's face and she began to shiver, as the shock of what had happened

---

[111] Philippians 4:6-9
[112] Psalms 46:10

penetrated into her being. Daniel looked over and saw them approaching. He saw the tears on Sherry's face and started to run towards her.

"I'm alright," Sherry reassured him. "I'll let Manu tell you what happened."

Manu walked up to Daniel and gave Sherry's hand to him. He stepped back and began to speak. "I went into the house to look for Doctor Sherry. I told you I had questions I wanted to ask her. I heard sounds coming from the bedroom. As I got closer to it, I could hear someone in there singing the death chant. I recognized Riki's voice. I rushed in, and he had his club raised. Doctor Sherry was lying on the bed asleep. Riki was about to kill her. I threw my knife and killed him. He is lying in the dirt in your bedroom. I did not want Doctor Sherry to stay there alone while I went to get you, so I brought her with me. I will bring her to my house where she can stay until we get everything cleaned up. Noemi will prepare last meal for us and Leonardo's family. Edwardo, you will bring your family. We can have Bible study time also."

"Manu, that's a lot for Noemi to do," Sherry said, "especially after just having a baby. Maybe Connie and I can help."

"No, it is our feast to celebrate life, Noemi's life, little Juan's life, Ciba's life, Juan, our hunter's life, and now your life, Doctor Sherry. My mother will help Noemi. I also have a young girl who is helping her. It will be well."

Manu motioned to two men and told them what had happened. He told them to take the body to the burning ground and dispose of it properly along with the dead bird and feathers. He told them of the curse, and they knew what to do. He called two others over to clean up the blood. He again took Sherry's hand and led her to his house. She had never been there before. It was a house similar in structure to the others close by, but somewhat larger. That was to be expected because he was the chief, and also his mother lived with him. While they were walking, Sherry decided to try to help Noemi. "Manu," she asked, "do you think Noemi is too thin?"

"Yes," he answered emphatically, "she worries me she is so thin."

"Manu, your mother has convinced Noemi that being thin would make you happy. She said you would lose interest in her if she gained weight. I told her it was bad for her and the baby that she was so thin, but she would not eat. I'm sure your mother meant well, but it would help if you told her she needed to gain some weight and that she looked too thin."

Manu looked so surprised. He said, "My mother was just saying to me that Noemi looked too thin. She did not really care for Noemi when I married her. I think I will ask my mother to go and stay with Riki's family. They now have no mother or father. Noemi does not need her kind of help. She now has a young girl from the village helping her. You need one also. I will fix it. Tomorrow you will not have to cook or clean house. She will also take care of the garden."

"Manu sure knows how to take charge," Sherry thought, but that is the role and responsibility of a chief. Sherry began to relax as she walked with him. The more she talked with him the more she liked and respected him. They came up to Manu's house and he called out, "Noemi, I am bringing people home for last meal. Where is my mother?"

"I don't know," answered Noemi, "she left after lunch and I have not seen her since then. Hello Doctor Sherry, would you like to see the baby?"

"Oh yes," said Sherry, anticipating a warm bundle to hold close. What she saw was a listless baby who responded weakly to stimulus. She looked up at Noemi. "What has happened?"

"I don't know," said Noemi. I've been trying to feed him but he doesn't seem interested. Manu's mother said 'He will eat when he gets hungry, and I should not worry. I was going to bring him over this afternoon for you to see him but I had to cook and clean first."

"What do you mean cook and clean," demanded Manu. "I had Suma coming over to help."

"Your mother said I didn't need her and told her to go home," said Noemi. "She said husbands don't like it when their wives are too lazy to cook for them."

"My mother doesn't know what I like. I got Suma to help you so you would get strong quickly and gain some weight back. I don't like to see you so skinny. Now, let Doctor Sherry examine Juan while you get us something to eat and drink. I'm going to watch, to make sure you eat and drink too. Then I'm going to get Suma back here to help you. You should be resting."

Sherry laid the baby on the table, and unwrapped him. He was dry. "Noemi, when was the last time he was wet?"

"Not since this morning," Noemi answered.

"When was the last time you had anything to eat or drink?" Sherry asked.

"Not since yesterday. I was going to have some tea and eat breakfast, but Chabuto reminded me that too much drink and food are bad for the baby, it gives me too much milk and causes the baby to choke."

Sherry could see that some prenatal classes were in order. She could also see that it looked as though Manu's mother had some malicious intent, wanting to cause harm to Noemi and the baby. It appeared that Manu felt that way also. He was very angry and said, "My mother will be moving to Riki's house to care for his children. His wife died and now he is dead also. I just hope she does a better job there than she has done here. She has been lying to you. I don't like skinny girls. I think that she was jealous because she could not give my father any children.

"My father, the old chief, was really my grandfather, Doctor Sherry. He adopted me when I was a baby. He married Chabuto later. She was not a good mother to me. I now realize it was because she could have no sons of her own. She came with a daughter to the marriage, but it was an adopted daughter. Chabuto bought her from the shaman. She was actually his daughter. Her name was Fuego. She no longer lives here in this village. She was caught consorting with devils. They voted to burn her, but she escaped by marrying the local missionary, and we have never seen her again. That was over thirty-five years ago. She left behind a daughter Luna who she sold to the shaman. Luna followed the dark gods also, and was even more wicked than her mother. She has not been seen for over fifteen years. It is said she went in search of another tribe. She did not want to worship our gods, she wanted to worship devils."

Sherry was quiet for a moment, trying to decide how to respond to such a revelation. "I'm sorry your mother had so much sadness in her life, but I think you made the right decision in sending her away, and maybe it is just as well that Luna is gone.

We don't want to be bothered by devils. Now we serve the one, true, and living God. He will keep us safe from evil.

"Now I will try to teach Noemi how to care for your son. If it meets with your approval, I will give classes to all the young mothers who have no experience with babies. I will instruct them about feeding and caring for them."

Sherry thanked Manu again, and told him she would stay with Noemi and help her get lunch ready. Then they would talk about caring for the baby.

After lunch was eaten, Manu went back to the compound to see how everything was going, and Sherry was left to instruct Noemi in the Art of Motherhood.

"Noemi, first thing you need to know is that eating and drinking are good for you and your baby and helps you produce good milk that will make him strong. You are not making any milk and little Juan has given up on getting a good meal. Let's find someone to feed him for a day or two until your milk comes back. Then you can take over. Do you know someone you can ask to feed little Juan?"

"Yes," Noemi said, "Erecia, lives next door and had a baby last month. Her baby is doing well and I don't think Juan would eat much yet, so her baby won't be hungry." Noemi frowned and then said, "Why do you think Chabuto told me those lies. Could my baby have died?"

"I'm not going to lie to you. Yes, Noemi, he could have died, and you could have died with him. Proper diet and drinking enough fluids are very important while you are pregnant and then later while you are feeding the baby. Didn't you see the baby getting weaker?"

"Yes," answered Noemi, "but I was afraid. Chabuto said she would tell Manu that I was a bad mother." Noemi hung her head in shame. "I did not want to be a bad mother. I did what she said; I trusted her. Was I wrong?"

"Yes," Sherry said. "But thank goodness we were in time to save you and the baby. From now on, if you have a question, ask me."

Noemi smiled shyly, "I do not have a family. My family is all dead. I have no mother to help me, to show me what to do. Will you be my mother, Doctor Sherry?"

Sherry took a moment to consider the question and what it would involve. In her world, she was young enough to be Noemi's older sister, but in Noemi's world, she was old enough to be Noemi's mother. If they spent time together, she could instruct Noemi in the things of God as well as motherhood. Sherry looked at Noemi and smiled, "I would be proud to be your mother. I have to tell you, you're going to have a younger brother or sister in around seven months."

Now it was Noemi's turn to smile. "I will make sure you don't get too skinny," she said, and laughed; but Sherry thought back to Chabuto and what she had done, and it wasn't funny. She was glad Manu was sending her away from his family. She only hoped it was far enough away.

They both sat and rested the remainder of the afternoon; then people and food started arriving. They ended up with around fifteen adults and several children, but there was more than enough food to go around and there were enough laps for the children to sit on. Daniel asked if he could speak a blessing over the food and their time together. Manu nodded and Daniel prayed. "Dear God, thank You for all You do for us. Thank You for healing Ciba, for bringing life back to Noemi, and for sending Manu to save Sherry. We ask You to bless this food and cause it to bring health to our bodies. Bless our time together. Help us to learn more about You and Your Son Jesus. In His Name we pray. Amen."

There was much talking and children laughing and large amounts of food consumed. Then it was cleared away and children were quieted. Edwardo stood and began to tell them all about Jesus. He started with the Bethlehem story. Everyone listened closely. He told how the prophets foretold the coming of Jesus, and that the angels announced His birth to the shepherds. He talked for about thirty minutes and then said they would pick this up again. "When would you like to have another Bible study about God?" he asked Manu.

"Tomorrow night after last meal; we will meet in the gathering area for more room. Thank you all for the time you are taking to share about your God with all of us."

Lara had come to listen also. She had a very thoughtful expression on her face. She took the two babies and Maria home to put to bed. She knew she would also have to clean up after the little puppy; but he was such a good companion for little Maria that she didn't mind.

Edwardo and Connie followed Daniel and Sherry home to prepare for the phone call from Maine. It had been a day filled with terror because of Riki and what he had tried to do. It was also a day of thanksgiving for the faithfulness of God in saving Sherry. Life was always busy and things were always happening in this mission field, but the pace seemed to have picked up in the last few days. There was an urgency in the air that could not be denied.

CHAPTER FORTY-ONE

OGUNQUIT, MAINE
JUNE 9

Bekah arrived at The Lobster Pot shortly after six, both hungry and thirsty. Even though she was early, Jean had a pot of coffee and a tray of cookies set out for her in a matter of minutes. As Bekah sipped the coffee and nibbled on her second cookie, she reflected on the happenings these last few days and slowly shook her head. It was almost too strange to believe. On top of that, she would most likely board a plane for Paraguay tomorrow. Paraguay, of all places, was a landlocked country, having little to distinguish itself or attract much of a tourist trade. But it had attracted the attention of God, and because of that, four people were going to head south to join up with four others God had chosen to help in this quest.

She looked out the window and saw the park across the street. There were children playing, mothers with infants in strollers, dogs cavorting, and all seemed right with the world. She thought of the good friends she had. She thought of her garden and the food bank and all the people it provided for. She thought of her store, and of Roberta and Sylvia. Lastly, she thought of Nana Sara and the wonderful life they had had together. She was truly blessed. She felt a peace wash over her and said a quiet, "Thank You."[113]

Everyone else began arriving at the restaurant a little early. They came with expectancy and excitement about what God was doing. They came for fellowship and encouragement. They came for the short time of prayer before the phone call, and they came for cookies. Everyone in town agreed that the chocolate chip cookies at The Lobster Pot were the best they had ever tasted.

After everyone had arrived, Bekah introduced Sandy, Kay and Shirley to the group, explaining that they were going to be praying on a regular basis with Sylvia and that to be effective, they needed to know what was happening. She explained that the phone calls would continue at seven o'clock, even after they were in Paraguay. This was to keep everyone informed of what was going on, share if they had any needs, and just to all pray together in unity.

Then Bekah said, "Roberta has talked to me concerning the fact that she and Joe believe that they are not supposed to go with us to Paraguay. They believe that their mission was to put us in touch with Daniel and Sherry, and that now they are to join with the prayer team in keeping up our defenses there, and here. Roberta and Joe are also going to stay in my house and take care of the garden and food bank, which will remove a big worry from me. She turned to Josh and Renato and Ted, "Did Joe talk with you? How do you feel about this? Are you in agreement, or do we need to talk about this further?"

Josh responded slowly and thoughtfully, "We certainly do need to be in agreement, and yes, Joe talked to Renato, Ted and

---

[113] Philippians 4:6-8

me at lunch today. We discussed it and we prayed about it. We're all in agreement that if they feel they have heard from God, then that is what they should do. We also feel that a smaller group going to Paraguay might be better, and would attract less attention. But the decision is theirs." He looked at Renato and Ted, "Do either of you have anything to add?"

They both shook their heads, "No".

"Another thing we prayed about this morning was that we feel we need to get down there as quickly as possible, and so Renato, Ted, Bekah and I will leave tomorrow afternoon. I know its short notice, but God has put this urgency in us that cannot be ignored. If we forget anything or leave something undone, we'll hope that it can either wait, or one of you can take care of it. What does everyone have to say about this change of plans? Also, do you ladies have a good idea of what has happened and what is going on?" Josh asked. "Do you know about the dreams?"

Sandy spoke for the group. "Yes, we were told about the dreams. I can understand Roberta and Joe thinking they were called to Paraguay, but like them, I feel they were called to be part of the home team. We have discussed it, and we want to be part of the team also. We are willing to give whatever time is necessary to get the job done. All three of us are widows, and this would give us a wonderful sense of fulfillment and of being useful. We are so glad that Sylvia asked us. You can trust us to be faithful to the quest and discreet in all we say and do. Sylvia told us about the trouble in New York. We will all keep our eyes and ears open, watching for anything, or anyone looking or acting suspiciously."

"Roberta and Joe," Josh questioned, "are you both comfortable with everything that has been discussed? Ladies, are you all in agreement?"

230

All said they were in agreement. Then Josh said, "Just like on the day of Pentecost, we are gathered together. We may not be in an upper room, but we are in agreement, seeking the will of God, His direction for our lives, and for this quest in particular. Please join hands and let's pray."

After praying, they stood quietly, with eyes closed, waiting expectantly for something to happen. Finally Bekah opened her eyes and said, "I guess there isn't going to be a mighty rushing wind or tongues of fire.[114] I was kind of hoping there would be, but I suppose I can go on faith."[115]Everyone laughed.

Then they looked at the clock. It was seven-fifteen and they were late with their call again. They sat down and Josh placed the call. They heard someone on the other end pick up and Josh said, "Hello."

---

50 Acts 2:1-3
51 Hebrews 11:1

CHAPTER FORTY-TWO

THE VILLAGE, PARAGUAY
JUNE 9

"Hello," Daniel said, "Is this Josh?"

"Yes it is. I recognize your voice also. How are things going down there Daniel? They have been fairly quiet up here. We have a few surprises, but nothing life- threatening.

"I wish I could say the same for down here. Riki, the native whose wife was killed by the wild boar made an attempt to kill Sherry. If it wasn't for Manu's quick actions, Sherry would be dead instead of Riki.

"As a result of that, and the other miraculous healings that have happened, we had a Bible study tonight with around fifteen adults, plus several children. God is showing Himself strong to these people. I've spent a great deal of time with Manu these last few days, and have seen how he reacts under pressure, as the chief, and especially as a new Christian. I have come to trust and respect him. I think we need to tell him what is happening; tell him about the dreams and show him the crucifix. I feel this is a sign of trust to him and will work to our benefit later.

"Also, as an added benefit, Manu is helping us add on to the house and clinic at no cost to us. We just need to provide all the building materials, except for the roof. The jungle provides that. We had ten people helping today, and tore down the wall in the kitchen. We saved all the wood, so we can use it over again. We are also starting on one of the sleeping areas for when all of you come down."

"Great," said Josh, "that's something we want to talk with you about. There has been a slight change of plans. As much as they want to see both of you, Joe and Roberta feel that they should stay here and be part of what's happening at home. They prayed about it and are at peace with that decision, even though they won't get to see the family they have been missing for so long. We all prayed and are in agreement, so it will be four of us coming, myself, Bekah, Renato and Ted. We'll be leaving tomorrow after lunch. Also, we have three extra ladies here, who are going to be part of the prayer team. We have told them everything. The only thing that concerns me about telling Manu is that he is such a new believer. When you tell him? Will you have to show him the crucifix? Edwardo has known Manu longer than you have. What does he think of the idea?

"We really haven't discussed it in great detail. I only mentioned it tonight. Edwardo, what do you think about telling Manu?"

"I've known Manu all my life. I looked up to him as a boy. He's around fifteen years older than me. I always wanted to follow him around. He was kind to me, and tolerated my hero worship with a smile and a pat on the head. He's been chief for five years, and now he's in his mid-thirties. He has always been a person of integrity and of good character.

"He has a mother who is a trouble maker, but he has just sent her away from his home, due to her malicious intent to his wife and new son. In fact, she is actually his step-mother.

"He appears to have had a genuine change of heart and professes to believe in God and His son Jesus. We only started on the birth of Jesus, how His birth was miraculous and foretold by the prophets a thousand years before His birth, and that it was announced by angels. Tomorrow, we'll go into Jesus' life and ministry, but he appears open to the Gospel and hungry to know more. Not only that, but the little he does know he shares with whoever will listen.

"I don't know if Manu is ready to hear everything or how he will react to the golden crucifix, but I think it is better he find out from us rather than someone else. Maybe God wants him involved with us. It would be very helpful to have him on our side. Also, seeing God work would certainly strengthen his faith. I vote we tell him."

Daniel turned to Sherry, "What do you say?"

Sherry answered thoughtfully. "I got to talk to Manu, and spend more time with Manu today than I ever have before. His kindness and gentleness with me after he killed Riki really impressed me. I was also impressed with the way he handled the situation with his mother. He showed wisdom, and discernment. I don't believe he makes snap decisions. He thinks things over, makes a decision, and then follows through with it. I think we should tell him."

"Connie?" Daniel questioned.

"I do not know Manu well," Connie said, "but I know his wife very well. I saw her the day she was born. She was right when she said she did not know her mother. Her mother died giving birth to her. She was raised by her mother's sister. She was the youngest. There were five children before her. She was always thin, and didn't see much food come her way. Unfortunately, marriage hasn't changed things. She is still thin, only now it is because of her mother-in-law's spite and malice. Hopefully things will change for the better now that Chabuto is gone.

"But to get back to Manu, he has been kind to her. It was a marriage arranged by his mother, and then she changed her mind. Manu did not want to shame the girl and break it off, so he married her against his mother's wishes.

"Manu is kind and considerate and stands up for the oppressed. I think that speaks well of him. I think we should tell him."

"OK," Josh said. "Do you want to do it now, or when we get there?"

"I think we need to do it now," Daniel said. "If all of you agree, I will have Manu and Leonardo over for breakfast tomorrow. I think we need to tell Leonardo also. He is one of Manu's counselors and he is now a Christian. He displays the same quiet strength of character and steadfastness that Manu does. Are there any objections?" No one said anything. "Maybe these two will take the place of Roberta and Joe. We will have sixteen people, including our new prayer partners, actively involved in the quest God has given us."

"Alright, sounds good to us up here. The four of us will fly out tomorrow. We're still on the same time frame. How does that sound to you, Daniel?"

"I think that's a good plan. We'll leave it at that. Good luck with all your preparations," Daniel said.

"Wait a minute," Bekah interrupted, "I just thought of something. Do women wear anything special there? Is there some kind of dress code?"

"I'm so glad you thought of that," Daniel replied," Yes they do. Let me get Sherry or Connie to talk with you about that."

"Bekah, this is Sherry. Yes, they do not wear pants or shorts. Short sleeve blouses are alright, but nothing sleeveless; same thing for dresses. Right below the knee is fine. Skirts and jumpers are good. Tee shirts are also fine. Bring a few jackets and sweaters everyone; remember it's almost winter here. It's nice during the day, in the seventies and eighties if it doesn't rain. It's the start of the rainy season. At night it could get into the fifties. Bring sturdy shoes, boots, water shoes, flip flops, and sneakers. Due to the wet ground, we go through a tremendous amount of footwear. We get muddy and we have dirt floors. Welcome to the jungle."

"OK, thanks. I'm glad I asked. It looks like we will be shopping tomorrow morning. I look forward to meeting all of you. I think that's it. Anyone have anything else?" She paused and no one spoke. "If not we'll say good night."

Bekah breathed a sigh. They had been on the phone almost an hour. It had been a rather tense phone call with all that was happening. From the faces of everyone, she wasn't the only person who was tired. She only hoped that when she got home her mind would slow down and let her rest. Right now it was spinning with all the things she needed to do for tomorrow. At the moment, she could not even remember where her passport was. She thought she had seen it in the safe deposit box. Thank God the bank was open Saturday mornings. She would have to retrieve the crucifix also if she was going to bring it with her.

She said goodnight to everyone and told Sylvia she would call the The Eye in the morning to let her and Roberta know what was going on with the preparations. She needed to give Roberta a key so she and Joe could stay at the house. She thought about putting out fresh towels in the guest bath when she went home. She walked out to her car and the Three Musketeers were waiting. "You three go on to Renato's. I'm fine. I have quite a bit to do tonight and I do not want to be tripping over you Ted."

"I won't be in the way; I'm going to crash on the sofa like I did last night. You won't even know I'm there."

"Maybe that's true," said Bekah with exasperation, "but you will certainly know I'm there. I will be all over the house looking for things I will need to pack. I'll be making lists of things I need to buy. I'm on a caffeine high that's been fed by four cups of coffee after five o'clock. I feel like I may never sleep again. I don't need anyone extra there. They will just cause additional stimulation."

"After talking with Renato and Josh, the three of us have decided to accompany you home."

Bekah started to object strenuously. "No, I already told you that you can't stay there."

"Yes," said Josh, "we all heard that loud and clear. Now listen", said Josh with patience, "Let us all escort you to your house. We are going to do a walk through and make sure no one is there and nothing is moved or missing. If we are fully persuaded, then we will all go over Renato's and leave you alone. That's the plan. Can you live with it? Keep the backyard lights on and the front porch light also. That should discourage anyone from coming around."

"All right, "Bekah conceded, "Just don't take too long. You all probably have some packing to do as well."

CHAPTER FORTY-THREE

OGUNQUIT, MAINE
JUNE 9

Bekah drove out to the house and her musketeers followed. It was a beautiful spring night and there was the smell of rain in the air. Bekah lived twenty minutes out of the town of Ogunquit. It was the largest town around, but she actually had a Wells address. It was a pleasant ride and she felt herself start to relax. As she turned into the driveway, that sense of peace and relaxation dissipated. Every light in the house was on and the back door stood wide open.

They all pulled in the yard together. Josh stepped out of his car with a gun in his hand. No one appeared surprised but Bekah. "You three stay put. I'm going to see if the house is empty. Bekah, does the house have a basement or attic that someone could hide in?"

"Yes, both," she said. "Please don't go in there. Shouldn't we call the police?"

"Not just yet," Josh answered, "not until we know what we're dealing with, and have some idea of whom or what they were after."

Josh walked quietly to the back door and looked in. He was relatively certain that whoever had broken in was gone, but he was cautious just the same. He kept his gun raised as he went from room to room, surveying the damage and destruction.

Drawers were pulled open and contents scattered, closets were ripped apart.

In the office, Nana Sara's beautiful, antique desk had been splintered. It was completely demolished, and its contents gone. Someone had been very interested in its secrets. What did remain was now scattered. It was difficult to determine what was missing from it, or from anywhere else.

Josh wondered who was responsible for the wreckage and what they wanted. He had his suspicions, but had kept quiet thus far. It appeared they would not be learning anything from the contents of the desk, and he wondered if it was important to the quest or only to Bekah personally. Now they would never know. The odds of getting those things back were negligible.

He finished searching through the rest of the house and found it all in total chaos. Everything was smashed, furniture was ripped apart, and contents were strewn from one end of the house to the other. Someone had been very thorough. They appeared to take actual enjoyment in the path of destruction they paved.

Putting his gun away, Josh went back to the door and called Bekah. As she came up the steps, he stopped her before she went inside. He wanted to prepare her for what she was about see. "Bekah, you're going to have to be strong, you can't fall apart. No matter how bad it is, God will give you strength."[116]

Just entering the porch was distressing, seeing all the fruits of her labor smashed and stepped on. Even the dried herbs hanging from the ceiling had been pulled down and trampled on.

As she walked into the kitchen, the extent of the destruction began to cut her. Each and every possession that she

[116] 2 Corinthians 12:9

239

saw destroyed or damaged wounded her further. Before long her soul was hemorrhaging and she needed not only emotional, but physical support. Josh took her arm and guided her over to the stairs.

There was not even a chair left standing for her to sit in. She sat down on the bottom step and surveyed the destruction. It was hard to imagine one person doing all this damage. Then she spoke, "Josh, are we sure it was only one person? Maybe there was a group. Maybe they'll come back. Are we safe here, maybe we should leave until help comes?"

"I don't think anyone will be back. They've come and gone. Whether it was one or more, they accomplished their goal. They tore this place apart looking for something. I think you know what, and I don't think they will be back."

"Does the rest of the house look the same as down here?" Bekah asked. "If it does, I don't want to look at it yet. All my possessions, my mementos and treasures have been destroyed. My memories have been tainted. Any time I try to recall one, the first thing my mind will recall is a picture of this carnage. I feel as if my home has been brutally slaughtered. It had been alive with all my hopes and dreams, now it's dead. Please take me back outside. I don't want to see anymore tonight."

"Bekah," Josh asked, "before we go any further I need to ask you an important question. Where is the crucifix? I have to think that Haydon Carlton is responsible for this, and if he didn't find it, he may look somewhere else."

"The crucifix is in a safe deposit box in the bank. I put it there this afternoon."

Josh suggested, "Maybe we should call the police now."

Bekah went back into the house to place the call, but was unable to locate the telephone. It had been ripped from the wall and was most likely on the floor under some of the debris. She went back to her car and took her cell phone out of her purse. She sat in the front seat and called the police station.

After finishing the call, she walked back to Josh's car and announced, "The police will be here in fifteen to twenty minutes, and we're not to touch anything. What are we going to tell them when they ask if we know a reason why someone would break into my house? Also, we need to call Sylvia, Roberta and Joe and let them know what has happened. Roberta and Joe were going to move in tomorrow. Maybe they can help us clean up some of this so they have a place to stay. They can go through it all if they have time, and save whatever is salvageable. We can take pictures for the insurance company. I don't know if anything of value is buried, broken or stolen. Perhaps we can spend some time looking after the police leave." Bekah was almost babbling, saying the first things that came to mind to whoever was listening.

Renato walked over to her. "I called Joe and Roberta as soon as we got here. They stopped by to pick up Sylvia and should be here any minute to help." As he finished speaking, a state police car pulled into the yard. Right behind them were Joe, Roberta and Sylvia.

Josh walked up to the police car; everyone else went over to Bekah and huddled together. "Good evening," he said. My name is Joshua Randall and I'm a friend of Bekah Ryan's. She's over there being consoled by some of her other friends. She's had a tough time lately with her grandmother dying, and now this. The house is totally trashed. I can show you around, if you want a guide. I've already been through it to make sure there was no one

241

hiding or injured inside. I can also introduce you to Bekah if you'd like."

"I'm Sargent Hathaway of the Maine State Police Department, and yes, I'd like to meet her. You took a quite a chance going in there by yourself."

Josh replied, "I wasn't totally by myself, I was armed. I'm connected to the CIA, and licensed to carry a weapon." Josh took out his wallet and showed his license. My friends aren't aware of that fact, not that it would make much difference. If it's alright with you, I would like to keep this under the table for now. I didn't think they needed to know, but circumstances have changed and now I need to tell them."

"There's no problem," Sargent Hathaway answered, "as long as it doesn't pertain to the break-in. This is not in Ogunquit proper, or Wells so it's the State Police, not local, that will handle the investigation. I just want to go over and meet Ms. Ryan. Then if it's fine with her, you can show me around."

They both walked up to Bekah. She had separated herself from the group and was sitting on the back steps. "Bekah, this is Sargent Jim Hathaway from the Maine State Police Department. He's willing to let me take him through the house and around the property if you don't want to go back inside."

Bekah looked at Josh questioningly and said, "Whatever you would like to do is fine with me. I would rather not look at it again if I don't have to, at least not right away."

Josh and Sargent Hathaway turned and headed into the house. Josh let him go first. When he opened the door, he stopped to survey the damage. "Wow! They really trashed the place. Is the rest of the place this bad?"

"No," answered Josh, "it's worse. I walked through the whole house first to make sure it was safe. Bekah walked through downstairs. By the time she had finished there, she didn't have the heart to go upstairs. This was like the rape of a property; nothing was left unbroken or untouched. It was almost as though someone wanted to not only rob her in a physical sense, but also to hurt her spirit as well. All her memories of her childhood and her grandmother were encompassed in this house. This is equivalent to a house fire, but with malice. Instead of ashes which the wind can carry away, or water washes away, these remnants of a life must be thrown away. There is nothing left to save. Even her clothes were ripped to shreds."

Josh and the officer finished looking at the lower level, and taking multiple pictures. Now they walked upstairs. Touring through the whole house and taking pictures of everything took the better part of an hour. It was a sad sight. Even the attic and basement were a shambles. When they finished, they stood in the kitchen and looked around again. Then Sargent Hathaway turned to Josh and questioned him. "I see her old friends over there consoling her, but who are you? You're not from around here, you're CIA, and you're packing a gun. By the way, what are you carrying? May I see it?"

"Sure," Josh replied. He bent down and took his weapon out of an ankle holster and handed it to him. It was a Glock 30S, .45 caliber.

"Wow! You don't believe in fooling around, do you?"

"No I don't," said Josh. "If you are not prepared to act decisively, someone can get hurt, and I don't want it to be me. I've dealt with a number of bad guys, and I learned a few lessons the hard way. Now, I don't fool around, and I believe the person who did this was a bad guy."

"Thanks," said Sargent Hathaway, returning the fire arm. "Now if you don't mind, I'd appreciate you telling me why you are here."

Josh thought for a moment and then said, "I feel that God has sent me here. All of us here had a dream we think was from God, sending us on a quest. Four of us are supposed to leave for Paraguay tomorrow."

They walked back out into the yard and started walking over to the group. "Wow! That's some story. I assume they will all confirm this?" Sargent Hathaway questioned.

Josh responded in a tired voice, "You'll just have to ask them yourself."

Bekah stood there amidst her friends, leaning on their strength, and drawing on the last of her courage to finish this interview so the night could be over.

Sargent Hathaway walked up to Bekah and said, "I'm sorry for your loss, and I know you must be hurting, but I have to ask you some questions. This doesn't appear to be a random act of violence. Whoever broke in had a motive. Why would he pick your house and ransack it the way he did? Do you know what he was looking for, and is there anything you can tell me that will help our investigation?"

"We don't even know if anything is missing, other than the contents of the desk. I didn't see anything at all from it: no papers, ledgers, or envelopes lying around. The thing that makes it difficult is that Nana Sara was very secretive about her desk and its contents. She kept it locked at all times. I took one drawer of the contents to the store today to go through. It was mostly

244

receipts kept over the years. It appears that in this area, Nana Sara was a hoarder. To make matters worse, four of us are scheduled to leave on a mission trip tomorrow afternoon to Paraguay. My friends are going to help me pick up the pieces here. I can't even put in an insurance claim until I get back and go through what they find and determine what is missing or broken. I really find it hard to make any decisions right now. I feel totally numb and emotionally drained."

"That's understandable, but I really need for you to answer my question, "Do you know of anyone who would have a motive for doing this?"

"As you know, my grandmother recently died. She left me an unusual piece of jewelry she said came from my mother, who was from Paraguay. My father was a missionary there. Anyway, we took it to a jeweler, Haydon Carlton, in New York City, who Ted, my ex-husband, had known. We just wanted to have the piece authenticated. The man was very friendly and helpful until he saw the piece. Then all he wanted to do was buy it from us or sell it for us.

"We even had some trouble with him in New York. We had a limo coming back to pick us up in front of his shop. When we were across the street the limo pulled up. This man, Haydon Carlton, came out of his store, talked to the limo driver and appeared to give him some money. Then the limo left without us. We assume he told the driver we didn't need him. We felt a sense of urgency to leave the area right away, so we took the subway and a bus to get back to the airport. I don't know if this man is responsible for the break-in, but he is my best guess."

"Wow! That's some story. Don't you worry about it Ms. Ryan," Sgt. Hathaway said. "We'll take care of everything. We'll probably have additional questions. Can we reach you in Paraguay, and who do you want to act on your behalf here?"

"My friends, Roberta and Joe Albright were planning to stay here while I was gone, to tend and harvest the garden, and see to the food bank that I have operating through my store. I've organized a small food bank with the produce from my garden, and we're just starting to harvest some of it now. I would hate to see it go to waste. I need to ask if they still want to stay here. Maybe we can clean one room out for them to sleep in. I'll have to purchase a new mattress and box spring because the ones that were here were torn up. It's a bit much to ask anyone to live in a situation like this, no less a friend. Roberta is also an employee of mine. I own The Eye of the Needle, a shop in town. Roberta, and Sylvia Jessup, both work for me."

"Yes, I agree, this is a big task," said Sgt. Hathaway, "and call me Jim. I feel like I already know you. My wife is Audrey Hathaway. She's spends quite a bit of time and money in your shop. I knew I recognized your name from somewhere. We will work with you here Ms. Ryan. Will Mrs. Albright be in contact with you while you are gone, and is she willing to act on your behalf?"

"Yes, we will stay in the house, and we are more than willing to act on Bekah's behalf," said Roberta, who was standing right behind her. "I'm more than a friend and employee, we're almost sisters." With that, she gave Bekah a big hug and said, "You seem to be acquiring more family than you ever had before. Come Christmas you will have to rent out a hall to accommodate us all for Christmas dinner."

There were tears in Bekah's eyes as she hugged Roberta. "I don't know what I'd do without you. If you and Joe hadn't already decided to stay home, there would be no way I could leave tomorrow. Now I don't even know where I'm going to spend the night. Renato, do you have one more bed in your house? Maybe I should stay at the guest house in town; at least they have spare tooth brushes and toothpaste."

"No," answered Renato softly as he put his arm around Bekah. "But I have a spare tooth brush, and you can sleep in my bed, I will sleep in the recliner. I usually do most nights anyway. This way you can sleep undisturbed, and I will feed you when you arise. We will do what we can tomorrow. Let's not worry about it now.[117]

"What we don't have time to purchase here we can get in Paraguay. In fact, we may do better shopping there for clothes for you because they will have the kind of clothes you need for the season they are having down there."

Josh spoke up, "That's a great idea Renato; maybe we should all wait to shop until we get down there rather than having a shopping frenzy tomorrow. We can also get the gifts for the chief and the village down there. In addition, it will save us from carrying large amounts of luggage."

Sargent Hathaway said, "I'm going to head back out on patrol now. Let me give you my card, and you can call me in the morning after you have had some rest. I have a few more questions, but they can wait."

Bekah put out her hand, "Thanks for all your help and kindness, and tell Audrey I said hello."

"I will. Good night." He got in his car and drove away.

Joe, Roberta and Sylvia said good night and then drove off also. It was just Bekah and her Three Musketeers. She walked over and sat on the front seat of her car while they all just stood

---

[117] Matthew 6:25-34

there and took in the sounds of the night. Josh questioned Bekah, "May I ask why you volunteered all that information to Sargent Hathaway. I thought we were going to try to keep a low profile."

"You're right," Bekah answered, "but I couldn't lie. Even though it might have helped us to keep this all quiet, in the long run, a lie is a lie, and I couldn't condone it; especially if we want God's blessing on what we are doing.[118] God will keep quiet what needs to be kept quiet."

"I think you're right about that Bekah," Ted said. Then he added as an afterthought, "Hey, are we ever going to eat dinner? Renato, do you have anything in your house to eat? I'm beyond hungry."

Renato replied with a laugh, "I'm sure we can find something. I don't know how good it will be, but I'm sure it will be filling."

Then Bekah heard a scratching noise and began to laugh. Josh, Ted and Renato looked at her with concern thinking she was about to lose control, but she reached over and grabbed a Styrofoam box that had been in the back seat. "If anyone still wants dinner, I seem to remember buying four lobsters and some potato salad for dinner tonight. It appears the lobsters are still alive and well."

Josh drove Bekah over to Renato's. Ted and Renato followed in Ted's rental car. Josh carried in the box with the lobsters and potato salad. Renato had an up to date kitchen with all the bells and whistles, but it had an old world charm. There were beautiful cherry wood cabinets, muted gold walls, and purple and teal accents. The room was warm and inviting. Renato's wife had died over thirty years ago but her spirit was still

---

[118] Matthew 15:18-20

there. The china was hers, the pictures were hers. He even had two or three needlepoints she did hanging on the wall. They were of grape vines and orchards. Renato got out the large lobster pot and put water on to boil. Bekah melted some butter.

"I wish we had something to celebrate with this meal," said Bekah sadly. "I can't believe what's happening to me; what's happening to all of us. We seem to be living in a dream world and it's starting to turn into a nightmare. It was bad enough having Nana die, but now all this is happening. I just don't know how to deal with it all. I need help, and I don't feel like I know how to get it. My world is falling apart. I have all these questions and no answers. Does anyone know what to do?"

Renato spoke up, "Come on over here and sit down Miss Bekah and let us pray for you. You need to remember that God wasn't taken unawares by any of this. He knows everything that is going to happen, from the beginning to the end. Remember anything bad that happens; God can turn to good.[119] Ted and Josh, please come over here and help me pray for Miss Bekah?"

They all put their hands on Bekah's shoulders. "Dear Lord," Renato prayed, "You said that if we would think on good things Your peace would come to us.[120] Miss Bekah needs that peace right now, but she's having trouble thinking on good things because of all that has happened. Her mind needs to be renewed.[121] She needs Your help, to look to the hills where her help comes from.[122] She can't be wondering what she should do, she needs to ask what You want her to do. We all ask, Lord, that

---

[119]Genesis 50:20
[120] Philippians 4:6-8
[121] Romans 12:2
[122] Psalm 121:1-8

You again show all of us what You want us to do, lead us and guide us. We pray in Jesus' Name. Amen"[123],[124]

"Bekah," Josh spoke in a soft voice, "Satan always tries to derail us when we are on a mission from God. He tries to put obstacles in our path and bring confusion into our lives. We can't let him have his way; we can't let him win. Remember Satan is the author of confusion and God is the author of peace.[125] Let's just keep going with our plans and trust Him. Remember we have to fight the devil no matter where we are.[126] If we stand up and fight, he loses because God is on our side."[127]

"Bekah," Ted spoke timidly. He took one of Bekah's hands in his. He was still not very knowledgeable concerning the Bible and felt uncomfortable speaking up. "I know I don't have much in the way of Bible knowledge. I think the only Scriptures I know are John 3:16 which I read when I got saved, and Genesis 1:1, which says, 'In the beginning;' but I know some principles, and one I've applied to my life is don't give up,[128] and keep trying."[129]

Bekah put her hand up and grabbed his and gave it a squeeze. "I want to thank you all for your prayers. Just acknowledging the presence of God brings peace. This last week has been more stressful than any other time in my life. Yet, as you say, God is with me and will walk me through it. I may be walking through 'the valley of the shadow of death;'[130] but through is the

---

[123] John 14:14
[124] John 16:26
[125] 1 Corinthians 14:33
[126] James 4:7
[127] Romans 8:31
[128] Ephesians 6:10-18
[129]Philippians 3:13-15
[130] Psalm 23

operative word. I'm not staying there. I know that even in dark times, God is with me, and He will never leave me or abandon me."[131]

Bekah took a deep breath, put a smile on her face, and said, "Now let's get these lobsters cooked. Other than two cookies, I haven't eaten since breakfast. I hear the water boiling. Renato, do you want the honor, or should I put these lobsters in the pot?"

Renato laughed, "As much as you love lobster, you go right ahead. I'll set the timer. How big are they?"

"Around two pounds apiece. These are pretty big dudes. I figure they'll need about twenty minutes. I thought if there was any left, we could have lobster omelets for breakfast tomorrow. Maybe we could even stop at the Lobster Pound tomorrow afternoon and get a lobster roll to go before we head to the airport. If so, that will be three times in less than a week. Not a bad average for a newcomer, is it Josh?

"Renato, do you have anything to drink in the refrigerator? I'm usually a water drinker, but maybe we'll splurge. Do you have any Coke or Sprite?"

"Bekah, you make me laugh. I have both, you will have to choose."

"OK, let's show our class. Get the Coke, and we'll serve it in glasses instead of out of the can." Bekah laughed for the first time that night. It felt good.

God had restored her joy and her peace. "Thank you Lord," she whispered.

---

[131] Hebrews 13:5

CHAPTER FORTY-FOUR

OGUNQUIT, MAINE

JUNE 10

Bekah was startled from her sleep by an incessant knocking on the door. She looked around, somewhat disoriented and then remembered the events of the previous evening. "Miss Bekah, Miss Bekah, are you alright?"

"Yes I'm fine. What's the matter?"

Renato spoke from the other side of the door, "It's after nine and I've knocked several times. I was worried something had happened to you."

"I'm sorry. I don't usually sleep this late. I'll be right down, as soon as I wash my face and brush my hair. Didn't you say you had a new toothbrush I could use?" Bekah queried.

"Yes," answered Renato. "I put it in the bathroom along with some tooth paste, soap and towels. Let me know if you need anything else. I've got biscuits in the oven and everything cut up for the lobster omelets."

"That sounds great. I'll be down in a few minutes. One thing about having no clothes to choose from," Bekah laughed, "is you can get ready in less time."

Renato chuckled. "That's true, and you usually found it difficult being on time. You always loved nice clothes and had so many to choose from. We'll be waiting. Come down when you are ready."

Renato went back downstairs, walked into the kitchen, and poured himself a cup of coffee. Ted was sitting, looking out the big window that faced the apple orchard, enjoying his cup of coffee. "How many trees do you grow in the orchard?" Ted inquired.

"Anywhere from one hundred seventy-five to two hundred trees are producing. This year we also planted twenty-five young trees. The orchard supports us all and turns a small profit. Between the store and the orchard, Bekah is a woman of means." Renato picked up his pipe and cleaned it out for the first smoke of the day. A short smoke before breakfast always improved his appetite, not that his needed improvement; especially if Bekah was cooking.

Bekah came down the stairs looking a little worn and wrinkled, but well rested. She saw Renato and Ted and asked, "Where's Josh? Aren't we all having breakfast together?"

"He went back over to the house to look around. He said to call him on his cell when breakfast was ready." Renato drew on his pipe a few times to make sure it was well lit. "With all the turmoil of the previous evening I didn't get to ask; did any of you see Josh carrying a hand gun last night? I was sure I had seen it and was going to question him about it, but we started talking about Nana Sara, and it slipped my mind."

"A gun!" exclaimed Bekah. "Why would he be carrying a gun?"

The kitchen door squeaked and everyone turned to see Josh coming into the room. "I was wondering when someone was going to ask. To answer everyone's question, I'm former military, and almost former CIA. I have a license to carry a concealed weapon. That license is honored by every state.

"As to why; God told me there was an evil tribe warring on peaceful tribes and sacrificing infant children to their evil gods. He was sending us to help them. It sounded like a serious situation, and I wanted to be ready in every way possible, in the natural and in the spiritual. David had a weapon to kill the giant, five small stones. It was a weapon he was skilled and familiar with. This is my weapon of choice."

"Why didn't you tell us?" Bekah demanded. "We had a right to know."

"I was hoping there would be no need for it, that it wouldn't come up. Obviously, that is not the case now. I'll tell you a little more of my story, and you can ask questions later. Why doesn't someone start cooking while I talk? We are under a little bit of a time constraint."

Josh leaned against the counter and began his story. "When I was in first grade a new family moved into the neighborhood. They were from very far away. My father showed me on the globe the country of Iraq. They had a son my age. It was summer and we were out of school. We were together a lot, but we didn't talk much because he didn't speak English and I didn't speak Arabic. That summer he started learning English from me and I started learning Arabic from him. Kids pick up languages quickly and by the time school started we weren't fluent in each other's language, but we could understand most of what was being said. By the end of that next year, we both sounded like natives of each other's homeland.

"His father worked in the oil industry and the family was here on an extended visa. His father was here to gain experience in the production of oil. Eventually, he and his wife had to return to Iraq, but Akeem lived with us until we graduated college. We both went to Oral Roberts University. I told you my degrees were in sociology and Biblical studies. I did my doctoral thesis on unreached people groups. His were in Oil Field Engineering and Biblical studies, and a Master's Degree in Geology and Plate Tectonics. We both graduated with honors. I came to find out later that Akeem's parents paid for my education as a thank you to my parents for caring for their son.

"After attending college for six years Akeem wanted to go back to Iraq to see his family. They had stayed in touch over the years in spite of everything going on in the area. Iraq had already been at war with Iran for a number of years. During that time Saddam Hussein rose to power, but they still managed to get two or three letters out every year.

"Akeem got a job with a government agency doing geological studies all over the world. He seemed happy, but was very worried about his family. In his last letter to them, Akeem told them he wanted to come home. They replied back with their current address, tickets, and papers he would need to enter the country. That was in 2001, before the bombing of the World Trade Center. It's been almost fourteen years. I haven't heard from him since then.

"After I graduated, the Iraqi war was going on and I enlisted. I went to Officer's Training School and was given a job in covert operations because of my linguistic skills. I saw time in and out of country for four years and then the CIA wanted me. It's hard to say no when your government pressures you. I made a compromise. I would work for them occasionally while I completed my doctorate in unreached people groups, and if they footed the bill I would give them four more years.

"So here I am today, I have my doctorate, and the government still hounds me. I carry a weapon because I need to be prepared to go if they give me the call. I owe them less than one month. It's ironic, but on Fourth of July, Independence Day, I will be free." Josh took a deep breath and looked at everyone. "Any questions," he asked.

"Wow! That is some story. I don't know what to say," said Bekah.

"Well I do," said Ted. "Is there anything else you haven't told us? I don't want any more surprises. That was some bombshell."

Josh looked at Renato. Renato sat there smoking his pipe and looking thoughtful. Finally he spoke. "Isn't it just like God to answer questions we haven't even asked, to help us when we don't even know we need help. I think we should thank God for giving us someone like this, skilled in areas we are not, not only armed with the weapon of prayer, but also, skilled in physical combat and armaments. I'm sorry you felt a need to keep this information from us, but I'm glad it is out in the open now. I see this as a positive and not a negative. It's good to know we have extra firepower."

Josh walked over to Bekah. "I have one more thing I want to say. I found this taped to a piece of wood in that pile that was once your grandmother's desk." He handed her a safe deposit box key.

The color drained out of Bekah's face. "Oh no," she whispered. In a louder voice she continued, "I can't believe it; more secrets. I don't even know what bank it belongs to. We have to leave here by one, it's already after ten, and I don't even have a suitcase. Also, my passport is in the bank and I need to get

256

it and the crucifix. I guess I can buy a suitcase down in Paraguay. I now have a toothbrush and tooth paste thanks to Renato, and my hairbrush was in my purse. I don't think I'll be needing makeup where we're going; that's a relief. I have a suggestion, you guys go pack what you're taking, and bring your suitcases down. I'm going to finish making breakfast, and then we can eat and head for town. Renato, where do you keep the paper plates?" Bekah asked. "We don't have time to clean up a big mess."

They got to town by eleven thirty and headed straight for the bank. Bekah retrieved her passport and the crucifix. They had decided to bring it with them, and pack it in one of the carry-ons. They asked the teller if she recognized the key Josh had found. She looked at it closely, and then said, "We have a rack of safe deposit boxes that are very old; they have a different type of key. Maybe it fits one of them. The number on it seems to have worn off. Do you know what it is?"

Frustrated, Bekah answered, "No I don't. How many are there?

"One hundred," answered the teller.

Bekah thanked the teller for her help. They left the bank and got back in the car. "I can't handle this now. I'm going to call Jim Pritchard and see if he can manage this for me. Maybe I can verbally give Roberta and Joe Power of Attorney. Let's go over to the shop. I'll call from there; then we need to pray before we leave."

Ted, Renato, Josh and Bekah all walked into The Eye. Everyone was there: Roberta, Joe and Sylvia, plus Sandy, Kay and

Shirley. Here was God's mighty army, ready to go forth and destroy the works of the devil.[132]

"We have run out of time. Will you pray with us? Then we have to leave," Bekah asked.

"Of course we will pray for you," replied Roberta, "but first, take these," and she handed Bekah a bag. "I went out and purchased some clothes for you; I knew you wouldn't have any time to get some for yourself. Go hurry and change. Joe's already gassed the truck and it's parked out front."

While Bekah went to change, Renato told them of the loose ends that needed to be tied up. Roberta and Joe agreed to accept power of attorney, and Roberta looked up Jim Prichard's number to have it ready for Bekah.

Bekah came back into the room. "Thank you so much, this was so thoughtful. I didn't like the idea of traveling so far in dirty clothes. I see you even bought an extra set. Where did the sweater come from that was in the bag?"

"It came from me," Roberta said. "I was going to give it to you for your birthday, but need took precedence. Bring your dirty clothes with you; I'll give you another bag for them. This way you will have an extra set. I also got you a pair of sneakers and some socks. One of the guys can put these bags in his suitcase. How many carry-ons do you have?"

Renato answered, "We only have three carry-ons. Bekah's clothes can fit in one of them. Bekah, don't forget to give Roberta the key to the safe deposit box."

Roberta held out her hand. "Here, give it to me," and she put it in her purse. "I've got Jim Prichard's number here;" Roberta

---

[132] 1 John 3:8

said. "Call him and let's get that taken care of. If we run out of time, go, we'll be praying for you all afternoon."

Bekah dialed the phone and waited while it rang. "Hello, Pritchard residence," said a female voice.

"Is that you Angie?" Bekah asked. "This is Bekah Ryan."

"Hi, Bekah, how are you doing?"

"Well I have some things that have come up and I need to talk with Jim. Is he there?"

"Sure, let me get him for you. Hold on."

Bekah waited. She could hear murmuring in the background, and realized they had already started praying.

Jim picked up the phone. "Hello, Bekah, what can I do for you?"

"Jim, I'm sorry to bother you at home, but I've run out of time. I'm leaving for Paraguay on a mission trip. I'm going to talk while we're in the car, we're already late."

She paused a moment and blew a kiss to everyone and mouthed, "I love you all."

"I don't know whether you heard, but my house was vandalized last night. They tore everything apart, even my clothes. The place is a total shambles. The State Police were out, Jim Hathaway, and he was very nice. I need to call him too, before I get on that plane. Anyway, in looking through the carnage, we found a key to a safe deposit box. I was at the bank and the teller said it looked like one that went to their old boxes, but the number was worn off. I've asked Roberta if she will go try the key and see if it opens any of those boxes. Can I give her and Joe power of attorney orally? There's no way I could stop by, and it may be a few weeks before I get back."

"Don't worry, we can do it orally. Just let me get my recorder and we'll take care of this. All right, just state today's date, who you are, and what you want to do." When they were through Jim asked, "Is there anything else I can help you with today?"

"No," Bekah said, "that was it. Thanks again, I'll call you when we get back.

"Now one down, one to go." Bekah said as she got out Jim Hathaway's business card and dialed the number.

"Good afternoon, Sargent Hathaway speaking, how can I help you?"

"Jim, its Bekah Ryan. I wanted to touch base with you before we left. We're running late and are on our way to the airport. I just talked with Jim Pritchard and gave Roberta and Joe Albright power of attorney to act on my behalf. We will usually be in touch with them on a daily basis. They have a satellite phone where we're staying. Our cell phones won't work. We will basically be out in the jungle."

"Sounds like a great trip. I think we can handle most things from here. I'm in the process of getting the rundown on Haydon Carlton. Maybe we can solve this mess before you get back. If I need to I can get Roberta to call you, or find out when you have calls scheduled. If I only have a question or two, I can tell her and she can ask you. You go have a great trip. Don't worry about us back here."

"Thanks so much, Jim," Bekah responded. "I'll stop by and see you when I get back." When she ended the call Bekah handed the phone to Joe and said, "Don't forget to take this back to The Eye, it's the store phone."

It took less than an hour and a half to get to the airport. Bekah sat rigidly, hands grasped tightly together. She felt like she was a rubber band ready to snap. Bekah thanked God it was not too crowded when they arrived. They got checked in, and went through the long security line with fifteen minutes to spare. When they boarded, the flight was not crowded and they could spread out with a seat in between. Bekah and Josh were in one row and Renato and Ted in the row across the aisle. Bekah looked out the window during takeoff, and then laid her head back on the headrest. She closed her eyes and was immediately asleep.

It was a three and a half hour flight from Boston to Miami. Josh, Renato and Ted could not really discuss much of their business, but they could discuss what they would need to purchase when they arrived in Asuncion. Renato had a pad and started writing things down. "I don't remember much about Paraguay, and I am sure it has changed in over fifty years, but cities are cities and they always have stores. I'm sure we will be able to get whatever we need there. We should probably get several pair each of loose fitting pants, and several short sleeve and long sleeve work shirts. Also we will need several pair of socks and changes of underwear. We all have our own toiletries, except for Bekah. All she has is a tooth brush and tooth paste. We will all need work boots, wet shoes, a few pair of sneakers, so some can dry out while we are wearing others. Bekah will have to do her own shopping, but I think we all agree, she should never be left alone. None of us should go anywhere alone. Remember Jesus sent His disciples out by twos."[133]

Since no one was sitting near, Josh felt safe to ask, "Do either of you know how to handle a gun? I think it's a good idea to

---

[133] Luke 10:1

have protection. We don't know what we are walking into. Also a knife would be a good idea, not just as protection, but as a work tool. I'm even thinking of purchasing a rifle. I wonder if there are licensing laws."

Renato spoke up first. "That sounds like a good idea; and yes I can handle a hand gun and rifle. Maybe before we make these purchases we should ask Daniel about it. We can call him tonight from Florida. I also want to hear how it went when they told the chief the whole story. I hope it went well."

"It will be almost eight p.m. when we get to Miami. Let's try calling home to see if they called Daniel, and what they found out. If they didn't get through, we can call as soon as we get to Asuncion, tomorrow morning. We get there around ten a.m."

Josh turned to Ted. "What about you? Are you comfortable with firearms?"

"The only danger I ever knew was in the boardroom from the hostile takeover of another company. No one ever threatened me bodily. I have gone to a shooting range on several occasions for target practice. I've also done some skeet shooting. I did pretty well at both."

Josh asked, "What type of handgun did you fire?"

"You have to understand," said Ted sheepishly, "I wanted to be a 'Dirty Harry', and carry a .44 Magnum handgun. Seriously though, I think what Renato said about talking to Daniel first is a good idea. For all we know, he may have several weapons there already."

They talked trivialities for a while, and then each one sat back and closed his eyes. The next thing they all knew, they were starting their descent into Miami and they needed to put their seats up. Bekah sat up with a smile on her face. "I can't believe I slept through the whole flight. I was really exhausted. We should be out in the terminal quickly. As soon as we take potty breaks and find a quiet spot, we can call Roberta and Joe and find out how things went with Manu and Leonardo. Then we can get something to eat."

CHAPTER FORTY-FIVE

THE VILLAGE, PARAGUAY
JUNE 10

Sherry rose early. They had sent word last night and invited Manu and Leonardo for breakfast. She was baking flat bread to make a frittata. She hoped the chickens had cooperated. She needed at least a dozen eggs if it was going to be successful. She had all kinds of veggies from the garden, and would use locally made goat cheese to top it off. Her stomach started rumbling just thinking about it.

She took a basket, and went out to the chicken house Daniel had built last year. They had been losing too many chickens to predators and this was the perfect solution. Now Sherry didn't have to look for the chicken's favorite spots in the jungle to lay their eggs. They lay them in the morning and then she lets them out to wander and eat lots of good, nourishing bugs. At night, she would lure them back into the chicken house with food scraps and corn. She currently had around twenty-five chickens, so even if each of them didn't lay an egg, she should still have enough.

After collecting the eggs, Sherry found she had sixteen eggs. Enough that she would be able to send a smaller frittata home for Lara and Edwardo's children. He and Connie had decided to leave them home. Since there was so much to be discussed; they did not want to be distracted.

Daniel was already making his first trip to the river to get water for the day. He would probably make several more before the day was over, or find a willing young man who would do it for him.

While Sherry was preparing breakfast, she thought about the events of the previous day. She thought about how bad things could have been if God had not taken a hand. She did not believe in luck. It was not luck that had brought Manu to her bedroom door at just the right moment. God leads us into situations. Manu had not known he was being led by God. He did not know what was transpiring, but God knew. His timing was perfect and tragedy was averted. Her being here, making breakfast was testimony to that.

Sherry assembled the frittatas, and dropped pieces of fresh goat cheese on them. Then she put them in the oven for around twenty minutes. It was a wood oven, and cooking time varied with how hot it got. She got her herbal tea mix that the native women made and brewed up a large pot. She and Daniel had given up coffee most of the time in favor of that. It was refreshing and tasty and it seemed to give her a lift.

Sherry went outside and saw Edwardo and Connie walking up the hill, and heard Daniel talking with Manu. She walked over. "Come on to breakfast," Sherry said, "all I have to do is remove it from the oven and pour tea."

"Thank you for inviting Leonardo and me to breakfast. Usually we just have tea, bread and fruit," Manu said.

"How are Noemi and Juan this morning?" Sherry asked. "Did Ericia feed little Juan last night and this morning?"

"Noemi is doing well," said Manu, "and she had a small amount of milk this morning and tried to feed him. He lasted for around ten minutes and then started getting impatient. She gave him back to Erecia to finish. She is going to keep trying until she has a steady supply of milk. She doesn't think it will be too long."

"That's great. She just has to keep eating and drinking," said Sherry.

"Everything is ready, and everyone is here but Leonardo. Is he coming?" Sherry inquired.

"Yes, he is very happy to come. He just needed to make sure that Ciba had her breakfast. She still has a hard time because she is still in quite a bit of pain," Manu said.

"I'll stop by after breakfast to check on Ciba and see how she is healing. I also need to check on Juan, the injured hunter. Here comes Leonardo now. I see him walking up the path," Sherry observed.

Everyone came into the kitchen and Edwardo said, "Let's join hands and bless this food and our time together."

When he finished, Sherry put a plate of fruit on the table and cut the frittata as you would a pizza. Everyone had a nice large piece. Connie poured everyone tea, and the table was quiet as each of them enjoyed the breakfast.

"That was a wonderful breakfast Doctor Sherry. Do you have this for breakfast all the time?" Manu questioned.

"No, it's more for when we have friends over or holidays. I wanted to do something special today because of your new commitment to God and to Jesus, His Son. We also wanted some time to talk with both of you. We have some things we need to tell you."

266

"Well Doctor Sherry, we are always glad to listen to you," Manu answered with a smile.

"A few nights ago, eleven people had a dream they felt was from God, and all the dreams were very similar. Seven people were from the U.S. and the other four were Daniel and me and Edwardo and Connie. God told us there was a tribe of people who were calling Him to help them, and that there was an evil tribe who was taking their babies and sacrificing them in fire to their evil god. One of the people who had the dream was Daniel's brother Joe, and God told him to call us. In the dream, God told the people in the U.S. that they needed to come to Paraguay to help fight this evil tribe and protect the babies and the people. He wants them to tell the people the good news of God, His Son Jesus and the Holy Spirit. He wants everyone to hear this good news, this message of hope; even the evil tribe. "

Manu and Leonardo sat there stunned into silence; their eyes wide with amazement. They looked at each other, and then back at Sherry and Daniel. "Who told you of this evil tribe?" questioned Leonardo. "How do you know this?"

"God told us in a dream," Edwardo repeated. "Connie and I and Daniel and Sherry had similar dreams. God also asked me to raise an army to fight this evil tribe, with the regular weapons we have, or can make, but also with our spiritual weapons of prayer and the Word of God. That is one of the reasons we study God's Word. Then we can use it to fight the enemy.[134] Connie had a dream also and God asked her to get people together to pray for our success and for protection from that evil tribe."

"Do you and Leonardo remember the day we found the baby in the river?" asked Daniel.

---

[134] Hebrews 4:12

"Yes," said Manu, "it was the day you got back from your trip, and Edwardo asked if he and Connie could adopt the child."

"That's right. But we need to show you something else we found in the basket the next day. Sherry, would you go get the crucifix."

Sherry walked into the bedroom, praying for grace and favor from God. She asked that Manu and Leonardo receive this information with an understanding attitude, and not with anger and suspicion, believing that they had been deceived. She retrieved the crucifix and carried it out into the kitchen. She laid it on the table in front of Manu and Leonardo. She watched their reaction, and saw that they were astounded.

"We had taken the baby out of the basket without really examining it," Daniel explained. "The next day we went back to look the basket over and see if we could find any clues as to where it might have come from. The crucifix was in the bottom of the basket, under a wild boar hide we assume was there to keep the baby warm. We think that this crucifix and the one you offered Sherry are very similar. Maybe they came from the same place, or the same people."

"There is another astonishing thing," added Sherry, "we think one of our friends who will be coming down from the U.S. has a similar crucifix to the one you have. Her mother was from Paraguay and died in childbirth. Before she died, she gave it to her husband to give to their daughter, Bekah. He shortly remarried, and brought his infant daughter and his new wife, who was also from Paraguay, home to the U.S." Sherry went on with the story, and told of Nana Sara's death and the letter that contained the crucifix.

Manu gripped the table. "Who is this woman? You must tell me more of her," he ordered.

Daniel replied carefully, seeing the tension and anxiety in Manu. "She is a very good friend of my brother Joe. We don't know her well. We have only talked to her on the telephone since all this began. She is leaving the U.S. today with three other people, and coming to Paraguay. They will get to Ascension tomorrow morning. Then they will fly to Puerto Bahia Negra where I will meet them. They are bringing us some tools and supplies. I will have to rent another boat or two to bring all of them and the supplies back here. We had already talked about this Manu. It won't be a problem, will it?"

"No," Manu stuttered over the word. "She must come. I need to see her. This is all very strange, and I am very confused. You do not know the whole story, and I cannot tell it to you now, but I must see her. It is very important. You must pray to God for her to be safe. Evil has been stirred up and danger is lurking all around. I will send five strong men to go with you to bring everyone here safely. It is a long boat ride and much can happen."

It was Daniel's turn to stare in amazement. This was not the response he had expected. He looked around and saw that everyone was apprehensive. Daniel asked everyone to join hands and pray. He prayed for God's protection, and for God's angelic army to fight on their behalf and protect them from the enemy. He also prayed for the Holy Spirit, the Comforter, to bring peace to all their hearts and minds.[135]

When they were through praying, they remained standing still for a moment, and then looked around at each other. It was apparent to all of them that they had been touched by God. The

---

[135] Philippians 4:6-8

anxiety and confusion they had been experiencing appeared to have been washed away. Manu and Leonardo looked at each other, each with surprise on their faces. "Did God do this," he questioned? "Leonardo and I are not worried any longer."

"When people come together and pray in faith to the Father God, and in the Name of Jesus His Son, God can perform miracles.[136] Remember how we prayed," Daniel said, "and God healed Noemi and Ciba. With God, nothing is impossible."[137]

"Yes," Manu said with excitement. "We will talk more about God at lunch time. Now we must go to work so everything will be ready when your friends come. Some of the men are already working. The rest need instruction. This is a big job, but we will get it done in time. Also, Doctor Sherry, I will have Paloma come over to help you every morning. She will stay until last meal is prepared. She is very bright and intelligent. She can help you in the clinic also. I will send word for her to come now and she will make lunch for all of us. If there is nothing for her to do here, you can send her down to help Miss Connie. Paloma is a very hard worker."

Connie finally spoke up, "I appreciate the offer of help Manu, but I have Lara to help me, and she is so good with the children."

"That may be so," stated Manu, "but she needs children of her own. I am looking for a good husband for her." After that last remark, Manu and Leonardo left.

---

[136] Mark 11:23-24
[137] Luke 1:28-37

CHAPTER FORTY-SIX

THE VILLAGE, PARAGUAY
JUNE 10

Daniel spoke up. "There were many responses I might have anticipated, but that was not one of them. Now all our cards are on the table and Manu has a secret. I'm just glad they are not angry or suspicious of us and that this didn't work against their new belief in God. I'm not going to even try to think of what Manu needs to talk to us about when everyone gets here, and why he was so interested in Bekah. I wonder if it has something to do with the fact that she was born in Paraguay."

"We can't spend the morning stewing over it, we have lots of work to do," Sherry said. "Connie and I will make an inventory of house supplies and clinic supplies. We will make a list of what needs to be picked up. It's a good thing it's still the rainy season and the river is running a little high. Even with two boats, they will sit low in the water because of their load. What are you and Edwardo going to be doing?"

"First," Daniel replied, "I'm going to see if Manu can get us two young men or older boys to clean out the chicken house before I bring back the new chickens. Put down cracked corn on your list. With fifty chickens, we're going to use up our store of corn faster. Next, I'm going to check the building supplies, I know we always need more two by fours, one by sixes, and nails for anything we build. I might pick up a few more hammers, since we seem to have so many workers. I'd also like to give everyone who helped a hammer as a thank you. They're a handy tool to have around. We'll also need several more flashlights, and a large quantity of batteries. On my way by, I'm going to check on the water barrel, and also fire wood. Burning that stove continually uses up a lot of wood. We could employ someone full time for just water, wood, and chickens. Those are three hard jobs that consume a great deal of time. Unfortunately, they are essential to us and can't be eliminated. Maybe we could barter with someone? I'll think on it."

Daniel and Edwardo walked out the door, talking quietly, their minds already on the other tasks of the day. Connie turned to Sherry and said, "I know we have a lot to do, but would you mind sitting and having another cup of tea? We can be making a list while we talk."

"Sure," Sherry said as she put water in a pot for tea. "Are you alright? I know there's a lot going on and you have the burden of three small children. Is it too much for you? Do you need more help?"

"No, I'm doing fine, and Lara is a big help. She is the one I want to talk to you about. You heard Manu say he is going to look for a husband for her. She has confided in me in no uncertain terms that she does not wish to be married. She does not have a very good perspective on marriage. Our father was abusive to our mother during the later years of their marriage. I escaped most of it by marrying Edwardo, and our marriage is wonderful and we love each other. My parent's marriage was arranged. Though they were together many years, they never learned to love each other, but instead resented each other. They would always argue about how much better life would have been if they could have married someone of their own choosing. Now it appears Manu is going to put Lara in the same situation. I would like to see her healed of this hurt in her heart before she is asked to marry anyone."

Sherry thought for a moment and then said, "Lara and I had a talk the other day and she told me she did not want to marry and was happy as she was, living with you and helping you with the home and the children. She didn't mention anything about your mother and father, but she was quite adamant about the issue. Has anyone shown any interest in her, any of the young men of the village?"

"Not that I am aware," said Connie, "They may have spoken to Edwardo, but he has not mentioned it to me. Lara is well liked by everyone, but none seem to have singled her out for special attention. Maybe if someone does, she will change her mind. Sherry, would you pray for her with me?"

"Of course I will," answered Sherry. She took Connie's hands in hers and began to pray. "Heavenly Father, Connie and I come to You in the mighty name of Jesus, and thank You that You care for us, from the big details of our lives to the small inconsequential things that seem insignificant to us; but nothing is insignificant to You. Your Word says that You even know the number of hairs on our head.[138] We come to You now, lifting up our friend and sister Lara. She has grown up in an unhealthy environment, and because of her experiences, has an unhealthy view of marriage and relationships. We ask that the Holy Spirit, the Comforter, bring peace to her heart.[139] We pray that she sees the truth; that not all marriages are like her parent's marriage. We pray that she see that they can be warm, loving, and fulfilling.

---

[138] Luke 12:7
[139] John 14:26

Lord, show her the loving marriages of those around her to open her eyes to the truth. We ask that she be freed from the fear of entering into a relationship because of what she has seen in the past.[140] We thank You in advance, knowing that You hear our prayers. Again, as in everything, we pray in the mighty name of Jesus. Amen"

"Thank you so much, Sherry. I know there will be an answer to this prayer shortly."

"Please Connie, any time you have a care or concern, let me know and we can pray together, and I will do the same with you."

Sherry and Connie finished their tea and went back into the clinic and started inventorying there first. Sherry checked her supply of antibiotics. She used them mostly for her pregnant mothers to combat infections during delivery in a less than sterile environment. With the possibility of conflict before them, she decided to order extra stock. She checked over all her inventory, and ordered twice as much as she usually did as a precaution. She also ordered more sheets and blankets and ten extra cots. They could be used by the guests that were coming, and also for additional patients as the need arose. The clinic was becoming more than a birthing center. It now served as a hospital also. Sherry put down a generator on the list, and two large pole lights she could use during almost any procedure, surgical or just an examination. She had mentioned it several days ago, but was unaware of whether or not those items had made it to anyone else's list.

Sherry was getting weary. It had been a long time since breakfast and her stomach was talking to her. Just as she was

---

[140] John 8:32

about to go into the kitchen to see what there was to eat, Paloma, the young woman Manu had mentioned, walked into the clinic and announced, "Lunch is ready."

Sherry offered up a silent "thank You" and followed her back into the kitchen. On the table was a pot of chicken soup, some corn bread, and a bowl of local fruit. "I could get used to this," Sherry thought.

Everyone again sat down to lunch. They blessed the food and began to eat. Nothing was said about the meeting this morning. They were all talking about the progress of the house and clinic expansion. Tomorrow the walls would be finished and then the roof could be started. The roof would go quickly, for it was a type of thatched roof, and the supplies were all local, jungle grown. Thankfully the weather had been dry the last few days, so the thatching would go quickly.

"Manu," Sherry said, "I want to thank you for sending Paloma. Connie and I had been working all morning and I had nothing prepared for lunch. She had the perfect lunch."

"You are welcome Doctor Sherry. She has agreed to do lunch and dinner, tend the garden, keep the house clean, and anything else you may require. If there is nothing to do here, she will go down to Connie's house and help there. This is a good thing."

"This is a very good thing. Manu, I notice Leonardo is not here. Is something the matter? I was going to go by after lunch and see Ciba to check on her wounds."

Manu replied slowly, "I don't believe anything is wrong with the wounds, she is just in considerable pain and Leonardo is tender hearted. He stayed to keep her company for a while to help take her mind off the pain."

Sherry stood up, "I've finished my lunch and I'll go right over," Sherry responded. "I should have been more attentive. I might have something I can give her that will help with the pain. I'll see you when I get back and let you know how she is."

Sherry did not keep narcotics on hand, but she had a mild sleeping pill that would relax Ciba, and in turn ease the pain. Once relaxed she would be able to sleep, which is healing in itself. Most of the native people living out here had no experience with drugs of any kind, and so they responded to small doses well.

Leonardo was there comforting his wife when she arrived. He held her hand as Sherry examined the wounds. Again, there was a slight inflammation, but no discharge or heat. Sherry told them both, "It is looking good. Ciba, you can get up with help and sit in a chair, even outside, as long as you have help nearby. Why don't you invite Noemi over to sit with you? She and the baby need to get out also. I think you would both enjoy the company."

Sherry waved as she left, and walked back to her house. Connie had gone home to feed the babies and give Maria lunch. She did not like to depend on Lara all the time. Lara had her life to live, and she did not want to be the one to hold her back. No one was around and Sherry decided she would lie down for a short nap.

Two hours later Daniel was calling her name and shaking her awake. "Sherry," he said softly. "Sherry, honey, come on and wake up. It's dinner time. It's a little early, but everyone is here and Paloma fried up some fish and yams and steamed some mixed vegetables. She seems to be a very good cook. They want to have time to find out more about God and His Son Jesus before we have the phone call. They are excited to be here and be

276

invited to listen. I told Manu and Leonardo that they can make comments if they care to.

"Here's a wet cloth for your face. Your comb is on the dresser. How are you feeling?" Daniel asked.

"I feel fine; I'm just tired all the time. It's a normal occurrence in early pregnancy. I'm just glad I'm not experiencing morning sickness also."

Sherry walked into the kitchen and everyone was there: Manu and Leonardo, Edwardo and Connie, the three children, Lara, and several others who had been at the Bible study. They had all brought dishes of food. It appeared to be a party or celebration. In a way it was; we were celebrating the new birth of Manu, Noemi, and Leonardo, and hopefully more to come.

They ate their dinner cheerfully, everyone laughing and happy, even the children. Then Daniel got up and shared a simple message on the saving grace of Jesus.[141] "A sacrifice had to be made for sin," Daniel said, "And God sent Jesus, His son, to be that sacrifice.[142] After He suffered and died, God raised Him from the dead. The Bible says we have all sinned.[143] If we acknowledge this and ask God to forgive us, He is willing to do so. Not only that, but He will also welcome us into His family as His sons and daughters."[144],[145]

When he had closed his Bible and put it down, he raised his eyes, and four men and three women from the village stood up. "We want to know your God and His Son Jesus also."

---

[141] Ephesians 2:7-9
[142] John 3:16
[143] Romans 3:23
[144] Galatians 4:7
[145] Ephesians 2:19

Daniel had a sense that revival was breaking out in this small village. He prayed that it spread like wildfire. Daniel and Edwardo prayed for the men, and Sherry and Connie prayed for the women. There was much rejoicing in the room and in Heaven.[146] Everyone laughed and hugged one another, and then most of them left for home. The six of them were left. It was almost seven o'clock, and they sat on chairs near the telephone, patiently waiting for the phone to ring. Manu and Leonardo appeared to be very calm.

---

[146] Luke 15:10

CHAPTER FORTY-SEVEN

THE VILLAGE, PARAGUAY
JUNE 10

Right at seven the phone began to ring. Daniel reached for it and put it on speaker phone. "Hello, this is Daniel. I'm here with Sherry, Edwardo, Connie, Manu and Leonardo. Everything is good here. How are all of you up there?"

Joe answered, "We are all doing well. Ted, Renato, Josh and Bekah are on their way to Miami. I have Roberta, Sylvia, Sandy, Kay and Shirley here with me. We have been praying all afternoon for Bekah and her group and all of you down in Paraguay."

Daniel replied, "We spent the morning explaining to Manu and Leonardo all we know about the crucifixes. We made lists of all the supplies we need to purchase, and we had a Bible study. Four men and three women dedicated their lives to God the Father, and His Son, Jesus."

"Well that's great news!" Joe said excitedly. "Our news is a little more somber. When Bekah arrived home last night, her home had been broken into and vandalized. Everything, and I mean everything, was destroyed. So far as we can tell the only things missing are things that were in her grandmother's desk. We have a strong feeling it was arranged by the jeweler who examined the crucifix. I'm glad Bekah is going out of the country and that she has the crucifix with her. Their flight leaves Miami around midnight. It gets in around ten o'clock, barring any delays.

Thankfully, the state police were very kind and understanding. They may call if they have any questions for Bekah. I hope you don't mind, I gave them your number. Roberta and I are staying at Bekah's house to help with the garden, and to try to sort through some of the debris left from the break-in. Bekah also left Roberta and me with power of attorney. What prompted that was a key Josh found taped to some wood that was part of her grandmother's desk. Monday we are going to the bank to see if it opens anything. They have one hundred old safe deposit boxes that the key may fit, but the number is worn off."

Daniel thought a moment then said, "I'm leaving tomorrow with Leonardo, one of Manu's counselors, and three other men. Manu felt we needed them for protection. We will have at least two boats coming back, most likely three with the additional passengers and supplies.

"Manu says he feels like evil has been stirred up. We have prayed and felt the peace of God concerning this, but would appreciate your prayers also. Please keep a prayer diary to record anything you feel God has spoken to you. Call us any time you feel there is a need and we will do the same. The only other thing I have is good news. Sherry is having a baby and it will arrive around Christmas."

"Well congratulations," said Joe. "Tell her to be sure to get enough rest. Making a baby is hard work. Well blessings to all of you down there. You'll probably hear from Bekah in the morning."

"She will most likely be talking with Sherry as we are leaving at the crack of dawn," said Daniel. "We will probably get to Puerto Bahia Negra before they do, since they have lots of shopping to do. I have a cell phone I use in the city if I need to. I just buy minutes. She can call me on it." He gave Joe the number. "Good night to all and be at peace."

"You also," Joe said.

"We know," Joe spoke to the group, "the Bible says that the devil is like a roaring lion seeking whom he may devour.[147] Well, it won't be us. The Bible also says that the One who lives in me is greater than the one who lives in the world.[148]

"We all have each other's numbers, don't we? Let's be sure to keep in close contact. Things seem to be going well down there. Seven saved is a wonderful thing. I wish I could be there to see when everyone meets. It will be very exciting. When I hear from Bekah, I will call Sylvia and she can start up the prayer teams. See you all tomorrow."

---

[147] 1 Peter 5:7-9
[148] 1 John 4:4

CHAPTER FORTY-EIGHT

THE VILLAGE, PARAGUAY
JUNE 10

Manu looked at Daniel, and with concern in his voice questioned, "Is Miss Bekah safe? Explain to me what has happened."

As Daniel spoke and tried to make it clear to Manu what had taken place, he could see fear start to rear its ugly head. He stopped talking and went over and took Manu's hand. Daniel spoke calmly, and with confidence. "Manu, we need to trust that God will do what He said.[149] God cannot lie.[150] Lying is evil, and God is good and cannot do evil. Satan, the devil, is the father of all lies, and he lies to us continually to bring fear, and to try to get us to doubt God."[151]

Manu interrupted. "You do not understand, and I cannot explain it until I talk with and meet Miss Bekah. I need to see if she is the one. That is all I can tell you right now. I helped God before; I want to help Him again. I can send ten men down with you to keep you safe on your journey there and back. There are many dangers out there."

"Thank you Manu. I appreciate your concern, but as we discussed, I think Leonardo, and three others will be more than enough. That will be one to two extra people in each boat in

---

[149] Isaiah 55:8-11
[150] Titus:1:2
[151] John 8:44

282

addition to the driver. God has people everywhere who can assist Him. We need to do whatever God has called us to do, unless we hear otherwise. Right now God is calling you to be chief of your people, and to lead and guide them. We have to learn to trust Him. Bekah has a calling from God to come down to Paraguay and go on a quest for Him. He has the power and ability to get her here and be with her as she fulfills this quest. You are part of this quest now. Put your faith in God that He will show you what to do."

"I will try," Manu said unenthusiastically. "God is not always easy to understand or obey."

"That's true," answered Daniel, "But we all get better at it the more we do it."

Manu looked up and smiled, "I have not been doing it very long, I need to get some more experience." He lifted his hand and waved as he walked out of the kitchen.

CHAPTER FORTY-NINE

After talking with everyone at home the night before, finding out that things went well in Paraguay, and that there was no problem with Manu and Leonardo, Bekah, Josh, Renato and Ted began to relax. They had been wound up tight for over forty-eight hours and it was hard to let go, but sheer exhaustion does win out. All four of them slept most of the way to Paraguay. They awoke to the sun as the plane starting to descend.

Bekah looked out the window and wondered what the next few days would bring. She had been born in this country, and in a way, was returning home, and not only her, but Renato was also returning home. She was excited; she was not nervous. She didn't know if she could describe what she was feeling; maybe anticipation. She felt that something astounding was going to happen down here and she was part of it. The people she was with and the people she was meeting were part of it also; but first and foremost, God was the focus of it all. They all needed to keep Him their principal emphasis. In all of life, God needs to be number one.[152]

They exited the airplane and walked through the terminal. The plane had been fairly full, so there was a crowd around the baggage carousel. Thankfully, all they had were carry-ons. Renato

---

[152] Matthew 6:33-34

and Ted both carried duffel bags; Bekah carried her purse. They went through immigration quickly, and customs wasn't a problem because of their small amount of luggage. They did not even look through the bags. Bekah was relieved, because she did not know how she was going to explain the crucifix if it became necessary. She had prayed and put the care of it in God's hands. It appeared He had resolved of the situation.

They stopped to decide what they should do first. Everyone had the same idea, breakfast. They called a taxi and Renato asked the driver to take them to a good place for breakfast. Ten minutes later they were all standing in front of La Tortilla, or The Omelet.

Walking through the door, the rich smells of cooking food assaulted their senses. Being hungry increased their sensitivity. The restaurant was far from new, but it was clean and inviting. There was no sign to wait to be seated, so they walked to the back and took a booth. Bekah and Ted sat opposite Renato and Josh. They all ordered coffee, and it came quickly, steaming and fragrant. Bekah added cream, the rest took it black, and they all groaned with the flavor of it. There was no menu, so they all allowed Renato to order for them. After a rather lengthy exchange which they didn't even try to follow, the waitress left to put in the order. Renato sat there with a grin on his face, looking like a Cheshire cat. "We're all getting the special; and no, don't ask, just anticipate and you'll all be pleasantly surprised."

Ten minutes later food began arriving at the table. First were two large steaks with four fried eggs on each, next was a platter of empanadas, small fried meat pies; and then came a baking dish of sopa paraguaya, a casserole of fried vegetables, corn meal, milk and cheese. Finally a large container of warm flour tortillas was set on the table, along with a large pot of coffee. The waitress smiled a big smile and said, "Disfrute de su comida, or as you would say, enjoy your breakfast."

"She is certainly right, we will enjoy this meal," Bekah said. "I just don't know how we will eat it all. Why don't we start by giving thanks for our safe arrival into Paraguay and then let's bless the food."

After they had prayed, they divided the steak and eggs among the four of them and then passed around all the platters and took a sampling of each. Renato told them, "Steak isn't typical for breakfast, but just like Josh needed to eat lobster in Maine, we need to eat steak in Paraguay. Meat is very popular here. Paraguay is a carnivore's paradise, especially in the city and countryside. We will not get much of it in the jungles, so eat up. The rest of the dishes are traditional, and could be eaten any time of day. Usually breakfast is a light meal of some kind of bread and maybe fruit, and a drink of an herbal tea or coffee. Midday meal is the large meal and served midafternoon. Supper is also light. Snacks are eaten throughout the day as hunger requires and availability allows."

"These dishes are delicious," Bekah said with enthusiasm, "I'm going to try to get some local recipes to take home with me, and the steak almost melts in your mouth."

They were all quiet while they devoted their attention to the eating of this wonderful food. After a time, they started pushing the food around on their plates, having lost the capacity to swallow another bite. A sizeable dent had been put in the amount of food that had been served, and they felt pleased with themselves and their efforts.

Finally Ted said, "This seems like a good place to make a phone call; we are by ourselves in this corner of the room. Let's call Daniel."

"Good idea," answered Josh. "Everyone get out their list and hopefully we'll get all our questions answered and the list covered." The breakfast rush was over and the restaurant had emptied out considerably. There was no one sitting in the tables next to them, so they had some privacy.

Josh dialed the number and waited. It rang six times and then a breathless Sherry picked up and said, "Hello."

"Hello Sherry, this is Josh. I'm here in Asuncion with Bekah, Ted and Renato. Our flight went well. We have just finished breakfast and are calling from the restaurant. Is Daniel there, or has he left already for Puerto Bahia Negra?"

"They left before the sun came up. It's about an eight to ten hour ride, depending on the river. The river is flowing well, so they shouldn't have any problems."

"Sherry, we had a few questions to ask before we started shopping for supplies. First, do you know if Daniel has any firearms?"

"Yes he does; now let me think a minute because he has several pieces. I don't know makes and models, but he has five handguns, three rifles, and two shotguns. That was my latest count. He may have sneaked one or two in since I last counted. He likes his guns."

"Great," replied Josh, "Then he shouldn't mind if we bring some. We're going to pick some up here. Does Daniel have a special place he likes to shop?"

"Yes, there's a shop near downtown called Excelsior. The taxi drivers will know it; they will take you right to the front door.

Jose is the owner. Tell him you are a friend of Daniel Albright and he'll treat you fairly."

"Next, do we need to buy tents, cots, bedding, towels and all those essentials?"

"No tents," said Sherry. "We had shelters built for you. It's basically a large room. You'll be covered, and have one window and a door, but that's about it. Also, we will have a room for Bekah. They are finishing up an addition to the house and clinic. We're putting in an extra bedroom and doubling the size of the kitchen. We're also enlarging the clinic with a private patient room and an all-purpose room. Best of all, we put in a new outhouse.

"Before I forget, you will need mosquito netting for all four of you. Don't go cheap, get quality netting, and get sheets, blankets, towels and pillows. Also, get some cots; seven or eight should do. We won't need them all right away, but wherever this quest leads us, we may need to house more people as time goes by. We have a bed, but cots and hammocks are the best we can do for company. It will save Daniel from having to purchase them. Daniel has a list of the regular supplies we need to purchase in Puerto Bahia Negra on a monthly basis, but I mentioned to you about the generator and two large pole lights to help me see what I am doing. It's hard to stitch someone up, or deliver a baby by a kerosene lamp."

"No problem," Ted said, "we can get that here. We're going to charter a plane and meet Daniel either late today, or early tomorrow, depending on how we do with our shopping. Anything else on your wish list I can help you with?"

"Wow, this is sooo tempting. I have a wish list a mile long, but I am believing God to help me," Sherry replied.

"You don't understand Sherry, God is using me to answer your prayer, to meet your needs. Besides what we already talked about, what are the top three things you need? I don't guarantee I can get them, but I'll sure try."

Ted's enthusiasm was infectious. Sherry felt her faith rise. "Alright," she said, "You asked for it. I need an autoclave, running water in the house and compound, and cement floors. The dirt and dust generated by dirt floors is so hard to deal with, and very unsanitary also. I don't expect you to come up with any of this, but thank you for caring enough to ask."

The phone was silent for a moment as it changed hands. "Sherry, this is Bekah. I need to ask you where I should go, in fact where we all should go to get our clothes and personal supplies for this trip. We came down basically with just the clothes on our back. Is there a shopping center or mall in the city, or will we have to go to several different places? We need working clothes, hiking clothes and relaxing clothes. We also need work shoes, wet shoes, boots, and hiking boots."

"Anderson's is where you want to go, and it's on the same street as Excelsior, maybe a block down from it. They specialize in jungle trips. You'll be able to get everything you need there, and we keep a supply of things if you run out of anything.

"Sherry, I'll also need underwear, toiletries and ladies essentials. My home was broken into last night and everything was destroyed, even my clothes."

"Joe told us about that. I'm glad you're alright. Anderson's will have whatever you need."

"We told you we're going to charter a small plane to take us up to meet Daniel and transport all our supplies, so space won't be a problem. Is there anything else you can think of you might need?"

"It may not be a problem there," Sherry replied, "but getting back here could be a problem. There will be at least eleven people coming back, plus all the supplies. We planned on renting another boat or two, but that may not be enough, depending on what you bring with you."

Ted spoke up, "Don't worry about the expense, I've got that covered. We'll hire ten boats if we need them. Also, we wanted to bring gifts for the men and women of the village. We thought tools, such as shovels and picks and axes, hatchets and saws. Do you think that's a good idea? We have no idea how well supplied they are or if they would even use these."

"Yes they would. Their main concerns are always food and shelter. Storms and floods destroy homes and other buildings, and feeding everyone takes tremendous time and energy. Most people are misinformed about the jungle. There isn't fruit growing on every tree. You'll understand more when you get here. The jungle is also tenacious. It keeps trying to take back the land that we have cleared. The edges of the fields are constantly patrolled and the men hack away at the jungle with whatever tools they have.

"Machetes would also be very handy, if you're comfortable buying them. Maybe these could be a tribal gift, not just for one person. Five or six would work for that purpose. The women would appreciate small, sharp knives for digging roots and cutting vines. Everyone here wears their hair long, so combs and brushes are important, as well as material for clothes, and just tee shirts of assorted sizes. The children would love balls of any size, hand balls, soccer balls. The little ones might enjoy bubbles. But I must tell you, everyone enjoys sweets of any kind. Just remember if you do get the sweets, make sure they are packaged well, because insects are terrible here and we lose too large a percentage of our food supply to them.

"Again for a tribal gift, chickens and goats are greatly appreciated. We keep chickens ourselves, and barter them to get food, or to get work done. They also provide eggs for eating and bartering. Occasionally, a chicken ends up in the pot. That's a really good dinner.

"Living on the edge of civilization, we try to live as the people do as much as possible. We do have a house that's fully enclosed, but we have dirt floors. We have lizards running around, but they are our bug patrol. The people, for the most part are warm and friendly. We have a local shaman who tries to stir up trouble now and then, but now that Manu is a Christian, he may be more cautious about what he says and does. His grand-daughter was the real problem. Her name was Luna, and she was a trouble maker. She was pretty good at it too. She enjoyed causing every kind of strife between people; friends fighting with friends, neighbors fighting with neighbors, husbands fighting with wives. She would instigate these fights with gossip, lies, and suspicious actions which sparked anger and jealousy. She was finally confronted by Manu and his counselors, and warned to stop, or face the consequences. That was about five years ago; right after Manu became chief. She left, and we have never seen her again. But right before she disappeared, we had a fire in the village. Several houses were destroyed and four people died. No one knows for sure whether Luna was the culprit, but a dead chicken, and black feathers were found in the doorway of one of the houses, and blood was smeared on the doorposts. I think she solicited the help of the devil, and he seemed to be working through her in ever increasing ways.

"Well I've told you enough to keep you thinking and praying. We're told in the Bible to pray without ceasing,[153] and we practice that down here. We stay in close communication with God, and we hope you all will also. Call if you need to. I'm usually close by. I'm looking forward to meeting all of you and figuring out what we are supposed to be doing. Hopefully, I will see you soon. God bless you all."

"Thanks for all your help," Josh said. "We look forward to meeting you also; and don't worry; we are staying in prayer too. God bless you Sherry. "

---

[153] 1 Thessalonians 5:16-18

CHAPTER FIFTY

ASUNCION, PARAGUAY
JUNE 11

They left the restaurant and took a taxi to Excelsior. It was a rather large store with a glass front. Several customers could be seen through the glass. They walked into the store and immediately the atmosphere changed. Everyone stopped talking and turned to look at them. Renato was standing next to Bekah and she grabbed his arm, feeling security from his closeness. They walked up to the counter and Josh asked for Jose. The man behind the counter was about five foot five inches tall, and must have weighed at least three hundred pounds, all of what appeared to be muscle. He had a bald head and a large, dark moustache. He appeared to be in his late forties or early fifties. "I am Jose. What is your business?" he asked curtly.

Josh replied, "Daniel Albright told me to come here and ask for you; that you would be most helpful in getting me what I need."

"Daniel sent you here?" Jose's face lit up and his whole attitude changed. "Why didn't you say so? He is one of my very best friends. If you are a friend of Daniel's then you are a friend of mine. What can I do for you?"

Josh smiled back. Apparently the name of Daniel Albright opened doors around here, and he was glad of it. "I'd like to purchase some fire arms and ammunition."

"I am at your service. Tell me what you need. If I don't have it, I can probably get it for you."

"That sounds good. I'd like four, Glock 30's with three magazines each, I'd like a Beretta A300 Extrema semi-automatic, and a Sig Sauer M400.300 semi-automatic. I'd also like the cases for the rifles, and five hundred rounds of ammunition for each. In addition, I want scopes for the Sig and the Beretta.

"Wow! That is a big order. Let me see what I have in stock. I know I have the Glocks, it's a popular model; but I'll have to check on the other two."

Jose went over to his computer to check his inventory. They all stood together waiting. Jose may have changed his attitude, but no one else was smiling. After ten minutes he came back. "You are in luck. I have the Beretta, but not the Sig. But I called a fellow I know and he has one, brand new, and with a scope already on it. He also has two hundred rounds of ammunition and an ammunition case. He is willing to let them go for fifteen hundred American dollars, cash. He can have them here by four o'clock. I can have everything packaged up for you at that time. Is that satisfactory?"

"Do you have a firing range in the back so that I can test the rifle, and the rest of the weapons?" Josh said.

"A very wise idea, and yes we do have a firing range. You are welcome to test all of the firearms if you wish."

"Thank you," said Josh, "I'd like that. Also, can you arrange for this to be transported to the airport? We are going to charter a plane to fly out tonight."

"No problem. If you are back by four all the merchandise will be waiting for you to examine and test as you wish."

"Great, we'll see you at four then," said Josh. "Thank you for your help."

As they all turned to leave, one of the other customers came up and blocked their path. He was tall and slim, around thirty years old. "Just where are you planning to go with all that fire power," he inquired? "Someone could do a lot of damage with everything you just bought."

"Yes, they could," said Josh with a cold sounding voice. "But that's not our intention, and it's none of your business."

Josh went to walk around the man, trying to avoid a confrontation, but the man put his hand out a grabbed Josh's arm. Josh stopped and said, "Mister, you're making a big mistake. I don't want any trouble, but you're not going to push us around."

Suddenly the man let go and took a step back. Jose came out from behind the counter carrying a shotgun. He pointed it at the man and told him to get out, and not to come back again.

The man said, "I didn't mean to cause trouble, I just wanted to know who he was after. I have a business to protect and I didn't want him trying to take over any of my cases."

Jose gestured with the shotgun towards the door. "That may be the case, but you don't go around threatening people in my store; now out!" The man glared at all of them and muttered under his breath, but he left.

Jose spoke apologetically, "Keep your eyes open, he's a mean one. His name is Esteban Montero and he's a bounty hunter. His reputation is that he only takes the dead or alive cases, and he always brings them back dead. He hangs around here hoping to pick up extra work. Most of the people he is assigned to bring back haven't even gone to trial yet, but they have run from the law, and have been accused of a serious crime.

If he takes them on, they have no chance. You gave me a good reason to ban him from my store. Now the problem will be that I will need extra security for a while until he cools off. Watch your backs my friends. He is a mean one and doesn't like anyone getting in his way. I will see all of you at four."

As they left the store, Bekah glanced across the street and there Montero sat with a malicious grin on his face. He got up, waved, then turned and walked down the street. "Josh, did you see him across the street. He really gives me the creeps, but I guess that's what he wants to do. Well the devil may be out there like a roaring lion,[154] but he's not going to get me. Father, I put You in remembrance of Your Word,[155] which says that no weapon formed against us shall prosper.[156] We thank You for Your protection."

Excitedly, Bekah said, "OK, let's go shopping. I can see the sign for Anderson's down the street on the left. They all hurried down the block, aware of the time constraint they were under. As they approached the store Bekah announced, "I'll handle the toys, material, personal items and candy. Also, everyone is responsible for their own personal gear."

"That's right. But remember, no one goes off on their own. Bekah, I'm coming with you to shop. I'll leave it to Renato and Ted to get whatever else we need."

"Wait a minute," Ted said in an agitated voice, "why are you going with Bekah, you need to shop too."

"Once I found out where we were going I had my supplies sent here. They are waiting for me at the airport. Remember, it's

---

[154] 1 Peter 5:7-9
[155] Isaiah 43:26
[156] Isaiah 54:17

two thirty now, we meet at the check-out counter at three thirty. Come on Bekah," Josh grabbed her hand, "let's move. We don't have much time. Where are the toys?"

"I see them over there," said Bekah. We need shopping carts. They are at the front door. Come on, we'll each need one." Bekah went up and down the aisles looking at merchandise, selecting some and discarding others. The balls alone took up almost one shopping cart. She got the bubbles and some jump ropes. She got toy trucks and story books, crayons and coloring books. They went to the candy department and Bekah went wild. "I'll get lots of hard candy for everyone, but I'll get lots of bubble gum for the children. Butterscotch and caramel are good also. I would love to get chocolate, but in this heat and humidity, I don't think it would keep well. Let's get some popcorn, I don't know if they have ever seen popcorn." Bekah was like a child let loose, roaming the aisles and getting more excited as she went. "Let's go look for the women. There's the material. I'll just buy several bolts of cloth and they can share. I'll also buy ten pair of scissors. I'll bet that's a luxury they don't have. Let's pick up ten frying pans. Even if they have one, they can always use more."

Josh just followed Bekah and smiled. "Over here are toiletries. The little girls will love hair ribbons; the women will like the big clips to gather their hair. I'll need a few of them myself. I also need to get my personal toiletries." They shopped there for another ten minutes. They had fifteen minutes to go and Bekah still needed clothes and shoes.

They hurried to sporting goods and got a pair of rubber boots, and water shoes. Then she picked out two pair of sneakers, and some hiking boots. They ran to clothes department and

Bekah picked out some underwear. Josh said they had four minutes left.

Bekah turned around and saw a display of tee-shirts and picked up an assortment in each size. Then she saw some skirts. She just went to her size and picked out ten. She stopped by some loose pants and grabbed four. "Maybe I can wear them under my skirts," she said to Josh. "I'm not going to worry about what I'm going to wear, God will provide, especially since I'm serving Him with everything that is in me."[157] On the way to the checkout they passed a large table of flip flops. Bekah put two armloads in the cart. "I can give some as gifts," she laughed as she pushed the overflowing cart across the aisle.

Renato and Ted were waiting for them. "You're five minutes late," Ted said in a disgruntled voice."

Renato rolled his eyes. "Ted, quit your pouting and let's get checked out."

Josh smiled, "Well I'm shopping with a woman. What would you expect? I don't see how I could have made it any quicker, but the next time we have to shop, you go ahead and try."

Ted and Renato both laughed. "We already checked ours out and, we told them to take this all to the airport and hold it there for us. Let's get you two checked out, and then we can go back to Excelsior and get that issue taken care of."

The four of them walked out of the store and into the sunshine. Walking down the street Bekah thought it looked like any other large city, big and sprawling, filled with traffic and people on the move. She yearned for the comfort and solitude of her house and the apple orchard, but she turned her focus to the

---

[157] Matthew 6:25-34

quest that God had given to her, and prayed that He would find her faithful to the end.[158]

Renato looked around through eyes filled with nostalgia, but could find no memory, or reminder of his past in the scene that was before him. He remembered God's Word that said not to look back, but to keep pressing on toward what God had called you to do.[159]

Ted looked at the city and saw business opportunities. There was money to be made down here, and when he was finished with this job, he would look into it. Yet something else called to him. He had made a choice and he must stick to it. He had changed the focus of his life and would not look back.[160]

Josh saw yet another assignment on foreign soil, and longed for the end of his service so he could return home and finally be free of commitments and responsibilities; but he knew that was not possible. He had now been recruited into the Army of God, and it was a lifetime commitment.[161]

They hurried back to the Excelsior, knowing they were running out of time. They decided to split up. Ted and Renato would head for the airport to charter the plane and get their purchases and belongings on board. Bekah and Josh would finish with the gun purchases and meet them at the airport. Josh still wanted to test the weapons to assure himself they were in proper working order. When they walked into the store, Jose was all smiles, but he still had his shotgun on the counter. That spoke a

---

[158] 1 Corinthians 4:2
[159] Philippians 3:12-14
[160] Matthew 6:24
[161] Luke 9:62

warning to Josh that Montero was a serious threat and that he could not afford to let his guard down.

They went out to the target range behind the building. It was an open field, with a fifteen foot high concrete wall going across the back. It was approximately fifty feet long. The wall was set back from the store about one hundred yards. Jose had given Josh the rifle to examine in the store; now he would fire it several times to test its accuracy, and whether there appeared to be any defects in it, or if the scope needed recalibration. Everyone picked up a set of headphones to protect their ears. Josh looked through the scope and fired several rounds at the target that had been set up on the wall. Jose sent a young man down to retrieve the target. Josh was pleased with how the gun performed. He had not gotten all bullseyes, but achieved an excellent score. He finished testing the rest of the weapons and they all performed well.

Ted had given him cash for the purchase of the rifle which he gave to Jose. He put the rest on his credit card and left instructions that it all be sent to the airport within the hour. Josh decided to keep one hand gun with him. He purchased a shoulder holster, put a full clip in the gun and placed it in the holster. Now he felt more prepared to meet any threat that came their way. He thanked Jose for his help and he and Bekah left the store to find a taxi.

Across the street, Esteban Montero was watching from his car parked down a side road. He saw Josh and Bekah leave, but he also saw their purchases being loaded into a delivery van, and he knew the driver very well. He waited until the driver was finished loading and had traveled down the block. He then started down the street and pulled up next to him. He beeped his horn and the driver recognized him and waved. Montero motioned for him to pull over. "Where are you taking this shipment?' Montero asked.

"I'm taking it to the airport. They're chartering a plane," said the driver.

"Do you know where they are going?" Montero asked.

The driver smiled. "I saw you hanging around and had a feeling you would want to know, so I tried to stay close and hear what they were saying. They are flying up to Puerto Bahia Negra. Do you know of anything going on up there that would call for that kind of fire power?"

Montero ignored the question. He just took out his wallet and gave him a U.S. hundred dollar bill. "Keep your eyes and ears open. Let me know if you hear anything else." The van pulled out and Montero sat there thinking for a while. He was unaware of anything happening up in that region of the country, but it was a little out of his area. He would make some inquiries. He now had phone calls he needed to make and more questions he needed to ask.

CHAPTER FIFTY-ONE

NEW YORK CITY
JUNE 11

Haydon Carlton was sitting in his office admiring all the beautiful artwork and jewelry collected over three generations. His office was tastefully decorated with unbelievably valuable pieces that caused him to smile and sigh pleasurably.

He had Carlos Rampone stay in the Ogunquit area to keep tabs on everyone. He must have been a pretty good snoop because he learned that Bekah Ryan and three others had left for Paraguay.

He made a few more phone calls and got the name of Esteban Montero. He came highly recommended. After speaking with Montero, and agreeing on a price, Haydon set him following the four and keeping tabs on them. He was to take the crucifix if he could, without any blood shed; but if it was necessary, use any means at his disposal. He decided to also send Rampone down tonight to give Montero whatever extra help he might need.

Just then his private telephone started to ring. "Hello. This is Montero. I have some information for you."

"Well, what can you tell me?"

"The group you described to me has come. I saw them in a store purchasing a surprising amount of weapons, two rifles, a shotgun, several hand guns, and a large amount of ammunition. They had it transported to the airport. They are chartering a plane to take them to Puerto Bahia Negra, which is around three hundred and fifty miles to the northeast. Who are these people? Are they associated with any organization? I tried to intimidate them, but the big guy would not back down."

"His name is Joshua Randall. I'll make some calls and see if I can find out something about him. Just keep following them."

"This is turning out to be more than you asked me to do. I will require extra people to help me, and we will have to travel. I will also require further payment."

"Yes, yes, no problem," Haydon said. "I'll double your price and pay you an extra thousand for any travel expenses you incur. I'm sending an associate of mine, Carlos Rampone, to lend a hand. He's not afraid to get his hands dirty. Now just get the job done. Call me with an update tomorrow."

The connection broke, and Montero sat, looking thoughtfully at his phone. First of all, he didn't like the fact that an outsider was coming down and nosing into his business. Second, something was going on here. He didn't have all the information concerning this job, and he was determined to get it before he went any further. There were too many unanswered questions, and he didn't work that way. He was going to get some answers, one way or another. First, he was going to make some calls of his own. If that didn't work, he had other means at his disposal. He was not in a hurry.

CHAPTER FIFTY-TWO

OGUNQUIT, MAINE
JUNE 11

"Hello. You have reached 'The Eye of the Needle', how can I help you?"

"Sylvia, is that you? This is Ted. I'm trying out my new satellite phone. Can you hear me clearly?"

"Yes Ted, loud and clear. Where are you? How are things going?"

"We're about twenty thousand feet up. We chartered a small jet and we're heading up to Puerto Bahia Negra. We did most of the shopping, and will pick up anything else we need there. Barring anything unusual, we should get there about the same time Daniel does. Things went pretty smooth in Asuncion. Sherry told us the places we should shop and we filled this plane. We're going to need more than two boats, probably closer to five. I'll let you talk to Bekah."

"Hi Sylvia, I can't believe we're here. It seems like it's taken forever, when in fact, it's been less than a week. How are things going there? Have you had any problems?"

"No," Sylvia answered, "everything is going smoothly; but one unusual thing happened, we had a phone call from a relative of yours who read Nana Sara's obituary in the paper and wanted to know more about her. It seems his mother was one of her nieces and he-"

"Wait a minute Sylvia," Bekah interrupted, "Nana had no family; it was just her and me. Did he give his name or leave a number? Did he ask any questions?"

"Well let me think; I didn't answer the phone, Penny did. She was helping out that day. She's here; let me get her on the phone for you."

"Hi Bekah," came a bubbly voice. "How is everything going? Do you have a tan yet? Are there beaches in Paraguay?" Penny bubbled till she overflowed.

"Penny, I want to ask you about the phone call the other day. Do you remember much about it?"

"Sure," said Penny. "It was your cousin Sam Smith. He said he saw Nana Sara's obituary in the paper and realized he was related. He said your families had lost touch. He wanted to talk with you, get back in touch and stay in touch. I thought that was so sweet of him. He asked if you were here and I felt bad I had to tell him you weren't. I said that you were gone on an extended vacation to of all places Paraguay. He was real surprised and said he would call back in a few weeks when you got back. Did I do OK?"

"You did great Penny. Thanks. Now put Sylvia back on."

"Oh, I forgot to give you a message from him. He said to say, 'Hey, see you soon.' He sounded real glad to find you."

"I'll just bet he did," Bekah said. "He seems pretty sure of himself, doesn't he?"

Sylvia took the phone. "Hold on while I find someplace quiet to talk." She walked back into Bekah's office. "Oh Bekah, I'm so sorry. I didn't hear her conversation until now. I hope this doesn't cause a problem."

"I hope so too. Whoever it was knows we are in Paraguay; and given the deceptive way he got the information, it doesn't sound like a good thing. I think the 'Hey' wasn't a greeting so much as a flag as to who was speaking, Haydon Carlton. I don't like the fact that he said he would see me soon. If ever a man personified evil, he did. Let's hope he stays in the states and we keep many, many miles between us. I just hope he doesn't find someone down here to do his dirty work. Come to think of it, maybe he already has. It was kind of interesting that an Esteban Montero showed up out of nowhere to hassle us. I wonder what his background is. Well keep praying. We need God with us in all His power and might. We'll talk tomorrow." When she hung up she turned and asked, "Did you all hear? It sounds as though this Esteban Montero might be a trouble maker."

"Well maybe this is where my background comes in handy," said Josh. "I don't really want to get in touch with the C.I.A. and alert them to where I am. They always seem to come up with a project for me, wherever I go; but I could ask a friend in the agency to look up Montero's background and how it would pertain to us. Maybe he can keep quiet about it and not alert anyone to my whereabouts."

Ted said, "We've got about thirty minutes until we land. Do you want to make the call now, or after we land?"

"It's around five thirty bureau time. Let me call now." Josh used the new satellite phone and punched in a number. After a moment they heard someone pick up the phone. They were on speaker phone.

"Hey my friend, how are you, and what are you doing in Paraguay?"

"Well I always told everyone my life was an open book; I guess I didn't know just how right I was. How did you know I was here?"

"A flag went up when you made a large purchase of firearms. Are you planning to start a war?"

"You know better than that. Did you think I went mercenary?"

"You're right, I do know better than that, and no I don't think you went mercenary. I'm just curious about why you need all that fire power down there in the boonies. You hear any rumors we need to know about?"

Josh questioned, "Why the third degree, do you know something I don't know that maybe I need to hear about?"

Isaac answered back, "You tell me your secrets, and I'll tell you mine."

Josh told him, "I want you to know, you're on speaker phone. I'm here with three other missionaries on what we feel is a quest from God. We are going to meet up with other missionaries who live in a village in the north east jungle of Paraguay, along the river. There has been rumor of some villages being destroyed by a warring tribe, and babies being sacrificed in fire. Does that sound like a reason to have some weapons? We only have them for protection, and intimidation if needed."

"Wow!" said Isaac. "That is some tale. How much of it is true?"

"All of it," Josh replied, knowing that he was leaving out part of the story, but unwilling to reveal everything. The C.I.A. had basically owned him, and yet, he could taste freedom, knowing he only owed them one more month. He did not want to get embroiled in anything on their plate at this late hour. He wanted to stay under their radar as much as possible, and was angry with himself for not thinking that they would get a flag when he purchased the firearms. "We even have a woman in the party who is not, and has never been on anyone's watch list. She owns an apple orchard and a knitting store. The foreman of the orchard is here with us. He immigrated to the U.S. from Paraguay when he was a teenager. He's now in his mid-sixties and a respected citizen. We also have a business man who came along for the ride. He is funding the mission trip and is being a helping hand wherever he can. Then there's me, almost ex-C.I.A and Mission Director of a church in Claremore, Oklahoma, which you already know. Now, if you would be so kind as to answer my question."

"Alright, and I'll tell you only because I don't want you stumbling into something that could get all of you in deep trouble. We think there's a middle-eastern Islamic extremist training camp code named La Muerto Negro, or The Black Death somewhere in the jungle where you are headed. We've been hearing lots of chatter about it for the last few months, but nothing has yet to surface. We don't know for certain, but there have been several groups of middle-eastern men entering the country for the last four months, and none of them have left. Also, they all seem to have vanished. We believe they are out there somewhere, recruiting followers and inciting trouble. There has also been an influx of young men from several other countries including the U.S., and we think they are recruits also. Remember, this is under the table, so all of you need to keep your mouths shut about it."

"I have one other favor I need to ask you," Josh said. "What can you tell me about a man named Esteban Montero, presently residing in Asuncion?"

"Hold on," said Isaac, "let me run him through the computer." He paused a moment and then replied with surprise. "He's a pretty bad dude. He's been up on several charges for murder, or attempted murder, but the charges are either dropped because the witnesses were missing, or they were found dead. His occupation is bounty hunter, and he only takes on dead or alive pursuit. So far no one has come back alive with him, and he's got a long record of successful apprehensions. How did you come in contact with him?

"He was at the store where we were purchasing the firearms. He got snotty, wanting to know our business, why we were there, and why we were needing guns. He tried to intimidate us. I was in the store with Ms. Ryan, and my other friends, and he tried pushing us around. The owner of the store came over with a shotgun and ordered him to leave. He was still hanging around when we left and looking very unhappy. Thanks for the heads up on him. Hopefully, he won't feel like coming our way and heading out into the jungle. Maybe we've seen the last of him, but we'll stay on our toes.

"As far as The Black Death goes," Josh said, "if I hear or see anything, you'll be the first to know. Forewarned is forearmed. Now, I've been warned, and I'm also armed. Thanks for your help buddy. I'll be talking with you soon."

"Not if I don't talk to you first, and you know that may happen. Be safe, my friend."

Everyone was silent for a moment or two, taking in the shocking things they had just heard. None of them had had any idea they were walking into such danger, and perhaps they would be luring an element of danger named Esteban Montero right into the jungle. That was a thought no one wanted to consider, but one that they could not easily ignore.

Ted tried to lighten the tension saying, "Maybe I need to do some target practice, just in case you need me. I want to be more than just a pretty face. Right now I'm feeling like dead weight. In my dream, God told me to fund the quest. He didn't say 'Go'. I really wanted to go, and no one disagreed. Now I'm wondering if that was such a great idea."

"Ted," answered Josh, "we were all in agreement that you should go. I'm sure if God didn't want you here, at least one of us would have heard His voice. I don't want you to feel that you are not needed or appreciated. We all have different skills and gifts that God has given us for a purpose, His purpose. One of your gifts has already helped us tremendously. If it wasn't for you, none of us would be here. You were right, car washes and garage sales just wouldn't have done it. Do you know the Bible talks about the gift of giving?[162] Almost anyone can carry a gun, but not everyone has the means, and is willing to give as you have. You will receive a reward for what you have done.[163] Also, I believe that this trip will be a pivotal point in your life, something you can look back on and say, 'Look, I helped slay the giant.' That's just what these obstacles are, they're giants. We've all been given a weapon to use against them, and I don't mean a gun. When the time comes, you will use your weapon, and we will all use our weapons in the name of the Lord. Now we're almost on the ground. Let's sit back and try to relax."

It was almost nine o'clock when they taxied down the runway. It was a very small airport, and the runway was the only

---

[162] Romans 12:6-8
[163] Matthew 25:14-30

thing paved, as far as the eye could see. The busiest road around looked to be the road of the river. It was trafficked by small barges, small cargo boats, motor boats and canoes. There were lights on the river, shining up and down its watery pathway, and traffic looked brisk for this time of night.

They disembarked from the plane, and stood watching while their cargo was transferred to pallets. It took five pallets, stacked about five feet high to hold it all. For the first time, they saw it all in one place and were intimidated by the size of it. "I don't know how we're going to get it all up there," Bekah said.

"Don't worry," Renato responded. "Remember the Bible assures us that with God all things are possible.[164] We need to concentrate on His abilities, not ours."

"Look over there," said Renato. "There's a tall, blond, white guy with four natives. I wonder if that is Daniel. Maybe we should go over and see."

As they turned and started walking toward them, the group turned and started heading their way. The white man was in front of the rest and as they got closer, he held out his hand and smiled. "I'm Daniel," he said. "You must be Renato, Ted, Josh and Bekah." He shook hands with each of them. Then he turned to his companions and introduced them. This is Leonardo, Axel, Giancarlo and Maitie. Manu sent them as protectors. Looking at the amount of cargo you have, and the supplies I am getting, we will need to hire at least four extra boats. We can't get the bigger boats because by the time we get to where we are going, the river will be smaller and shallower. Thank God it's the rainy season and the river's flowing well. During the dry season boat traffic up where we are is questionable. We have a number of large canoes,

---

[164] Mark 10:27

and three or four are motorized, depending on whether the engines are working or not. I came down in a small, twenty-five foot flat bottomed boat that I use to make monthly supply runs. What we are able to hire will hopefully be comparable.

Renato spoke to the native men in their native tongue, and thanked them for coming to meet them. He thanked them for all their help. He told them he had been a boy when he left Paraguay, but remembered traveling down a river, and then taking a long truck ride. It had been around fifty-five years ago, and time erases even good memories. They all shook his hand and welcomed him home. Turning back to his group, he had tears in his eyes. It certainly was a strange homecoming, but it was a homecoming none the less.

Everyone had been watching, and now Josh extended his hand. "I think I can speak for the rest of us when I say we are all glad to be here. It feels like we have been working for weeks towards this moment, when in fact it is less than a week. I know that we have had things to overcome just as all of you have, but God has been with us, protecting, and leading, and guiding us to this point in time. I feel as though we have rivers to cross and mountains to climb before this quest is ended, but it is for such a time as this that we have all been born,[165] and our lives have all been a precursor to this quest. God had a plan and purpose for them[166]and He is putting it into play. I have a feeling this is only the beginning, and we will get to know each other on a much deeper level before this is through."

Daniel spoke from his heart, "I can't tell you how gratified I am that God has taken it upon Himself to help all the tribes in this

---

[165] Esther 4:14
[166] Jerimiah 29:11

area, especially the tribe that was just recently attacked. I also feel that God wants to extend His hand to the tribe that has been committing these atrocities. They are walking in darkness and God is sending a light. I am humbled by the fact that He has chosen us to be His hand extended – for peace or war, or both. I don't know which right now, but as we go forth, God will reveal his plan."

Everyone stood quietly in awe of the moment; then Ted spoke up with enthusiasm. "Let's go rent all the boats we'll need so we can get loaded and start up river at first light. I can't wait to meet everyone and pray together so we can seek the will of God on how to accomplish His purpose. I want to complete the quest He has called us to."

As one, they turned, and united in spirit, they took their first steps to fulfill the quest, not knowing all the answers, or all the repercussions of what was going to happen, but just happy and fulfilled with completing The Call and anxious to begin The Quest.

BIOGRAPHY

Lorraine and her husband Mike started out as high school sweethearts. They have now been married forty-seven years. They have two children and two grandchildren who help keep life exciting. Lorraine was raised in New Jersey and relocated with her family to Oklahoma in 1977. At that time she hoped there was a God, but had no faith to support that belief. That hope was turned into a firm belief in 1981. She subsequently developed a burning desire to share God's Word with those around her. Unfortunately, she had very little knowledge of the Bible. This prompted her to attend Rhema Bible Training Center where she received a two year degree. She served in her local church in a number of positions and was eventually ordained into the ministry.

Lorraine has a heart for missions and has been on several mission trips over the years, including trips to the Philippines and Ivory Coast. Her last was a two week trip to Paraguay at the end of April, 2016. There she got to experience what she had only imagined and meet the people who already lived in her heart.

Lorraine is also a registered nurse. She has incorporated her nurse's training and experience, plus her love of gardening, cooking, and needlework into the tapestry of her book, The Call. It is the first book of the series, And Then the End Shall Come

Lorraine is currently working on her second book of the series, The Quest, which should be out shortly.

To order the second book in the series, contact me at lmcafasso@gmail.com. This book will be available on Kindle shortly.